THE SPARK BETWEEN US

STACY TRAVIS

FAST TURTLE PRESS

THE SPARK BETWEEN US

STACY TRAVIS

Cover Design: Shanoff Designs

Copyediting: Evident Ink

Publicity: Social Butterfly PR

CHAPTER ONE

arah

THE SPARKLING RED lights all around me would have looked so pretty flickering on a Christmas tree or beaming through a stained-glass window.

But since I was staring at a sea of brake lights on the interstate, I didn't feel much like caroling. More like yelling obscene things to the drivers next to me and delighting in the fact that they couldn't hear me.

"Call Tater Tot," I told my hands-free phone on the dash. My sisters had nicknamed her after the fried potato nuggets our mom served us way too often as kids because that's how five older siblings tortured the youngest.

I knew Tatum would be at her desk. My other sisters had unpredictable work hours, hobbies, and social lives. For Tatum and I, our jobs filled the roles of work, hobbies, and social lives.

"I detect a pissy tone. Are we having a bad day?" my phone asked in its British baritone. Cheeky little thing. Tatum was developing emotion-recognition software at her tech company and had programmed my phone as a test subject.

"We are having the kind of day when we endeavor to ring our sister, you English twat," I fired back. But really, I loved the English twat, whom I fondly referred to as Nigel.

"Calling Tater Tot," he confirmed in a clipped accent. So obedient.

I imagined Nigel sitting beside me when I drove, looking a little like Henry Cavill and beckoning me to take long, sexy walks in the English countryside. "Off we go," he'd say in his clipped, jolly voice. "Another brilliant day for a sexy shag."

Nigel's voice, along with the fantasy of a hot Brit riding me sidesaddle, claimed bragging rights for the longest and most successful of all my relationships. Such was the life of a science professor.

"You're driving, aren't you?" Tatum's quiet laugh and reassuring voice immediately relaxed me.

"Yes, how'd you know?" I fiddled with the air conditioning to notch it down a few degrees.

"Because that's when you call me. When you're bored in the car and you know I'm working." Her sigh didn't make me feel apologetic. On the contrary, I knew talking to me was sometimes the only break she took in a twelve-hour workday, so I considered it a win-win.

"I'm driving to Carolwood and confirming why I can't do this commute every day. I just can't. I shouldn't. I'm making the right call here, yes?"

I could hear typing in the background. The steady tap-tap indicated either answering emails or writing lines of code. "Yes. It's the right call, Ms. Magoo."

My eyesight wasn't the problem. However, my mind had a tendency to wander, which had resulted in me hitting a few stationary objects—among them a neighbor's retaining wall, an idling garbage truck, and a mailbox.

It was a quirk. Everyone had quirks. My quirk just happened to result in high insurance rates. Unfortunately, one more slip-up would probably leave me fighting for a window seat on the bus.

The lane to my right started moving, but mine lagged like a bedraggled snail.

So. Annoying.

I hit my steering wheel in frustration, which had the effect of unintentionally honking my horn. The guy in the car in front of me threw up a hand as if to ask what I expected him to do. I waved and gave him a thumbs up.

"You just pissed someone off, didn't you?" Tatum's chuckle echoed through my speakerphone.

"Maybe. Is road rage still a thing?" I asked, recalling stories about angry drivers gunning each other down on freeways.

"It is, and you definitely have it, but you're sort of polite and passive aggressive about it, riding people's back bumpers then flashing a peace sign like you didn't mean it."

"I just don't want to make anyone mad enough to shoot me."

Over the past few years, I'd made traffic a non-issue by living a few miles from my job. Some days, I rode my bike. Unfortunately, that was all about to change.

Thanks to a career opportunity I couldn't pass up, I had two choices: commute an hour to work and risk bodily injury if another mailbox appeared in my path, or relocate to a small town where I knew nobody. I chose door number two.

"Well, this is it, then. My traffic swan song," I said.

"You already did it? You packed up and everything? Who's renting your house?" The typing stopped.

"Um, no one." I'd intended to find a tenant but . . . "None of the prospects worked out."

"Translation—you didn't like any of them enough to let them pay you thousands of dollars to live in your house." She was correct. I didn't have a rational reason.

I shouldn't have cared how much charisma the tenant had as long as the person could pay on time and didn't plan to tear the place up, but I'd somehow gone mother hen about my home—no suitor seemed good enough to date my baby, so I sent them all away, corsages and all.

Ah, finally my lane started moving. I unkinked the knot in my neck as my speedometer edged up to ten miles an hour. Then I came to a grinding halt again.

"Shit!" I gasped as my car's front bumper came within inches of the fender in front of me. The Toyota Camry I'd almost humped seemed to be lacking brake lights. "There's nothing in front of you. You don't need to stop!" I narrowly managed to keep from pounding the horn again.

"Still your fault if you hit him," Tatum sang. Her tapping on the keyboard resumed. "Wait, so no one's living in your house for six months?"

I shrugged even though she couldn't see me. "I mean, maybe I'll come back on the weekends some time, but pretty much, no—"

"Can I live there?" Her voice squeaked with glee.

"You live in Palo Alto. Near work. Which makes sense," I reminded her. She had a five minute commute, door to door. Blissful. What kind of person gives that up?

"I live in a cracker box. I'd commute an hour if it meant I could spread out in your house."

I slammed on my brakes again. "Just drive!" Almost as though he heard me, the man in the Toyota started inching forward. "Sorry again. So let me make sure I'm understanding. You want to put yourself through what I'm experiencing right now, just to live in a house you'll barely get to see anyway? You work a million hours a week."

"Not all of us are as squeamish about traffic as you are. I like driving. Give me a steamy romance audiobook or some true crime podcast, and I'll drive all day," she said.

"Are we even related?"

Then Nigel piped up, giving me instructions, telling me to take the next freeway exit. "North Carolwood Avenue" sounded like a storybook destination in his British accent. This was it, the beginning of . . . something.

"Hang on . . ." Tatum instructed. I heard muffled voices, and after a moment, she yelped.

While I waited to find out what had her so excited, I focused on the road and a future I couldn't quite fathom.

For the next six months, I'd be another local in Carolwood, California. Sure, the town likely had some kindly folks and operated at a slower pace, but I wasn't moving for the scenery. Carolwood had the distinction of being a short drive from Lawrence Livermore National Laboratory—basically NASA meets Hogwarts for physicists. Mind-blowing science fair nirvana. Researchers there dallied with things like national security and the nation's nuclear weapons. And they wanted me.

If all went according to plan, I'd break new ground in metals welding using friction and lasers.

Yup, my nerd flag flies high.

I hadn't done much planning in my abrupt decision to move my life away from Berkeley, where I taught college physics. My train of thought had involved picturing my commute, feeling nauseous at the amount of time I'd spend on the road each day, experiencing dizziness at the idea of running into more stationary objects, and making a frantic call to my brother, Finn.

Besides being an economist with a savant-like understanding of the stock market, Finn was my oldest sibling, only brother, and go-to savior when I got stuck.

He also taught at Berkeley, so it only took him a few minutes to get from his office to mine, where I was lying on the floor with my knees up near my ears to keep the blood flowing to my head.

Finn knew a guy. Calls were made. A roommate situation was procured.

I went home, drank wine from a can, and started packing.

That was a week ago.

Now I was obeying Nigel's directions and pretending he was guiding me to a charming bed and breakfast where we'd have a very proper British tryst. I diligently signaled and exited the freeway and turned on First Street, which took me toward the center of town. The main road featured a parkway down the center, and after a block, I reached an open green space with a burbling fountain and several benches. A few streets with shops fanned out in various directions, and . . . that was it. That was the town.

I hadn't expected a sprawling place like San Francisco or Oakland, but Carolwood was even slightly smaller than I'd anticipated when I pictured a place with a population of twelve thousand. No more views of the Bay Bridge or the bustle of students, bye-bye thirty coffee houses in a one mile radius.

This would be quieter. Much quieter.

I had mixed feelings about the move. Working at the lab checked every box on my career thrill spreadsheet, and avoiding the commute felt like multitasking gold. But since my family lived an hour away and I didn't have any friends in town, the next six months promised a lot of solo time. A lot of hours reading science journals and finding new, interesting ways to make salad dressing. For myself, party of one.

"Sorry, sorry," Tatum piped in. "We just got a new contract. Everyone's pumped." I could hear the excitement in her voice. She had startup culture in her genes. She never ran out of energy, and she loved technology.

"Don't worry about it. But I should call you later. I need to get my bearings before I get lost in suburbia." I was already passing the same wine shop for the third time.

"I can't believe you're gonna live in a cow town for six months. Do you even need a car there, or will you ride a pony to work?"

"It's not a cow town. If you ever bothered to detour from your tiny world on your state-of-the-art tech campus, you'd see it's a nice place. I heard they make wine here. Tourists come."

"Awesome. You'll be cow tipping in the grapevines like a local in no time."

"Small minded."

"Giddyup. Maybe you'll meet a cowboy."

"Not why I'm here," I sang, reminding her of what she already knew.

"Well, hopefully some burly cattle rustler out there will change your mind." Laughing at her hilarity, she said goodbye and hung up.

Turning on a side street took me past a bookstore, a bakery, and another wine shop. Okay! Pretty much all I needed was right here in the few blocks that made up the business district.

The roommate situation remained the only unknown, but I wasn't too worried.

Finn had lined up a spare room at the home of a guy he knew, Braden Michaels. They'd been best friends in high school and had stayed pretty close. Since he and Finn were four years older, my memories of Braden were spotty, other than him being a dark-haired menace who slammed a lot of doors and drove too fast. He may have had acne. And an attitude. No doubt he'd matured like we all did and was a fine upstanding citizen.

Finn said he worked for the city—probably meant he had a nine-to-five job. Nice and stable. Maybe even boring.

Boring didn't bother me. I was comfortable with boring. A person didn't need flashy clothes or a big personality to get by. The world needed some people to act normal, put our heads down, and get the work done while the hell-raisers and fun people created havoc. I'd always been the responsible, reliable type.

All Finn said was, "the kid turned out all right" and advised that I form my own opinions about Braden Michaels. "Approach your new roommate situation without assumptions or predisposition to bias." Irritating economist, that Finn.

"This is my life for the next six months. It's not an economic model." It annoyed me that he wouldn't give me a tiny nugget of information, but Finn clammed up and acted like I was the weird one for asking.

I rolled my eyes at the recollection before glancing outside at a peach colored brick library building with white columns. Under the pastel blue sky, everything looked much cleaner and more orderly than some of the grimier neighborhoods I was used to in the East Bay. I passed a health food market and an alehouse, picturing a friendly bartender who knew everyone in town by name.

I should have had my eyes on the road. If I had, I might have noticed the ever-diminishing gap between my front bumper and the back of a giant red and silver wall of metal looming in front of me.

Should have, could have . . .

Story of my life on the road. Too little, way too late.

I barely had time to attempt to slow down. Then, the screech of brakes . . . the scream that shocked me even though it was mine . . . the jerking of the steering wheel to no avail, then . . .

Bam!!

My car slammed hard into the stationary object with an impossible smack that provided no cushioning or the slightest bit of give.

It was Physics 101: the greater the force of a moving object, the greater the change in motion, i.e., I hit the gas hard and took all that speed with me. And also Physics 101: the larger the stationary object, the more negligible effect the force on it will have, i.e., I hit something massive, and it bore the impact like a flea flick.

Yup, my brain went there, down the science rabbit hole, thinking about energy transfer and kinetic energy, even as the entire front end of my car went concave. Crumpled metal, sounds of glass shattering, and a scream—mine. Then my head was thrust forward and back again by the impact and a zealous airbag.

What the hell just happened?

If I hadn't been able to identify the looming object in front of me before, the powdery marshmallow of airbag made it impossible now. I was aware of a burning sensation on my hands and an ache in my jaw. But I was alive.

Thank you, tiny Prius.

Peeking around the overinflated mess of airbag, I identified the looming red wall of metal that had turned my hood into an accordion—the back of a fire truck.

It had a hand-drawn placard above its bumper with three tiny, ironic words: Welcome to Carolwood.

raden

I HAD no idea what I'd gotten myself into when I said yes to Finn, but after he referred to his sister as a physics dork for the third time, I decided she sounded pretty harmless.

I pictured a female version of Albert Einstein with wild wiry hair and a slide rule in her pocket. I realized that stereotype made me sound like an uninformed Neanderthal, but Finn had painted a picture, and my imagination followed to an unimaginative place.

So, I agreed.

What else could I say to my oldest friend who'd talked the cops out of arresting me, wing-manned me into my first girlfriend, and defended me in front of my irate parents—all before we were sixteen? Not to mention bailing me out of the biggest shit show of my life just a couple years ago.

Even if he was too nice to say it—or think it—I owed him.

By transference, I guess that meant I owed his younger sister too.

I knew very little about her except for the whole science dork thing, which only told me she had nothing in common with me.

Probably better that way. If she and I had different interests and separate lives, we'd have less chance of getting in each other's hair.

"And dude, in case it wasn't clear . . . she's not your type," Finn said.

I laughed at the insinuation. Warning me to stay away from his little sister felt like a throwback to junior high school when I'd have jumped on any warm-blooded female. By high school, I had standards, and they didn't include studious Sarah, who rolled her eyes like a typical twelve-year-old and made it clear I bored her.

"I'm going to pretend you didn't say that," I said.

He laughed to cover the awkwardness. "Sorry, but I needed to put it out there. Sarah doesn't really date, so she's not the kind of girl you hook up with." I wondered how much he really knew about his sister. I didn't date anymore either, but I sure as hell hooked up. Probably not how he wanted to think about his sibling.

I also wished he were here so I could punch him.

Finn rattled off a few more details about Sarah, all of which made me confident that keeping my hands off her would pose no problem. He described an uptight workaholic who kept to herself and had her head so much in the clouds that she bumped into things and sometimes showed up at work in pajama bottoms.

"Stop trying to paint an awful picture, okay? I'm not some unhinged sex addict who won't be able to keep my hands to myself."

At the very least, I can resist a clumsy female Einstein.

I vaguely remembered her, always outside rigging up some science fair project that inevitably made a mess. I was from a family of boys, but if I'd had a sister, I imagined she'd act just like Sarah, timid around my friends because we were loud, sweaty, and generally up to no good.

I remembered her wide-eyed look when she saw us drinking beer once while still in high school. "But the drinking age is twenty-one. You're breaking the law," she'd said primly, hands on her hips like a schoolmarm. After that, I went out of my way to avoid her. I didn't need the judgement from a prepubescent know-it-all.

Finn had turned a corner when he got to college. That was around the time his dad was diagnosed with an inoperable brain tumor. His outlook toward himself and his family changed, and he instantly went from being an aimless college kid to an organized economics major who was already making plans to be the only man in the house.

When his dad died two years later, Finn took on the role in earnest, saved his first million by successfully gaming the stock market, and served as fierce protector of his mom and five sisters ever since. That included finding housing for his dorky sister now.

A week ago, I'd have greeted the vaguest suggestion that I get a roommate with a loud hell no.

And yet . . . here I was.

"I've got the extra bedroom just sitting here empty. Might as well put it to good use," I heard myself saying. I didn't bother to add that part of the reason it stood empty was that I couldn't bear to go in there. Finn didn't know I still wasn't over the shit my ex said when she left. But in two years, I hadn't set foot in that room. Each time I'd attempted it, my chest had seized up and I'd felt gutted all over again. Maybe it would help me move on if someone else used the space and I could view it as a spare room again.

"It's fine. Really. Can she cook at least?" I asked.

His bark of a laugh answered that question. "Not unless you like a lot of salads and baked potatoes with weird toppings like mustard."

"Nothing wrong with those, as long as they're next to a steak."

"My thought exactly," Finn chuckled. "I think you'll get along fine. You're opposite enough. You can stay in your separate corners, you shoveling down animal entrails and her eating some fake steak made from jackfruit."

"Is that food, or are you trying to be funny?" I asked. People didn't try to make steak out of fruit, did they? Finn's laugh told me that maybe his kooky sister did. "I'm glad you find this all so amusing."

Is his sister some kind of insane vegan hippie? She does live in Berkeley, so it's possible.

Finn cleared his throat in his professor-serious way, but the laugh didn't leave his voice. "I find it awesome. And truth be told, I'm a little jealous. We always said we'd room together after college—too bad it never worked out. Just be nice to her and show her around town. After that, you probably won't see her much. She pretty much lives at work." A fruity, robotic nun.

He thanked me a few more times, which somehow made me feel more indebted to him, and we hung up.

I raked a hand over the few days' worth of scruff on my face. I hadn't decided yet whether to let it grow back into a full beard. The guys at the fire station had been giving me shit since I'd shaved my beard a month ago, constantly touching my face like it was a miracle that I had actual skin under there. If I heard "like a baby's butt" one more time, I'd hand down a week of kitchen duty to the nearest asshole.

By my calculation, Sarah wouldn't arrive for at least an hour, which gave me time to get out of the house for a bit. I'd been crammed inside cleaning the place up for most of the day because I didn't want Finn's sister to bolt before she knew me well enough to embrace my clutter.

My bike sat basking in the sun, begging me to ride. I couldn't turn that pretty thing down when I had a free hour, so I grabbed my helmet and leather jacket and headed outside.

"You're as pretty as ever, Dolores," I said, rubbing a hand over her shiny red gas tank. No one was around to hear me talking to a motorcycle, but who cared if they did? A man's relationship with a beautiful machine was his own business.

I wasn't a Harley Davidson kind of guy, and I didn't belong to a pack or a club. When I needed to escape or clear my head, I went for a ride. A couple years ago, I bought a used Ducati with all the speed I wanted without the flash. No two-wheeled swinging dick to prove anything to anyone.

I pulled on my gloves and straddled the bike. Firing up the engine, I felt the seductive purr that always ratcheted up my heart rate a few notches. Perfect day to ride the winding roads past the vineyards outside of town.

I eased the bike out onto the road, keeping the speed down on the residential streets and into town. No one liked a loud, crazy motorcycle scaring the life out of people when they were out walking around. Once I got onto the road, I'd open her up.

It surprised me to find a string of cars idling for a couple blocks on Second Street. Traffic wasn't a thing in Carolwood. The place was too small. Had to be construction.

Splitting the lane on the bike, I passed most of the cars, planning to high-five the crew as I rode by. Probably guys I knew.

But I didn't see construction guys.

"Shit. That ain't good." I winced, watching the guys from my unit, Engine 97, circle a white Prius that had rammed into the back of their truck.

From the looks of things, it had just happened. The hood sat uselessly crumpled like an empty TV dinner tray. I could see someone in the car behind the cloud of airbag. "So much for the ride," I muttered, pulling my bike off the road, locking my helmet, and jogging over to the rig.

"What the hell happened?" I asked Logan, our driver-engineer who'd never gotten as much as a scratch on the paint in seven years. As he took photos of the scene, he made notes on a small pad. I knew he'd be stressing over getting the truck back into spit-shine condition, no doubt mentally polishing every inch of chrome while he grimly surveyed the damage.

"Just what it looks like. We were stopped, and next thing I know, there's a car glued to the back of the truck."

While he wrote his report, two of my other guys climbed through the backseat to try to get the driver out. I could only see them from the waist down.

"Objects in mirror may be closer than they appear," I grumbled.

"Way closer." He shook his head, his close-clipped yellow-blond hair not moving an inch. "I didn't even see her. She must've been following so close I didn't pick her up in the mirrors. Then, three, two, one, contact."

"For real, did you back into her?" I loved giving him shit.

He glared at me. Logan was the guy you wanted behind the wheel, but he had no sense of humor about his driving, which meant no one would pass up a chance to get in a dig—it was the culture of our unit. "Nope. Parked at the light. I dunno what the hell she was doing. Probably on her phone."

Probably. Distracted drivers caused nine rear-ends out of ten these days.

"You need to break out the jaws?" I'd have felt a little jealous if they ended up using the jaws of life without me, not gonna lie. There wasn't a guy in the department who didn't secretly love it when we could cut a car in half.

"Driver door's jammed. They're hoping to get her out through the back," Logan said.

Then, as if noticing me for the first time, he looked me over from head to toe. "You trying to pick up women in that?"

I looked down at my motorcycle boots, jeans, gloves, and leather jacket, which must've looked warm on a nice day and a little odd without the accompanying motorcycle. "Hilarious. I was headed out for a ride when I pulled up on your mess."

"When are you going to get rid of that death machine, man? Seriously, if I have to peel one more case of roadkill off the asphalt, I'm gonna hurl."

I huffed out an annoyed breath. "I'm careful."

"No, you're not, and we both know it. Been two years of this shit." He was right, and I didn't care. Riding the bike was the one place I acted irresponsibly, and I loved the rush.

"I didn't stop here for a lecture. Do you need any help?" I folded my arms and waited for him to let me take over.

"No. You're off duty. We've got this."

I didn't want to leave, though, so I conjured reasons why my guys might need me there. "You call an ambulance?"

"What kind of question is that?" Logan glared at me, looking about as vicious as a bunny.

"Well, I don't hear them," I said, straining to hear any sign of sirens in the distance.

He pointed. The ambulance was a block away, trying to navigate around the traffic.

"You might ask if we're okay, seeing as we're the ones who got hit, asshole," Mitch said, backing himself out of the Prius. He scrubbed a hand through his brown curls, which he'd slicked back with some kind of product. "Women love to touch it, never gonna cut it," he said way too often.

"I can see you're fine enough to run your mouth, so I'm not asking, jerkoff."

Mitch wasn't just a firefighter in my unit. He was also my half-brother, courtesy of our dad, who couldn't keep his pants zipped long enough to stay faithful to one wife, let alone three.

When I was five, my dad left us and married Mitch's mom. Left her a few years after that. Left his third wife after that.

The walking heartbreak of a man gifted me with a skewed view of commitment, but the silver lining was Mitch, two years younger than me and an inch taller, which he never missed an opportunity to mention.

I clenched my fists, needing someplace to channel my energy when I saw no obvious way to help. Stifling the urge to ask whether they'd turned off the battery to the Prius—they knew what they were doing—my eyes drifted to the mess of a car anyway to check for signs of a leak.

"You love us so much, you come on your day off." Mitch smacked my shoulder with the back of his hand and took in my outfit. "Loser, you'd rather skip a ride than miss out on any action?" I turned away from his smirk, unwilling to admit he was right.

Wriggling out of my leather jacket, I grabbed some extra medical supplies while a rookie named Cash and one of the medics slid the driver out of the car, laying her on a stretcher on the sidewalk.

The tow truck's backup signal beeped as it moved, and the woman let out a yelp. "Wait, I've got stuff in there I need. You can't tow it!"

"Oh, hey. There's a task for you, Michaels. Purse retrieval," Mitch laughed. The smartass was guaranteeing I'd be filling his running shoes with sand tomorrow.

"Relax and let them check your vital signs. I'll unload your car," I called to her, ducking into the backseat. I pushed past clutter and boxes of books to reach the front. Her cellphone sat in a mount on the dashboard. It felt warm from use, but at least she'd been hands-free.

The passenger seat contained a banker's box with a lid. I nudged it out of the seat, and, judging by its weight—more books.

People said books made good friends. If it was true, this woman had a lot of people in her corner.

I grabbed her purse off the floor, along with a small daypack and a brown paper lunch bag folded neatly at the top. Then I lugged the heavy box over the center console and out through the back door. When I emerged from the car with the purse and backpack over one shoulder and boxes stacked high, she was sitting up, frowning, eyes narrowed in my direction.

"What are you doing with those?" she asked, her eyes fixed on the boxes in my hands. I almost dropped everything, not because of her glare but because of the arresting blue of her eyes. The pale aqua color reminded me of a beach in the Caribbean Sea where I suddenly, desperately wanted to go. The drinks would have umbrellas, and I'd float on a raft and gaze at that soothing blue for days.

If I took vacations. Which I did not.

"Your car's not drivable, ma'am. I'm helping you remove your belongings." I wanted to be polite and not let her vacation eyes, her messy strands of honey-brown hair, or her plush, pink lips distract me from being professional. I swallowed hard and pretended my heart rate hadn't ticked up a notch.

But those eyes. Pale like aquamarine gemstones, they contained a hundred tiny flashes of color and light. I didn't want to look away —couldn't look away.

"But who are you? Where'd you come from?" she asked, pulling me out of my trance.

Oh. Yeah. I probably looked like a random biker who showed up and started manhandling her stuff.

"Technically, I'm off duty, but I'm a firefighter with these guys, ma'am."

She closed her eyes for a long blink and shook her head. When she opened them, her lips turned up into a smirk. "Okay, but please don't call me ma'am. I'm not a ninety-year-old woman."

"What would you prefer I call you?"

"I dunno. Anything. 'Damsel in distress' is better than ma'am." I took her sass as a good sign. Likely meant the accident hadn't hurt her too badly.

"Fine, damsel in distress, I'm going to keep emptying your car. Is that okay by you?" I grinned, pouring on a bit of charm to try to blunt her discomfort. I organized her boxes in a neat stack.

"Sure. Thank you," she croaked, grimacing. "Oh, and could I have my lunch?" She tipped her head toward the paper bag I held in my hand with her purse. I forked it over. She carefully unfolded the top, took a crustless sandwich on wheat from a baggie, and took a bite.

This woman had probably totaled her car, and her chief concern was eating her PB&J. I'd seen pretty much everything in my line of work, but I hadn't seen that. It wasn't until her eyes fluttered up at me that I realized I was still staring at her face.

"Check for swelling in her cervical spine. Something's pinching a nerve," I told the medics, turning away before my smile betrayed how much I liked looking at her. I went back to grab another load from the car.

In no way had I ever viewed a car accident as a means to hit on a woman—creepy and opportunistic was not my style. But I'd also never found it so hard to look away from someone. I suddenly wanted to know what else she had in that lunch bag and why she had all the books in her car. She had me intrigued after only a minute. What the hell was that about?

I heard Mitch laugh. "Too salty to be a damsel. Guess you're not in too much pain if you've got an appetite, but we still need the medics to check you out."

I stacked a few more boxes, all of them heavy.

"I told you. I'm fine." She looked from Mitch to Cash to me, and then she looked at the other two medics. The color drained from her face. "Actually, maybe I should lie down for a minute." She immediately shifted into a reclining position on the stretcher and curled her knees into her chest. "Sorry, vaso-vagal . . . it happens sometimes when I get nervous."

She hadn't seemed nervous. Was it the crowd? The attention? I felt an oddly possessive need to protect her from whatever was bothering her. The more we all hovered, the more she seemed desperate not to have people fussing over her. Here I was adding to the mess.

You're also acting like a lovestruck idiot.

I gave myself an invisible slap and went back to work emptying her shit out of the car.

The medics edged in with oxygen and started taking her vitals.

"Let's start with your name," Johnny, one of the medics, said.

"It's Sarah," she said, and I felt a stir in my gut at her name. Had to be a coincidence that Finn's sister had the same name . . . right?

"Do you know what day of the week it is, today's date?" Johnny asked. Standard question to assess whether she'd sustained any head trauma.

Out of the corner of my eye, I saw her lift her head. "Um, yeah. It's Tuesday. Thanksgiving Day. Nineteen seventy-two."

She was giving them shit. Unbelievable.

"Are you sure about that, ma'am?" Cash asked.

Her face cracked into a grin. "If you keep calling me ma'am, I'm going to keep giving you ridiculous answers. I told you, I'm fine." Her plump lips drew my eyes again, daring me to look away. She gestured to me. "If you're planning on unloading everything, I really appreciate it, but I'm afraid you've got your work cut out. The trunk is packed to the gills."

"Yeah? You moving your office or something?"

Or are you moving in . . . with me?

"Or something," she said, suddenly pressing the heels of her hands to her temples. "On second thought, mind if I lie back down? I just got a major head rush."

I looked down at the boxes of books I'd just taken out of the car, the gears in my brain starting to churn. Science books. Moving boxes.

"Sorry, what did you say your last name is?" I asked, dread crawling over my skin.

"I didn't. But it's Finley."

Of course it was. Shit.

I extended my hand. "Nice to meet you. Braden Michaels."

Her eyes grew rounder, tiny sparkles igniting amid the gorgeous aqua. "Braden, as in—"

"Yeah. As in Finn's friend. And your new roommate."

She looked the way I felt—confused, wary, maybe a little bit annoyed? It could have been shock from the accident, or maybe it just embarrassed her to meet me under these circumstances.

But I was wary for a whole other set of reasons, none of which had anything to do with a car accident. A brainy woman who looked like that spelled trouble. And I'd be living with her for six long months.

CHAPTER THREE

arah

WELL, fuck a duck.

If ever there was an inauspicious start to my new life in my temporary home, crashing into a fire truck fit the bill perfectly.

I'd probably lose my license. Or my insurance rates would skyrocket. To say nothing of having my new roommate show up purely by chance, acting helpful and gracious in the middle of my mortification.

Karma, meet Murphy's Law.

And on top of it, he was a far cry from the pale, doltish government employee I'd been expecting.

Damn Finn for his vagueness about details. Only an economist— and a guy—would describe a hot firefighter as a city employee.

He might as well have called him a data point.

Braden Michaels was a gorgeous, decadent dessert of a man who seemed to have zero control over his smolder. It emanated from his dark eyes, his lazy smile, and his sharp jawline softened by sexy stubble. I normally didn't get worked up over attractive men, but it was impossible not to notice this one.

Just try to ignore him, ladies. You'll fail.

His gaze made me nervous, which didn't help as I tried to keep myself from passing out. With a mind of its own, my tongue darted out and licked my lips.

Hello? Down, girl.

"So . . . I guess . . . nice to see you after all these years?" I cleared my throat and tried not to sound as mortified as I felt. The unsteadiness was new. I never went to pieces in a crisis. I was the one everyone else counted on to stay calm and rational. And I sure as heck never turned to jelly over a man. What? Was? Happening? "I sure know how to make an impression, huh?"

Braden grunted and nodded, turning even more into my image of a libido-driven caveman by the minute. "You hit the truck hard. Were you texting?" He still held one of my boxes in his large, strong hands, which almost distracted me from his frown.

"No, I don't do that."

"Good," he grumbled, looking away.

Is it my imagination, or was he a whole lot nicer before he knew I was his roommate?

The firetruck stood ahead of us, barely a blemish in sight. My shoulders slumped as I looked at my car, crumpled like used tin foil, and my boxes piled in a pyramid on the sidewalk. How would I get to work without a car? Would I even be able to rent one with yet another accident on my record?

Eyes burning, I realized I was truly stuck.

One of the medics had my arm wrapped in a blood pressure cuff and continued the drills to test whether or not I had a concussion.

I felt pretty certain I didn't, but I knew they wouldn't take my word for it. "I'm not seeing double. I don't have ringing in my ears. I don't feel nauseous." I knew the signs because I'd had a concussion last year, one more time when I didn't notice my surroundings.

I'd bent down to pick up some cereal that spilled on the floor in my pantry and stood up quickly, banging my head hard on the door handle. So hard, in fact, that it knocked me out for less than a minute.

Fine, it was more than a minute.

When I came to, I felt awful. Like, drag myself to the bathroom and vomit awful. That was a real concussion. It came with a headache for two days, nausea, dizziness, and vertigo. I'd had the good sense to get checked out by a doctor who did the exact battery of tests performed by the medics.

"I promise you, I'm fine," I insisted, wanting to retain some control over my circumstances. I hated having five different men assess my condition and debate the reason I'd plowed into a truck. It reminded me of so many science classes where I'd get the right experiment result, and my male classmates would gather, talking over me, certain they could prove me wrong. "Was she drinking?" "Did she have a seizure?" "Is she an awful driver?"

No. It was none of those things. I got distracted. Head in the clouds. Not the first time.

While the rest of the guys prattled on, I noticed Braden stood slightly apart from them, assessing me with his eyes. His cool expression gave no indication of what he saw until his voice cut through the chatter from his colleagues. "Leave her alone. Accidents happen."

As if guided by divine spirit, the men surrounding me stopped talking and quietly returned to the remaining tests on their checklist.

I shot Braden a look of gratitude with my plastered-on smile. "The main thing I'm suffering from is mortification," I muttered. The burns on my arms hurt more than anything, and I probably had some bruising on my face from the damned airbag. "Also, there has to be a way to make an airbag that can protect a person without kickboxing her head in the process."

"Not our area. You can take that up with the NTSB," Braden intoned, face devoid of expression. He stopped unloading boxes from my trunk and stood before me, arms crossed and staring like a very stoic Michelin Man. I think he actually had several stacked tires for biceps.

I sized up my new roommate a bit more, in denial that my heart raced at the sight of his face. Earlier, distracted by the hard line of his jaw and the sharpness of his cheekbones, I hadn't noticed the rest of him.

I'm not gonna lie—the rest of him was *nice*.

My eyes toured his features like he was a breakfast buffet—the muscled arms, tapered waist, dark head of hair which was slicked back yet nicely tousled. His gray T-shirt made sweet love to his broad shoulders, hard chest, and rippled six-pack.

All that muscle and capability made my heart ratatat with nerves. The people who looked like him belonged in Scotch ads or Avengers movies or, I supposed, at the fire station.

Not near me.

So even though I enjoyed the private tour, I tamped down on the adolescent butterflies and reminded myself I didn't get all flushed and breathless over guys like him.

I didn't. Most of the time.

And they didn't get breathless over me.

Any of the time.

I knew where I fell on the social hierarchy. Some things never changed. Even if there was no homecoming queen and king in adult life, people paired off the same way.

Like attracted like.

My brainpower drew me to intellectual people in drab garments because understanding the energy capacity of subatomic particles as they degraded was more important than knowing Jimmy Choo shoes were just as pretty as Louboutins but sometimes went on sale.

I'd admit to knowing a little about shoes.

My fashion-savvy sister Cherry made it her mission to keep me out of what she called the Fashion Dungeon, so I'd tucked away a few sexy dresses and some awesome designer shoes, but I rarely wore anything to work that wasn't practical. What was the point? My colleagues didn't judge me for wearing Chuck Taylor high tops. And my students thought they were cool.

I tipped my chin in Braden's direction, already feeling like I was imposing by living in his spare room. Now he was dragging my boxes around? "You don't need to deal with my stuff. I'll get it later."

"How?" His eyes glinted with a challenge.

I pantomimed carrying boxes. "Like this."

He shook his head. "No. You're not carrying five hundred pounds of books after a car accident. I'm already here. Just let me help. I'm going back to the house to get my truck. Okay?"

There was no dissuading the hero fireman from doing his rescue thing. Besides, I really had no plan for getting my stuff to his house. So I relented.

"Sure. Thank you. That's great." I hated how his gaze rested on me with a combination of pity and concern. I was a self-sufficient problem solver, and it bugged me that his first impression was of a helpless basket case. Even more, I hated that for the moment, I was one.

Amid the beeping of the machines the medics used to run more tests, I heard a motorcycle rev and saw Braden tear off into the distance. Of course, hottie fireman dude rode a motorcycle. And looked like a badass hero doing it.

I turned back to the medic, who had taken a pulse ox clip off my finger and was checking the reading. "Look okay?"

"Blood pressure's elevated, but that's normal in the circumstances. All other vitals look strong. No evidence of a concussion. We're done here, but if you start feeling worse, you should get checked out at the hospital."

"I'd just like to go home, er, to my new home, since I'm moving here today." I didn't want to go to the hospital, mainly because my head hurt, and my neck was stiffening up. I really hoped Braden's spare bedroom came with a bathtub. A little bit of soaking and a decent night's sleep, and I'd be as good as new.

The medic smiled and nodded. "Oh, that's what it was about with Michaels? I heard him say roommate, but it didn't make any sense since he's lived alone—"

"Hey, enough out of you," said a firefighter, whose nametag identified him as Mitch. My head began pounding in earnest, and I didn't bother to wonder what they were talking about. I'd have plenty of time with my new roomie to shoot the breeze and let him tell me all about his loner tendencies.

The medic dabbed some kind of ointment on the chemical burns caused by the airbag and wrapped my forearms in a swath of white bandages. I gritted my teeth against the sting of the ointment. "Sorry," he said. "You're lucky you shielded your face, or the airbag could have broken your nose."

I didn't remember doing that.

Fireman Mitch looked at me and nodded. "Anyway, if you're Braden's roommate, you've got nothing to worry about. He's a trained medic. He'll take decent care of you."

"You guys are friends?" I asked. Captain Obvious.

"Brothers, actually."

Before I could ask him more, a giant black truck pulled up behind my car. I saw Braden's motorcycle boots hit the pavement before he strode around and started loading my stuff into the back of the truck. Those boxes weighed thirty pounds apiece—I'd weighed them on my bathroom scale—but he tossed them around like feather pillows.

It had taken me seventeen trips to get everything out of my house and into my car, and he'd unloaded the whole thing in minutes.

Fireman Mitch waved at Braden, who sauntered over.

That's right, he sauntered.

The man didn't walk like a normal person. His long legs commanded respect as he moved, taking long, fluid strides while his broad shoulders led the way with an easy glide. He had a gait that said, "look at me," and at the same time said, "there's nothing to see here, nothing available to you, anyway."

Fascinating. I wondered if he'd had to master his carefree walk as part of his job. I glanced at the other firemen for comparison, but nope, they did not saunter.

Braden tipped his head in my direction as the medics helped me to my feet. "I swear, I'm fine," I told them. Then I disproved it by taking a clumsy lurch in Braden's direction.

The man's reflexes were sharp. He had his large palms on my shoulders in a split second and turned me to look up at him. I saw a tall, broad-shouldered, human version of a redwood tree. "You sure you're okay?" His gaze bore into mine like he was trying to see more than an acknowledgement of good health.

I nodded. "I'm good. Just a little head rush. Got up too quickly."

The tow truck had cleared a space behind my car and was lifting it onto the flatbed using heavy twin chains. The driver didn't even ask me where I wanted my car taken. Maybe in this town, there was only one auto repair shop. Or maybe he was taking it to the scrap yard. A problem for another day.

"Bye, car." I rolled my eyes at the situation and turned away.

Braden directed me toward his truck and pulled open the passenger door, where a step lowered so I could get in. The truck was gigantic, so I needed the extra step to avoid the kind of gymnastics I only did during the privacy of pole dancing classes I took as a workout. I certainly didn't want Braden lifting me inside.

He shut the door, said goodbye to his colleagues, and jumped into the driver's seat. If there was a step on his side, he didn't use it. He didn't speak much on the drive to his house, so I filled the dead air space with small talk.

"I heard Carolwood has a great rodeo in June. Guess I'll miss that, which is too bad because I do like to look at horses from afar."

"From afar?"

"Meaning I don't like to ride them—it just feels really awkward in my opinion to straddle something with that kind of girth." A garbled cough erupted from his throat, and I felt my face heat. "Do you ride?"

"Just my bike."

"Mountain bike? One of my sisters does that. Well, not really. She hikes. But she's near mountain bikers."

"Motorcycle."

"Oh, sure."

I had more to say, but within minutes we'd reached Braden's house. Then I was stunned speechless.

CHAPTER FOUR

arah

B<small>RADEN</small> <small>LIVED</small> in a house that could have been made from ginger-bread and frosting—it was that adorable.

We'd driven to the end of a short cul de sac with a basketball hoop in the street and a homemade skateboard ramp next door. The neighborhood had traditional prairie-style homes with pitched roofs, lots of windows, and pretty landscaping with flower boxes. I couldn't picture Braden coming home sooty after fighting a fire and weeding his geraniums.

And yet . . . there they were.

When Finn had sold me on his friend's spare bedroom, I'd pictured a box with beige carpet in a small two-bedroom apart-ment. I'd felt grateful. Any sparsely furnished bachelor den was fine by me.

Bare walls? Fine.

Few kitchen utensils? Expected.

My stereotype also included a giant weight set in the garage, some manly power tools, and the pervasive smell of musky body spray. I'll admit my concept came from picturing Finn as a teenager and aging up a few years. I hadn't dated enough in the past decade to know otherwise.

Braden's house had a white picket fence, a mailbox shaped like a dog, and a bird feeder hanging in a tree. I stole a glance at him to assess whether *he* thought the house screamed single man with a chiseled jaw and moody eyes, but unsurprisingly, he didn't say a word.

"This is beyond charming. Have you lived here long?"

He winced a little and looked away. "Bought it three years ago. Did all the work on it back then. Now, I just pretty much live in it." He ran a hand through his hair and sighed.

I realized I knew nothing about him. Maybe he wasn't single. For all I knew, Mrs. Braden stood waiting inside to welcome us home. Just because Finn hadn't mentioned a wife or girlfriend didn't mean anything. Finn tended to have half his brain focused on economic theory and didn't think to mention the obvious.

I stole a look at Braden as he put the truck in park and hopped out. His jeans hugged his legs like lovesick groupies, highlighting a very tight ass and muscular thighs.

I started to edge open the door on my side when he appeared and flung it wide, further proving his strength and land-speed capabilities.

He extended a hand to me, even though the helpful footstep lay at my feet. "Oh, thanks." In my thirty-three years, no one had ever offered me a hand out of a car before. Granted, he probably thought I bore some residual aches from the car accident, but still, it was sweet.

With a nod, he helped me down and put a hand on my lower back, walking me down the path that led to the bright yellow front door. His hand felt solid and warm, reassuring. It also sent a completely inappropriate surge of heat down my spine, ending between my legs.

Wait, what?

I did my best to ignore my body, which was telling me to lean into his hand. Instead, I focused on the neat row of terra cotta pots filled with succulents and how they tied the purple leaf plum trees into a cohesive color palate. I *really* focused. So much so that it took a second to realize all my boxes were still in the truck.

I glanced back toward the truck. "Oh, I should grab my stuff."

Braden shook his head, and I noticed his shoulders relaxed the closer we got to the front door. "Later. Let's get you settled. I'll bring it up."

"Oh, you don't have to do that. I'm happy to drag my own boxes out of the truck, really." I glanced back again, almost longingly. I wanted to move in and get settled. I also felt guilty about him helping me so much.

"You were just in a car accident. You're not carrying boxes," he said, coming around and fixing his dark eyes on me. My head ached, and I didn't feel like arguing. After unlocking the front door, he moved aside to let me walk in first.

Stepping into the entryway, I noted the faint smell of vanilla and a brief stillness, which was immediately punctuated by a stampede of feet sliding along the hardwood floors and the overjoyed whimper of a dog. A second later, a big furry golden retriever wagged its tail in front of me and pawed my legs.

"Bella, down . . ." Braden said in a stern dog-trainer voice. When his pup obeyed, he scratched her behind the ears and ruffled the fur on top of her head. "Good girl. Such a good girl." His voice went up an octave with his praise. Then he got down on his knees and lavished his dog friend with love. Maybe he was just slow to warm to humans.

"Sarah, meet Bella. Short for Lunabella Trouble Michaels. Four years old, still thinks she's a puppy, and kind of possessive of me," his voice rumbled. Bella began licking his chin as though he were covered in gravy.

"Trouble's her middle name. Someone a Bobby Vinton fan?"

His eyebrow quirked. "You know the song?"

I shrugged and smiled at Bella. "She looks too sweet to be trouble."

"When she goes through your trash and drags it down the stairs, you'll see it differently."

I stroked the top of her head, and she lifted her paw to shake hands. "Aw, she's adorable. Did you get her as a puppy?" Her soft ears felt like velvet.

He looked away when he answered. "Rescued her three years ago after a fire burned down her owners' home. They couldn't keep her at their new apartment, so we took her in. They still visit her when they can."

I caught his use of "we," but he'd seemed a little guarded, so I decided to focus on the dog for now. "Perks of the job, I guess. But also sad for them. Does that happen a lot, fires displacing pets?"

He nodded and ran a hand over his scruff. "More than you'd think." He cast a wary look in my direction. "Finn thought you'd be okay with a dog. This one's all fur. You're not allergic?"

"Nope. Love dogs."

He gave a quick nod. "Like I said, she's possessive, so don't be offended if she ignores you and clings to me."

"Aw, Bella. You won't ignore me. We girls need to stick together, right?" Bella's tongue rolled out and she licked my hand.

Braden's smile stayed fixed on his dog, but he tipped his head toward the rest of the house. "Lemme give you a quick tour." He rose to his feet, and I followed him as he walked me through a nicely furnished living room with overstuffed gray couches and navy pillows. There was no sign that a human bottom had made a dent in any of it.

On the coffee table, a painted ceramic bowl sat next to a stack of architecture books. In a corner, an upright piano stood with its bench pushed in tight, no sheet music on the stand.

Despite appearing untouched, the room looked cozy. In fact, it begged for use.

We moved down a short hallway past a staircase. Bella followed dutifully behind with a ball in her mouth. Instead of heading upstairs, we kept going into a great room where the modern kitchen and den were divided by a countertop island.

Judging by the flatscreen TV and the rumpled pillows, I guessed this was where Braden spent most of his time. He had a few magazines shoved onto the shelf of the rustic wood coffee table, sleek appliances plugged into the kitchen outlets, and Bella's food and water bowls near the French doors that led to the yard.

Braden pointed to the left. "Kitchen. Make yourself at home. Eat whatever you want. Don't worry about moving my stuff around to make room in the fridge . . ."

As if to demonstrate, he opened the refrigerator, moved a carton of milk to the shelf on the door, and left some space on the top shelf. "Just . . . do whatever you normally do."

"Thanks," I peeked into the fridge, noticing a six-pack of beer, several kinds of mustard, and a bowl of apples among myriad takeout containers. "Looks like you and I have similar eating habits. Takeout and fruit."

"Hmph. Yeah, sometimes I get lazy. And I'm at the station one out of every three nights."

"Oh, really? You sleep there?" I had no idea what kind of schedules firefighters kept.

"Yeah, twenty-four hours on, forty-eight off. But I also go in sometimes for day shifts. Anyway, you'll have the place to yourself some nights. Plus, I'm out a lot in the evenings." He left that tidbit hanging, but I assumed he meant he dated. Or hung with friends from work.

Fine by me. I was an independent person. And after living alone in Berkeley for the past few years, I felt relieved to have a roommate who'd be gone every third night.

Braden ran a hand through his hair, which drew my gaze there. He had good hair, thick and dark with some wave to it, and rumpling it just made him look better.

I rolled my eyes at myself, unable to stop ogling his various parts. Apparently.

From his comment about cooking for one, I concluded he didn't have a wife. There could still be a girlfriend—and let's be honest, from looking at him, he likely had a girlfriend or ten—but this wasn't going to be a *Three's Company* situation.

Bella sat at his feet with the ball in her mouth, eyes fixed on him with her tail wagging. He opened the back door, grabbed the ball from her mouth, and chucked it across the yard. Bella flew after it. I expected her to reappear a second later to continue the game, but she didn't.

"Where'd she go?" I craned my neck, but she'd gone off behind a row of hedges.

"She likes to bury stuff out there. That ball will be gone for a few days, then she'll dig it up and something else will disappear. She's not much of a retriever. Well, she does retrieve, she just doesn't relinquish the stuff she retrieves unless she feels like it." He gave me the hint of an almost-smile.

I made a mental note—the dog makes him happy. If conversation got awkward, I'd bring up Bella.

He continued his tour, pointing to the patio and the grass beyond it. "The yard's a nice place to sit if you have free time. I keep intending to build a fire pit out there but haven't gotten around to it."

"Free time, outdoors, check."

I took a look around the kitchen, which was clean but not overly tidy—there were dishes in the sink and dishtowels lying around, but nothing that screamed that he was either an incurable neat freak or a pigpen disaster. Straight down the middle—kind of like me.

His eyes roamed the room, fixing on the dishes, scanning the clean marble countertop, nodding at the pile of dog toys, almost like he was seeing the room through my eyes. He pointed at the TV. "No idea what you like to watch, but I'm pretty easy."

I held up a hand. "Okay, stop. Please. I know you're trying to be a good host, but really? I can eat all your food and move your stuff around? You're not weirdly protective of your mustard or something? You have no TV preferences? Come on, no one is that easy going." I beckoned him with my hand. "Give me something. An Australian-rules football obsession, cheesy reality dating shows? Do you sneak tabloids to read about English royals? Watch the Puppy Bowl instead of the Super Bowl? I promise I won't blab to your dudes at the fire station, so just spill it, roomie."

I had no idea if it was the ridiculousness of thinking of me as his roomie or the obvious gauntlet I'd thrown down over mustard, but Braden's face cracked into the first grin since finding out I was Finn's sister. And at the sight of his beautiful smile, I outright blushed.

If he noticed, he gave no indication. "Okay, fair enough. You might as well know that I'm a nut for March Madness, and I'll watch every game I can. But I watch some of them at the station, so I'm not like a cave bat here all day and night."

It was the most he'd said at one time since we'd met. "Okay then. I like basketball, but I don't know the college teams well enough to make picks for the tournament. Unless Cal makes it in, then I'm all about filling out a bracket and rooting for them to the death."

"They look good this year—maybe we'll have to have a little competition if they're in it," he challenged, rubbing his hands together, eyes ablaze.

"Competition? Oh yeah, now you're speaking my love language." As soon as I said it, the slight smile I'd earned disappeared, and he turned slightly away from me.

Was he shy? Grumpy? Socially awkward? Even though I barely knew him, it pained me that he kept shutting down.

So I backpedaled. "Anyway, I like basketball well enough. And the occasional episode of *Top Chef*. And *Bake Off*. Ooh, and *Chopped*. Okay, I'm a little obsessed with all cooking shows."

"Yet I hear you don't cook," he challenged.

I gave him a side-eye. "Finn told you that?"

"He might have mentioned." His smile returned as more of a smirk.

I folded my arms over my chest and jutted one hip to the side. "I *can* cook. I mostly don't cook for one because that's a waste of time, but I have serious salad skills."

He chuckled. "Don't worry. I don't cook that much either. I don't think it's a character flaw." He went over and collected stuffed animal carcasses with the fluff strewn everywhere and squeaky balls, dropping them in a basket by the door.

"I cook," I insisted sternly, narrowing my eyes at him.

"I believe you." His shrug made me think he didn't.

"I'll prove it. I'll cook you dinner, and you'll see I give those *Top Chef*s a run for their arugula." I tipped my head to the side and grinned. Besides having something to prove, I wanted to pull my weight around here.

He sighed, rubbing a hand over his face. "You don't have to do that. Really."

"I want to, and I will." I narrowed my eyes so he'd see the seriousness. When I set my mind on something, it would happen. He might as well understand that about me.

"Fine. I look forward to it," he conceded.

He motioned me to follow him upstairs. On the gray-carpeted landing, we faced several closed doors. The first opened to a laundry room. "There are towels here and sheets, but everything in your room is clean."

"Great. I like a clean towel," I chirped.

He pushed the door open to the next room and pointed. "Gym. Has everything. Feel free to use the equipment if you're into it." He was almost awkward in his deadpan presentation.

"I'm not into it. In fact, I hate it, but I know it would be good for me to use all the heavy pieces of metal, pain contraptions, and vomit machines."

"Vomit machines?"

"It's how I think of treadmills and bikes." He blinked a couple times, and I nodded enthusiastically. "Awesome, glad they're so handy. I won't even have to leave the house to suffer."

"You don't have to work out if you don't want to," he whispered kindly like he was trying not to frighten an insane person.

"Okay," I whispered back.

He led me to a third door and swung it open, then took a few steps back and pointed from the hallway. "Bed, dresser. Bathroom's over there. Little desk . . ."

It was no tiny beige box. "It's perfect." I couldn't hide my grin. The window shades were pulled high, and the warm afternoon light flooded the room. On the bed, a fluffy white comforter with a cream-colored throw blanket tempted me to dive among pillows and sleep for a week.

The desk was a slab of barn wood on two metal trestles, and at the foot of the bed, a brown steamer trunk with vintage straps completed the look. "This room is gorgeous. I can't thank you enough. It's really great."

Braden swallowed hard and crossed his arms defensively. "Glad you like it." I noticed his eyes, a little red with the beginnings of dark circles forming beneath them. His face was a mirror of how I felt, suddenly drained, probably the residual effects of the accident.

I wanted to talk to him and break through the awkwardness a little more. I wanted to play with his dog and find the cooking channels on his TV, but my body wouldn't cooperate. We stared at each other, both of us glassy-eyed.

"You should really stand in the shower and get some wet heat on your neck and back. It'll help your spine from locking up tomorrow. You have to be at work all day, right?"

I nodded, my body aching in agreement. "Yeah, I need to be there early. Shower's a good idea. I can do that tonight."

"You should do it now." He stared down at me, stern like an older brother. Maybe he thought this was how Finn would treat me.

"Okay." I felt too exhausted to argue. "I'll do it now. Soon as I get my stuff from your truck."

He blocked my exit from the room and shook his head. "I'll get it. You relax." He backed out of the room, and seconds later I heard his footsteps on the stairs. I heard Bella scamper up to him when he got down, and his voice went up an octave when he lavished her with attention. "Who's my good girl? Yes, you are. Want to come out to the truck?"

I was glad he had Bella in his life. I couldn't fight the feeling that there was something sad about him, and it made my heart ache, even if I didn't understand why.

I texted Finn.

Me: Hey, made it to Carolwood.

I didn't overexplain my grand entry into town. Finn would have a field day lecturing me about my driving.

Finn: Great! Getting settled?

Me: Yeah, about that. Anything I should know about Braden? Dark secrets?

Finn didn't answer immediately, and I stared at the phone, conjuring imaginary responses that confirmed my worst fears. Then I saw blinking dots.

Finn: None I'm at liberty to reveal. Why?

I had to put it delicately. They went back a long way, and I didn't want to throw Braden—and therefore myself—under the bus before I'd even unpacked a bag.

Me: He seems a little bummed out. I just don't want to cramp his style.

Finn: Lol. That won't be a problem. He has no style.

Me: Seriously. Don't leave me in the dark. You know I'll put my foot in my mouth.

Finn: He's fine. It's been two years. But if you're concerned, just ask him. Get to know your new roomie.

I could picture Finn smiling as he typed. He thought the idea of me having a roommate was so cute and funny. Jerk.

Me: What's been two years?

Finn: Talk. To. Him.

Fine. But I knew if he was anything like my brother, Braden wouldn't give me a straight answer.

CHAPTER FIVE

raden

I WASN'T TRYING to be a jerk.

I was trying to be a kind and polite host. But when I opened the door to the spare room, I nearly hyperventilated. In hindsight, it hadn't been a great idea to wait until Sarah arrived to blow the cobwebs off that room—the room where Ellie had screwed her boyfriend before breaking off our engagement.

Staying in the same house with her at the end and knowing she had no interest in marriage had nearly broken me. Once she moved out for good, I'd shut the door—literally—on everything that reminded me of her. If I'd been smarter, I'd have sold the house and moved. But a part of me didn't want to admit I'd gone to pieces, so I held it together and made the place mean something to me without her. Except for that room. I'd had no reason to go in there, so it sat like a shrine to a dead person.

Having Sarah as a roommate might breathe new life into the stodgy quarters. She was nothing if not bright and cheerful, despite my morose grumblings in her presence. I'd have to do better. She deserved a decent roommate who didn't act like a stiff bore, carrying a torch for a woman who was long gone.

And she deserved a roommate who didn't hit on her, no matter how much I liked looking at her pretty eyes and the pink in her cheeks when she blushed. I didn't need to mess with a smart, gorgeous woman who was out of my league. Been there, done that, put my heart through a meat grinder.

In the morning, she'd go to work and get busy, and life would be fine. Six months would fly by.

I mulled these thoughts three times over as I carried her boxes from the truck to where I stacked them outside her room.

"So, could I buy you some dinner tonight as a thank you?" Sarah asked as she came down the stairs. She hadn't showered.

Stubborn woman.

"Aw, you don't have to do that," I said, though I'd skipped lunch, and the mere mention of food had my stomach growling.

She waved a hand. "I'm not offering because I think I have to do it. I just figured I'm going to get pretty busy with work, and this might be our only chance to get to know each other a little bit. Don't you want to know the person who's freeloading in your spare bedroom?" Her pale eyes caught me, and I lost the battle. All I wanted to do was Google seas from around the world until I figured out an exact match for the color. Probably somewhere in the Caribbean where the sand would dust our feet like sugar.

Good lord, get a grip.

I nodded. "Sure, we can do that." She was right—we both worked a lot, and I should take the time to learn a little about her. One dinner would be harmless. "But let's get one thing straight. You don't owe me anything. I have the bedroom, no one was using it, and I'm glad to put it to use. So none of this 'freeloading' business. I'm happy to have you in my bedroom."

I could feel the heat rise on the back of my neck, and I squeezed my eyes shut. "I mean, my spare room is all yours."

She grinned. "I knew what you meant. It's all good."

It did not seem all good.

"You know, the only reason I plowed into the fire truck was all the wine bars," Sarah explained as we drove through town, and I pointed out various things—hardware store, grocery store, wine bar, wine bar.

"Why, did you stop off for a drink?" I eyed her suspiciously. None of my guys had said anything about her blood alcohol levels.

Her eyes went huge. "No. Never. I mean, I was fixated on how many wine places there are in a small radius. It's cool."

"Yeah. Surprises people who think all California wine comes from the Napa Valley."

She put a hand on her chest with a mock-gasp. "What blatant grapism. I'll admit I didn't learn much about Carolwood. I was too busy nerding out about lasers at the lab to research things to do around here for fun. Do you think I'm a grapist?" She crinkled her nose, and I couldn't help being charmed by her complete lack of pretense.

"I do not."

"Good. I'll have you know I'm an equal opportunity wine drinker, and to prove it, I'll drink all the wine with dinner."

"All of it?" I asked. She was adorable, which didn't bode well for my leaving her alone plan.

She waggled her eyebrows. "Well, I can't have you rescuing me twice in a day, so maybe I'll behave." Yup, she was going to test every bit of my will. Fortunately, fighting fires had gifted me with a lot of it.

I had the Uber drop us at Copeland Park and gave Sarah a history tour as we passed various shops on the way to dinner.

"There's a farmer's market here every Thursday." I pointed to the park that sat in front of the Copeland Library. Not wanting to remind her of the accident, I made sure to take us on a route that didn't go down that street.

"Hiya Braden," intoned a soft female voice as we passed a clothing store. I turned to see Anna, a preschool teacher I'd gone on one date with over a month ago. She flipped her blond hair over her shoulder, unleashing a cloud of perfume.

"Oh, hey. Good to see you." I didn't stop to chat, and I didn't bore Sarah with how I knew her. We continued past a few more shops, a nail salon, and a pub.

Carolwood wasn't big. In five minutes, we'd covered most of it. "This is Blacksmith Corner," I said, pointing to the iron arch over the entryway that said the words. The square had an open court-yard and a couple wineries and restaurants. "It was an auto shop a bunch of years ago, before I moved to town, and before that—"

"Lemme guess . . . a blacksmith shop?" She nudged me with her elbow, and I stiffened at the heat that coursed through my veins.

"Yeah, I think so." I picked up my pace to the restaurant.

We found an outdoor table at Carol's on the Corner, a wine bar with a brick façade and lots of windows. I knew the owners, and the place had a good, casual vibe—a bunch of mismatched tables and strings of tiny lights. Nothing about the place screamed 'date night,' and they had tapas and an awesome meat and cheese appetizer.

"So . . . wine." I signaled the waiter to put an order in right away. Maybe that would help the awkwardness. I picked out a bottle of red zinfandel I'd had before and exhaled a choppy breath. My rapidly-thumping heart clued me in to a feeling I hadn't experienced before.

Sarah made me nervous.

Of course she did. With barely any makeup and her hair twisted into a knot, she couldn't have looked less pretentious, and yet her subtle beauty floored me. But that wasn't the source of the nerves. I'd dated plenty of attractive women. She made me nervous because she was smart, and if anything revved my motor, it was intellect.

I inhaled a deep breath to slow my heart rate and focused on the menu.

"You good with sharing a few things?" Sarah pressed her fingers in three strategic spots on the menu like she was afraid the dishes would disappear if she didn't hold them down.

I shrugged. "Maybe. But we may not like the same things." Couples shared food. Platonic roommates who planned on staying that way should not.

She leaned back and squinted at me. "It says right here that all dishes are meant to be shared." Her other hand pointed to the top of the menu. I knew she had a thing for books, but did the woman have to read every word of everything she saw?

I put up my hands in surrender. "Sure. What do you see that looks good?"

"The cheesy bread. Do you like goat cheese? And the feta and fig jam and the artichoke dip, the sliders . . . Ooh, and the antipasto!"

I started to laugh. "So, pretty much the whole menu? I can see now why you want to share."

She raised an eyebrow. "Oh, I could probably eat all of that myself, but I'm *willing* to share. Up to you."

"Fine. Done. Let's get all of that." I pushed my menu away, eager to watch this petite woman put away the mountain of food she proposed.

"You sure? Is there anything you want? It shouldn't all be my decision." She chewed her bottom lip like she felt guilty about commandeering the menu.

I shook my head. "I like all of it. Honestly, there isn't a bad thing on the menu, so let's go big." Mercifully, the waiter returned with the wine and opened the bottle for me to taste it. "It's fine," I said, indicating he should fill our glasses.

Sarah held hers up for a toast. "To roommates who don't drive each other crazy." Her smile was already driving me crazy, but I clinked her glass anyway.

"How do you like it?" I nodded toward her glass after she'd taken a sip.

She took another sip, rolling it around on her tongue and licking her bottom lip. I almost growled.

"It's nice. I like it." Her voice suddenly sounded much more sultry.

I cleared my throat. "Are you a big wine drinker?" Normally, I brought my A-game to dinner with a woman, and tonight I felt lucky to string three words into a sentence.

She held her thumb and finger an inch apart. "Small wine drinker. I like it, don't know much about it. Maybe I'll learn a few things while I'm here. Seems like I could find a wine grower or ten if I look hard enough." She glanced around as if to find proof of that, which came easily with three wine shops in the surrounding area.

"I finally gave it a try a few years ago." I shuddered at the stiffness in my voice.

"Oh, right. I saw the grape arbor in your yard. Though you'd be hard-pressed to get a bottle out of that." Then she blushed. "Oh my god, worst pun!"

I pressed my lips together to hide the sheer delight I found in her. My grape arbor wasn't what I meant, but I didn't need to tell her I'd bought a few acres and planted a vineyard. We wouldn't be taking any romantic drives through the wine country, so what difference did it make?

Carol's owner came by with an appetizer, one of the few we hadn't ordered. "Hey Captain, always a pleasure." He dropped off a plate of black olive hummus, pita chips, and a breadbasket. "On the house."

"Hey, good to see you. You know you never have to do that, but thanks." We'd known each other for years, and I'd gotten called to more than a few kitchen fires there.

He pretended to rescind his offer, picking up the plates. "You telling me how to run my restaurant? Or just trying to impress your date?"

Sarah put her hand on the arm holding the food and piped up immediately. "Wait, not so fast with that. And I'm not his date. I'm the sister of a friend, and I'm crashing in his spare bedroom for a bit."

"Oh yeah? Well, welcome to town. Thanks for coming out to see us." He introduced himself and gave Sarah his card, which had a twenty percent discount for any wine in the store. She seemed delighted. Then he put the plate on the table and went to chat with another customer.

As soon as he was out of earshot, Sarah pinned me with a sharp stare. "He called you 'Captain.' And since I haven't seen you in any Marvel movies, I'm thinking...Captain and Tennille cover band? Or do you sail the seven seas?" Her wide eyes sparkled with mischief.

Why did she have to be smart and gorgeous *and* cute? I swallowed hard. "It's my job. I'm Captain at Engine 97," I told her.

She rearranged her wine and water glasses to make better room for the hummus to sit in the middle between us. "Is that something different than being a fireman?"

It made me laugh. "We don't refer to ourselves as firemen. Firefighter is the term we use. I'm a paramedic as well, but we have other guys with that training, so I don't do much of it anymore."

"Oh, firefighting and medical knowledge? I have tons of questions. Is that okay, or do you not like talking about work?"

"I don't mind talking about it. What do you want to know?" I rarely talked about it, mainly because most of the people I spent time with were people from work.

Every shade of blue in Sarah's eyes shimmered like a heatwave. "I want to know everything." Warmth spread in my chest at the way she said it, guileless and honest. "Then I'll return the favor if you want." She scooped a bite of hummus into her mouth, and I stared fixated when her tongue slipped out to lick the corner of her lips. "Ask me anything. I love talking about my work, but I hate talking about myself. So if someone asks about me, I pivot, so we end up talking about work instead. Little peek inside my brain." She bit into a chip.

"Why don't you like talking about yourself?"

She tilted her head to the side and blinked a couple times. "I'm still a work in progress. No conclusions to draw yet."

I'd never heard a person describe herself that way. I wanted to know more, but quizzing her didn't seem wise when she'd outright said she didn't want to talk about herself. Maybe once I knew her better.

Her pale eyes flickered with intensity, and I felt a little like an interrogation subject, but strangely, I didn't mind. "So to start, what do you have to do to become a captain? And how'd you pick this career? And why can't I call you a fireman? Sorry, I guess that's three questions," she laughed.

Before I could answer, Sarah's gaze shot past my shoulder, and I turned to see what caught her eye.

"Seems like they're trying to get your attention." Sure enough, on the other end of the patio, two women—both drunk, judging from the way they held each other up—were whispering to each other and burning a hole through Sarah with their stares."

I adjusted my chair to block them from her view and ignored them. "I know one of them. Not well. Don't worry about it."

"Someone you dated?" She shot me a knowing glance.

I shrugged. "Something like that. Okay, in answer to your first question, like every job, there are levels. Everyone starts out probationary—we call them probies. It's scut work, extra cleaning, the worst hours, et cetera."

"Do you haze them?"

"What?"

"Like fraternity pledges. They have to do all kinds of things to prove they're worthy. Sorry, I work at a university. I see a lot of pledge hazing."

"Well, no. Not in the way you mean. We are master practical jokers, and most have us have been locked out at night in our underwear at one point or another, but we don't make them eat onions soaked in Tabasco sauce or chug beer . . ."

"Sounds like you're familiar . . ." She waggled her eyebrows and smiled.

I gave a small salute. "Zeta Psi, UCLA, at your service."

"Nice. Okay, so once you're done being a probie, then what?"

I took another sip of wine. "Then you move through the ranks. First firefighter, then if you specialize, you can be an AO—apparatus operator—which means you're a driver engineer or operate some of the equipment and pump water."

She sat up straighter. This wasn't idle small talk to her—she was a knowledge sponge. The sparkle in her eyes told me she wanted me to keep going.

"Captain or lieutenant is the next rung up, but an engineer can pull rank and be acting captain if need be. Our AO was doing that earlier today until I showed up and confused everything. I probably shouldn't have done that, but it was hard to leave when I saw it was my unit. Anyway, captain is when you start moving more into supervision and management, but I still get to work every fire and emergency. The main thing that interested me was being able to control a scene and still do the work."

"So you like control." She winked at me.

"I do."

She raised an eyebrow. "Me too. But we'll get to that later." Her lips twisted into a sassy smile.

My mind immediately wandered to what she meant, envisioning her controlling me in all sorts of sexy ways. I took a deep breath and refocused on my firefighter lesson, but the words came out through gritted teeth.

"Anyhow, that's why I like being captain."

She nodded, seemingly satisfied with my explanation. "Okay, next question. Can I please call you a fireman?"

"Why do you want to call me a fireman so badly?" I ran a hand through my hair.

She took a big sip of wine and exhaled. "Finn had a fireman costume one Halloween with this awesome hat. *Fireman* sounds a little less threatening than calling someone a firefighter, which, for me, conjures all kinds of images of rushing into fiery buildings and burning forests and battling blazes."

I cast her a side-eye. "Well, yeah, but . . . going into burning places and fighting fires is literally what we do."

"Sure, I know that, but the image of running into an inferno is terrifying. It seems more dangerous and apt to get a person killed than my image of a fireman, which is Finn in costume playing with a hook and ladder truck."

"But . . . that's the job." I couldn't figure her out. She wasn't naïve, but she seemed to want to live in a kinder, gentler reality.

"I understand that, I do. But calling you a fireman sounds more benign. Firefighting sounds like something that would put you in danger, and I'll sleep better at night if I know you're safe."

It was charming. Also curious. Yesterday she'd never met me, and now she was worried about the dangers of a job I'd had for over ten years? "So you're saying you don't want me to get hurt?"

"Of course I don't. I realize I don't know you at all. But . . . no." She shrugged. "Please don't get hurt. I wouldn't . . ." She blinked hard and shook her head. "Look, I know what firefighting is, and I understand that you don't play with plastic firetrucks. Your job is real. And important. And now that I know you, I want you to stay safe, that's all. Promise me?"

Her genuine concern tugged at an errant scrap of my heart that had been boxed up and shoved on a back shelf for . . . years. I couldn't remember a time when someone put it that way, just laid out concern about my safety, and it stirred something up that was probably better left dormant. Even my ex had never put it that way, and I'd wanted to marry her.

"I promise. I'll do my best." I had a resting heart rate of fifty-five, and this was the second time this evening she had my heart thudding like I'd just hit the treadmill.

It unnerved me that this woman I barely knew had gotten real so quickly.

Because I didn't hate it.

Rather than think about what it meant or give it any sort of weight at all, I changed the subject. "Hey, how's your mom doing? I haven't seen her in a while."

"She's good . . . oh—" Her eyes got wide when the server came over with a shit ton of food. "Maybe I overdid it on the ordering."

Plates of charcuterie with olives and cheeses and dried fruit were placed on the table next to pulled pork sliders and cheesy bread. I'd lost track of what else we'd ordered, but I was pretty sure there was more to come.

Sarah blushed at the amount of food, and I found myself staring at her wide eyes as they took in the full plates that fought for space on our table. I allowed my gaze to linger on her face and take in her pretty mouth and long lashes while she was too preoccupied to notice.

Her skin was flushed and accented by soft curves from her cheekbones and a dimple in one cheek. It popped when she smiled. The pink swell of her lips that were already a little stained from the wine made me want to take a bite out of them. Right before I ran my tongue down the milky skin of her throat.

Stop. Just . . . stop.

Maybe if I told myself that enough times, the stubborn piece of my brain imagining all kinds of impossible things would fucking listen.

"You said you like to talk about work, so how about you tell me some things," I said, pulling a breadstick from the basket and breaking it in half. I didn't know much about physics, so I felt at a loss for what to ask. "What will you be doing at the lab?"

"Oh, you're going from zero right to a hundred. I thought you'd ask about my teaching job first."

"Sure, start with that. I majored in English, so everything I remember about physics comes from studying in high school with your brother."

She grinned. "So smug and arrogant, wasn't he? I'd ask him to help me with pre-algebra and he'd say something like, 'I'll try to get back to that simpler mindset.' Please tell me he annoyed you too."

"Finn . . . he was smart, sure, but he never used it to make anyone else feel dumb. He just didn't hide it."

"Of course he didn't. Guys don't do that."

"You saying that girls do?"

"Of course. If you're a high school girl and you're smart, like smarter than average, you have a choice. You can be smart and alienate ninety percent of your peers, go on very few dates, win lots of awards, and find your true calling in college. Or you can hide what you know, work hard to fit in, and have a good time."

"Which one were you?" I'd have put good money on the first one. She didn't seem like one to suffer fools, so I couldn't imagine her hiding.

She raised her eyebrows like the answer was obvious. "The second one."

"Really? You didn't let people know you were smart?" I frowned, disliking that women felt they had to do that.

She took a bite of a slider, and a little drip of barbecue sauce ran down her chin. It was all I could do not to reach over and wipe it away. Or lick it. I was evolved in my feminist thinking, but come on.

A second later, she caught it with a napkin and smiled. "I was smart quietly. I studied and did well on my assignments and the tests, but if I knew the answer in class, I kept it to myself. I never told people what grades I got. And I had a life—dates, stupid teenage fun, broke curfew, got grounded. All of that. Then I went to college and found other physicists who were way smarter than me, and I needed to work to keep up. I didn't give a crap what people thought anymore. I wanted to be a scientist. And here we are."

I had a feeling it wasn't quite as easy as that. "So you majored in physics?" She nodded. "Then you went to grad school?"

"Yes."

"Then what?"

"I've spent the last ten years studying and working on my PhD, then studying and publishing and teaching. It's been tough." She frowned at the recollection. Then she perked up and raised a finger in the air. "But! This fellowship at the lab could change everything. I'll be doing work in a new area of physics, which means I'll publish the shit out of whatever I discover, and that will earn me tenure track."

"And that's what you want? To be a tenured professor?"

"Yes. It's been my dream since I started grad school. I know it sounds dorky, but . . ." She tipped her hands to the sides and pointed her fingers at herself.

"You're not a dork. Tell me what you'll be doing at the lab."

This was a helluva lot more interesting than most dinners I had, which admittedly were just a small talk prelude to sex. If we even bothered with the dinner.

She shook her head and waved her hands like she'd rather shut down the line of questioning. "You're kind to ask, but we don't have to get into that whole thing. Trust me, it's a snooze if you're not interested in lasers and nuclear materials."

"Try me," I said, beckoning with my hand.

She took a deep breath and hit me with an enthusiastic grin. "Okay, so, the lab has a visiting scientists program, where they bring in people with specialized knowledge to apply it in a real-world study. So I'm doing something called diode laser-assisted friction stir welding."

My brain tapped out. That was too much science.

Not to mention that at the word welding, my brain was off and running, picturing Jennifer Beals in *Flashdance*, welding in a tight tank top before leaving work to dance in a club. "Um, okay, so what does it mean you're actually doing?"

She laughed. "Well, it's literally welding. You know, fusing two sheets of metal together, but the novelty is the process. I'm a physicist, but I also studied mechanical engineering. Then I got into friction stir welding, which is a way of joining two pieces without melting the metal. But the lab has these incredibly powerful lasers, and I want to use them to weld more efficiently."

The way she said it made it sound like she was adjusting the seasoning in a bread recipe, and I knew she was downplaying her intelligence. My mind was officially blown.

It was also still very preoccupied with *Flashdance*, only now I pictured *Sarah* welding in a tank top. "And just so I understand, what's the reason you need to fuse the metal without melting it?"

"It makes the bond stronger, and it allows us to join different types of metal alloys. Some of the private space exploration companies are really interested."

"So the work you're doing could end up in a rocket?"

She shrugged. "Maybe. Could be cool, right?"

"Wow. Yes. Very cool. I'm impressed, Sarah."

She blushed, and the creep of pink that spread over her cheeks made me want to brush my fingers over them. "Anyway, that's why I'm here, roomie."

I held my hands in my lap, far away from her cheeks. "Awesome. Well, it's a great place. I hope you like it. Lots to do here, outdoorsy and good weather most of the time." I speared some meat and cheese from the platter in front of us. "Don't know if you have any hobbies."

She nodded. "I do. I may have to take a break from it for a bit while I'm out here, but normally when I have a light day on campus, I go to a class . . ."

I waited.

"It's . . . pole dancing."

I stopped breathing, but at least I didn't choke.

Nodding, I took a sip of my wine to block my face, which I was pretty sure had turned the shade of a beet.

"So, like *Flashdance*? Welder by day, dancer by night?" I barked out, feeling a stirring in my pants that was wholly inappropriate for my roomie, who'd been talking about diode lasers a minute earlier.

She's a goddamn pole dancer.

She chuckled and crossed her arms over her chest as though trying to keep me from picturing her dancing. "Excellent movie reference. But no, that's not even close to what I do."

It hardly mattered. My brain was stuck.

Like a white-hot strobe had blinded me to everything except Sarah wearing lingerie and grinding on a pole under hot lights. For me.

Stop picturing it. Fuck!

"Cool," I finally managed to say with a straight face. Like it meant nothing.

She nodded. Like it meant nothing.

Then she spread some brie cheese on a cracker and took a bite. I choked out an excuse and went to the bathroom to get a grip.

This will be okay. It will. It has to be.

In the bathroom, I splashed some cold water on my face and took a hard look at myself in the mirror. What was happening? I hadn't been this jacked up over a woman anytime in the past two years. My emotions had been buried in caverns so deep I felt confident they were gone for good. I was fine with that.

It made no sense. Or . . . maybe it did. I've always been competitive as fuck. If I'm told I can't have something, I want it all the more and do anything in my power to make it mine.

That had to be what was happening here.

It was all in my head. I knew she was off-limits, so the competitive motherfucker in me started bucking against that. I just needed to get my head together and think of her like any other human who happened to be using my second bedroom.

When I got back to the table, Sarah looked up at me with a thin slice of Parma ham twirled around her fork and put the bit into her mouth. I had no defensible reason to focus on her lips or the soft contour of her jaw while she chewed.

She swallowed and smiled at me. "I figured I should get a head start on eating while you were gone. In case you had more questions."

"Good plan. Maybe we should focus on the food for a few minutes, or we could be here all night."

I bit into a slider and closed my eyes at how delicious the slow-roasted meat tasted on the brioche bun. Who needed to cook when someone else could make food that tasted like this? It was how I'd become addicted to takeout and why I rarely ate at home anymore. That, and I spent a lot of time at work.

Sarah finished the last of the cheesy bread and wiped her lips gingerly on a napkin before looking right at me with those gorgeous eyes. "This is weird, right? It's not just me?"

I tilted my head, trying to read her expression and decipher her meaning. "Could you be specific?

She waved her hands between us. "This. Us. We're in our thirties and we're roommates. I don't know about you, but I haven't had a roommate for about ten years. Does it freak you out a little bit?"

Yes, but not for the reasons she meant.

I shrugged. "Yes, it's . . . new. But we're both adults. I think it will be . . . fine."

"Well, okay . . . great." Her eyes came back to me. She leaned her cheek on one palm, elbow resting on the table.

I wanted to know more about her. "So in Berkeley, you live by yourself? With a boyfriend, or what?"

Subtle.

Her eyes had such a dreamy, pale blue cast, I had a hard time not staring again. She shook her head. "Nope. Neither. I don't date. No dates, no kissing. It's not the right time in my life for that. I have a plan."

The corner of my mouth hitched up in amusement. "Are you on a fixed calendar? When's go time?"

Those eyes pinned me like I'd missed out on understanding some law of the universe. "When I'm on tenure track and I've checked some career boxes. I like to have a plan. Probably why science suits me."

"What does science have to do with dating?"

"I just mean science is comforting because it has expected outcomes. I try to plan my life so I know what to do and what to expect. Right now, that's work, not dating or relationships. No unexpected detours."

"I get that. I don't do relationships either." For entirely different reasons. But hearing her lay out her "plans" only reinforced that I needed to stop gawking and let her pursue her career in peace.

Between my schedule and hers, we'd probably rarely see each other. Six months would fly by, and we'd have another dinner like this before I sent her home to Berkeley. I had plenty of women in my life. There was no sense in getting worked up over her.

She hadn't moved her cheek from her hand, and for a second, I saw her eyes droop. They shot open, and she jerked to an upright position, frowning. "Wow. I don't know what happened. I just suddenly got really, really tired."

"It's trauma. Mental, physical. Your body went through a lot, even though you've been doing your best to pretend it didn't."

She nodded slowly. "Personality trait. I like to be in control. So if I don't like the way something feels, I push it away. I didn't want to feel like an accident victim, and I really didn't like the attention, so the easiest thing was to say I was fine and get everyone off my case."

"But then what? What do you do if there's really something wrong?"

She shrugged. "I deal with it myself. Without all the drama." She stifled a yawn.

I signaled our waiter for the bill. "Let's get you home."

I could tell she was stiffening up. The wine probably helped in dulling the aches that would settle in later, but I had a feeling she had no idea the pain she was in for.

"How does your body feel right now?" My voice came out in a rumble. Her sleepy eyes widened a little, and she tilted her head. "I mean, after the accident. Are you hurting? You probably took a beating."

She exhaled and shook her head as though she was disappointed with herself. "Yeah, I calculated that at the approximate speed I was going, it was about nine hundred, seventy-five pounds of force on my body at impact where my head hit the headrest plus four-hundred twenty pounds from the detonation of the airbag." She cringed a little after she said it, then shrugged off her calculation. "You know, give or take."

I couldn't help but smile at her modesty. "'Give or take?' Something tells me your physics knowledge puts you a lot closer than 'give or take,' Damsel."

She flinched at the nickname, then smiled. "Damsel? Guess I had that coming, since I said you could call me a damsel in distress. But you know I'm not, right?"

"I do. That's why I like it. So over a thousand pounds of force, eh?"

"Yeah. And that's a lot." This woman was smart—there was no question—but it seemed like her high school habit of downplaying was still an active part of the way she interacted with people.

I nodded. "It is. So are you doing okay?"

Her eyelids looked heavy and unfocused. "I'm a little sore, but I'm fine. If I get some sleep, I'll be back in fighting shape." She smiled. "Give or take."

I poured the last of our wine into our glasses. "Finish your wine. It'll help relax your muscles. And I have some anti-inflammatories you can take before you go to sleep."

"Sleep . . . ah, that's a beautiful word. It might be past my bedtime." Her sleepy smile caused that dimple to pop. Her opposite cheek smushed into her hand, and the lazy way she stared at me made me want to think there was more to her look than just fatigue.

But I knew that's all it was. I didn't need to be a physicist to understand scientific fact. We were roommates. That's all.

raden

I SLEPT LIKE THE DEAD. That rarely happened. Usually, some errant thought woke me and kept running in a loop through my barely conscious brain until I gave up and went to my gym. But this morning, I woke up feeling surprisingly refreshed.

Sarah's door remained closed, so I quietly padded past it and headed for the kitchen.

"Morning, sunshine. Did I wake you?" Sarah sounded chipper, holding a cup of coffee with both hands, her elbows on the concrete slab kitchen counter in front of her. She didn't turn around when I walked up behind her, but she must have heard me coming.

My answer got caught in my throat as soon as I got close enough to see her tank tops and booty shorts. Women didn't wear those in my kitchen, mainly because women didn't spend the night.

Sarah's legs dangled beneath her chair, and I intentionally glanced away. Even without looking directly at them, I could see they were toned and long. I made a mental note to keep the heat turned low in the house so she'd be forced to wear pants all the time. And maybe a parka.

Moving around the island into the kitchen allowed me to see her face and blocked the mostly bare rest of her body from view. Her smile was easy and free, like she didn't have any place to be all day, even though I knew she had to be at the lab in a little over an hour. She sat with her back ramrod straight in a tall chair with an untouched slice of toast in front of her.

"Nah, I've been up for a while, working," I said. It wasn't the whole truth. I had been up for a while, but I'd mostly been staring at the ceiling.

Distracted by what I could see of her breasts through the flimsy material of her tank top, I didn't realize Sarah was talking to me until I noticed her silent stare. "Um, sorry. Just got lost in my head for a second."

She moved her eyes from her coffee to my face holding her head stiffly. "Say no more. Happens to me on the daily. I was just asking if you wanted some coffee. I used your French press. Hope that's okay."

I nodded, and she shifted her gaze to a second mug she'd already taken out. I filled it with coffee. "Of course it's okay. This is your home for the next six months. Please. Do whatever you normally do at home."

"Great. Well, normally, I walk around topless."

And I spit my fucking coffee all over the floor.

Then I caught her smirk. And a laugh. "Sorry. You just seemed so serious. I was trying to lighten the mood. You not a morning person? Apologies if you're not. I'm good in the mornings, but I'm kind of a basket case after nine o'clock at night."

I quirked an eyebrow at her. "Nine? So last night wasn't a one-off?"

She shrugged. "Last night, I was tired and sore from getting attacked by an overzealous airbag."

Rolling my eyes, I walked past her and grabbed a kitchen towel. "Hardly overzealous. If not for that airbag, we'd still be extracting your teeth from the steering wheel."

I caught her grimace as I mopped the coffee from the front of my shirt. "That's a horrible image. Okay, fine. Thank you, aggressive airbag, for saving me from having to wear braces into my forties."

She was too much—still in denial that she'd been in a bad accident. "So what time do you need to be at work? I have to go in, catch up on paperwork. If you're going soon, I can drive you."

Her eyes closed in a long blink. "That's right. I don't have a car. All morning I've been picturing the drive between here and the lab, walking myself down the route, and I don't even have a car." Her face fell in disappointment, and it made my heart ache. She shook her head and gave herself a pep talk. "It's gonna be fine, Sar. Just . . . focus on work."

Her eyes met mine, and she looked so vulnerable it didn't feel right to abandon her gaze.

Absently, she twisted her watch, a digital gadgety-looking thing that she probably used to time the degradation of radioactive isotopes or something. Yeah, I might have done a little research last night about physics and why she'd been brought out to Lawrence Livermore Lab.

It turned out she was a pretty big deal in the physics world—super smart, working on ground-breaking research that people like Elon Musk wanted to get their hands on, and now she was in charge of a giant project.

I noticed that she lifted her arm to eye level to see the watch instead of looking down at it. When she lowered her arm, she cringed a tiny bit. I'd worried it would happen.

"I'll go get dressed. I can be ready in ten. Is that good?" she asked.

I hitched a thumb over my shoulder to indicate she should head upstairs. "Perfect. I'll run you over, then I'll work out and grab a shower before work." I had no reason to tell her those things. She probably didn't give a shit about my workout and shower schedule, but I was testing her, seeing if she'd hop off the barstool and follow me.

She didn't move. I looked at her again, noticing how stiffly she sat, the unnatural straightness of her neck.

As another test, I walked slightly to the side while talking. "How are you feeling today? Any stiffness?" Her eyes tracked my movements, but she didn't turn her head.

"Good. All good." I moved even farther from her line of sight, and her eyes followed as far as they could until she wasn't looking at me anymore.

I came back in front of her and looked her in the eye. "You can't turn your head, can you?"

She blinked a couple times and took a sip of her coffee. Stalling. "I'm fine." Her eyes darted away.

"How long did it take you to get down the stairs and onto this barstool?" Given what I could see of her limited range of motion, I couldn't imagine how she'd hoisted herself on there.

She took a deep breath, then exhaled, her shoulders slumping in defeat. "A while."

"Why didn't you say anything?" I asked calmly.

She started to push herself up like she planned to get off the stool, but the movement caused her to suck in a sharp breath, and she lowered herself back down. "I'll be fine. I took an Advil."

She took an Advil.

"Why are you like this—so stubborn?" I tried and failed to keep the frustration out of my voice.

"I'm not stubborn. I'm self-sufficient."

She was stubborn. And I knew stubborn.

I'd been accused of being an immoveable chess piece willing to throw the entire game rather than admit I was on the wrong square. I used to take pride in my obstinacy, thinking it was grit. Now I knew it came mainly from not wanting to rely on other people, and I wondered if she was the same way.

My heart squeezed at the visible pain she was in, but it ached more at the amount of pain she was willing to endure rather than ask for help.

It was all too familiar, and seeing it from the other side made me feel worse for her.

"Damsel, an Advil isn't the answer. Your body's gotta recover." I reached for her, wrapping my hands around her hips.

"What are you doing?" Her eyes were wide with shock.

"I'm getting you down from the stool, so you don't have to wrench your neck doing it."

"Oh. Okay." She relaxed a little bit and let me pick her up and put her on the floor.

Gently, I put my hands on the slope of her shoulders and splayed my fingers across the back of her neck. "Are you completely locked up?"

"Yeah. I can't turn my head without a sharp shooting pain." I heard the defeat in her voice.

"Dammit." I could feel the muscles in spasm. They were hard as river stones. "I'm hoping this is just muscular. If you herniated a disk, you've got a bigger problem."

"Don't get mad at me. I probably just slept weird. I'm not used to the pillows. I'll go walk on your life-sucking treadmill, and it'll loosen up, I'm sure."

I took my hands away and came around to look at her. "I'm not mad at you. I'm mad at myself for not insisting you get checked out by a doctor or at least doing some preliminary physical therapy."

She pressed her lips together, stiffening at the obvious pain. She shifted as though she was going to reach and touch my arm, but the motion made her cringe. "It wasn't on you to force sense into my stubborn brain. I should have been smarter. The wine was helpful though."

"I'm glad. But I'm not getting you drunk and sending you off to work. Can you skip today?"

Her look of horror gave me my answer. "No way. It's my first day. I have the whole team meeting me. I need to be there."

"Fine. Here's what we're going to do. I've got an e-stim machine and some ice packs. I'll get you moving again so you can look people in the eye without grimacing, but you have to promise me

—promise—that you'll go straight to a neck and back guy I know in Pleasanton. If I can, I'll drive you."

"You don't have to drive me everywhere. I can take an Uber."

"That's hardly the point of this morning's lecture."

"Fine. Yes. I'll go. Where's Pleasanton?"

I shook my head. "You're kidding, right? You grew up in Oakland. Did no one teach you local geography?"

"Guess not. I know about Pleasanton. I've heard of it. I just don't know where it is relative to here."

"One town over. You might want to orient yourself."

"I'll do that." She dropped her voice down an octave, mocking me.

I pointed in the direction of her room. "Go, smartass. Put on a long-sleeved T-shirt and sweatpants. Do you have that?" I prayed she had that. Or better yet, a burka.

If I was going to work on her muscle aches, I wanted the least amount of skin exposed as possible. It would take an iron will not to enjoy putting my hands on her, but I'd prevail.

"I do. It might take me a sec to change since I can't see my feet."

I regretted the question as it was leaving my mouth. "Do you need me to help you change? Or carry you up there?"

She practically shrieked. "No! I can walk just fine. And dress myself. It's just my upper body that's messed. I'll manage. Be back in a minute."

When I heard her door slam, I went to the fridge and dumped a big dollop of creamer into my coffee, added three spoons of sugar, and slurped down the now-lukewarm sludge. It was awful.

Finn wasn't kidding with her not knowing how to cook. How does a person screw up coffee with a French press? There weren't too many options for how to use the thing.

Now for the bigger problem—the swelling dick in my pants.

I couldn't fucking touch her; I knew that.

Off. Limits.

She was my roommate, the accident victim who hit our truck, and a visiting physicist so out of my league that it felt ridiculous to consider anything but taking a very cold shower. So I did.

CHAPTER SEVEN

arah

IT TOOK me longer than I'd hoped to pull my sweatpants on because I had to lower myself into a squat while keeping my head facing straight ahead and barely moving anything above the waist. Getting a long-sleeved shirt on would be a challenge because I couldn't raise my arms over my head.

Since I'd crashed last night without unpacking a thing, all my clothes were still in various duffel bags and suitcases. Thankfully, I was an organized packer.

I used my foot to push a blue duffel bag out from behind the others and squatted to unzip it. Several pairs of pajamas sat on top, and I grabbed the first one I found. I also pulled out a running bra, which I could step into and pull up. There was no way I'd be able to reach around behind me to fasten an everyday bra.

Eventually, I gave in to screaming in pain for a second, but I managed to pull the bra up my body through the neck hole and only winced once as I put my arms into the sleeves of the pajama top and buttoned it.

It was no worse than what I'd gone through trying to use the French press.

When I came downstairs, Braden was ready with a black ergonomic-looking table set up in the room next to the kitchen. He had music playing from his phone, some hip-hop band I didn't recognize.

I was relieved. If he'd been playing some kind of spa music with singing bowls and birds chirping, it would have gotten very awkward, very fast. I didn't need a roommate who ran a massage parlor.

Though this roommate . . . he made me think twice about hot guys not being my type. They were absolutely my type, even if ogling represented the closest I'd ever come to dating one.

Yes, I'm objectifying him. Hot guy magic—check.

Bella came galloping in from the yard and started circling my legs, whimpering and doing her non-jumping jumping thing until I squatted and gave her a big scratch behind the ears.

"Good morning. I didn't see you before—were you still sleeping?" My dog-friendly voice came in an octave higher than my normal voice. I couldn't help it. Bella was adorable and sweet.

I wanted to believe the same was true of her owner, but Braden seemed reluctant to let go of his stoic facade. Then he'd do something caring and kind like he was doing now, making it impossible to dismiss him as a mountain of muscle who liked dogs better than people. His generous, grumpy, confusing nature intrigued me.

He was messing around on the coffee table with a gadget that had wires and small white squares of tape dangling from the ends. When I leaned against the massage table, he looked up. "Who knew I'd end up needing an in-home physical therapist? Are all your houseguests clumsy? Is that why you have this?" I asked.

"I don't have a lot of houseguests."

Okay. Maybe that was why he seemed a little uncomfortable when it came to having me here.

He went back to untangling the wires.

"I'm almost ready. Haven't used this in a while, and of course, it's a clusterfuck."

His swearing made me laugh, which made my neck hurt more. "Ouch. Stop being funny."

"Didn't realize messes entertained you." He shot me a stern glance, and I realized I'd already gotten used to the slightly peeved way he looked at me. It was almost a sexy scowl—if a person was into that sort of thing. And . . . I was.

Since I'd never lived in close proximity to someone of such spectacular physicality and I probably wouldn't again, I pushed my better behavior aside and continued objectifying him. I took the opportunity to assess the way his forearms and biceps flexed as he untangled the wires. A muscle in his jaw twitched when he got frustrated at the mess. He was . . . just so beautiful to look at.

I sighed. Then covered by clearing my throat. "I'd offer to help, but knowing me, I'd blow up your house."

He grunted without looking up. "I've got it. Can you get up on this table, or do you need a hand?"

"I think I can manage it." Courtesy of my pole dancing experience, I flipped one leg up onto the table, and the rest of my body followed.

Glancing back at the jumble of wires, I started to feel concerned. "What the heck is that thing? Are you planning to shock me into submission? Because you could just tell me to chill. Save the pain."

He looked up, seeming to focus on me for the first time. "Nice jammies." I couldn't dip my head to see what I'd put on, but I had two pairs that were the dark shade I pulled from my bag. They were either maroon plaid, or they were the ones with teddy bears cooking breakfast on them. "Okay, this is the e-stim I was talking about. It sends an electric charge at very mild frequencies and stimulates a response in your muscles. Helps them relax."

Those wires and the potential for some awful shock treatment scared the crap out of me. And the more stern and humorless he was, the more I wanted to get a rise out of him. "Electrocution as a calming technique. Wow, someone needs to introduce you to yoga, big guy."

"Cute." He actually smiled. "It sounds counterintuitive, but I swear it gets results."

With the wires now hanging from the contraption, he nodded to the table. "I need you on your stomach." I smiled, imagining him saying those words to legions of women under very different circumstances.

Then, in a total brain misfire, I imagined him saying them to me. I shivered at how it would feel when I obeyed.

So inappropriate. And . . . what else is new?

"I'm afraid I can't do that without screaming bloody murder," I grunted, unable to turn and look at him.

He placed a hand on the back of my neck and gently massaged with his fingers. "I can't believe how locked up you are. And you were going to go to work like this?" He sounded exasperated.

"What can I say? I like a challenge."

He didn't know me well enough to understand yet, but the more difficult a situation, the more determined I felt to beat it. I saw pain as something to be conquered, not my body's natural stop sign. So far, that mentality had gotten me pretty far, so I didn't see a reason to change.

"Here, can you roll to your side and get on your hands and knees?" My brain misfired with more errant thoughts of him commanding me onto all fours so he could take me doggie style. My neck revolted with a fierce bolt of pain as if telling my brain to shut up and behave.

He popped a head cradle up at the end of the table, and I managed to slide like a marooned seal and lie down flat with my face on the cushion.

"You good?" he asked, his voice gentle. His hand rubbed my back in soothing reassurance, and I blinked back the eruption of heat over my skin.

"I'm good now, but there's a decent chance I won't be able to get up. Like, ever. Fair warning." My voice came out muffled.

His deep, genuine laugh calmed me. "I'll help you. Now I'm going to lift up your shirt and put these stickers on your back and neck, okay?"

He was going to lift my shirt? I was glad to be face down so he couldn't see the blush rise on my cheeks. "Whatever you say, fireman," I joked in a mock-deep voice.

"Please stop it."

"What?"

"Just . . . think quiet thoughts and let me do this," he said.

"Fine."

I felt his warm hands lifting my pajama top partway, but mostly he reached under it and put the small patches in various places. "These might be a little cold. Bear with me."

They were cold, but then his warm hands brushed over my skin, and I could only focus on the electric burn of his fingertips as they moved expertly down my back. He placed two more of the cold stickers on my neck at the collar of my top, and then I heard loud crunching.

"Whatcha got going there?" I asked, wondering if he planned on eating a bag of chips while I percolated.

"Ice packs. These will be cold, obviously, but they'll help a lot." He laid them on my back, and I shivered. I didn't mind the ice. It helped turn down the furnace he'd ignited when he touched me.

This must be what all the ladies line up for. Hot hands, blazing feels.

"I'm good with the ice. Perfect for me. Ice queen over here."

"Ha. I don't get that vibe. Okay, I'm turning on the stim. You'll feel a tingling, but you don't want to be twitching. So tell me when you feel it, and I'll stop."

"Okay, boss. Hit me." It was a strange sensation. Tiny prickles turned into bigger tingles on my skin. Then I felt them deeper underneath. "I feel that. I don't think I'm twitching."

"You're not." He turned it higher. It was almost too much to bear, but then the feeling receded. I felt a twitch. "Yup, that's your threshold. We stop there."

He came around near the top of my head and put his hands on the muscles between my neck and shoulders. Then he laid what felt like a scorching hot towel across the back of my neck.

I might have moaned.

He took a step back. I could picture him there, admiring his work. "You okay?"

"Mmm-hmm." I felt weird but not bad.

"Good. I'll be back in fifteen minutes. You . . . just hang out there."

Over the next fifteen minutes, I let the strange combination of sensations work their magic on my tweaked muscles while Braden made noises in the kitchen. It sounded like he was washing dishes, opening and closing cupboards, opening the fridge. Then I heard his feet walking away and water running in the bathroom upstairs.

My body absorbed the jumbled mess of sensations—hot, cold, tingly—and my brain tried to process an additional feeling—lust.

It made no sense. He'd barely touched me, but that was enough to have every nerve along the surface of my skin firing and a flood of heat building in my core. The second he left the room, my body craved his touch, probably because my body was confusing medical attention with foreplay. Yes, it had been months—fine, years—since any man had touched me in the intimate way Braden just had, even if just for therapeutic purposes. Apparently, he'd awakened some dormant female urges.

And let's face it, the man was a hot rescue fantasy come to life, and I was caving to his charms like an expert spelunker.

That didn't take long. I'd barely been in town a day, and I already found myself abandoning my "like attracts like" theory and signing on for a brawny handsome firefighter. With great enthusiasm.

You're in trouble, lady friend.

No. It would be fine. The fantasy would stay in my head where it belonged. Noticing his physical beauty and inner kindness didn't need to make our roommate situation awkward. It was like appreciating a stunning work of art. I'd be crazy to ignore its beauty, even if I couldn't afford to own it.

I just needed to get off this table and ferry myself to work where I'd concentrate on the reason for moving here in the first place— science. If anything turned me on as much as Braden's hands on me, it was the possibility of a scientific breakthrough.

Okay, I may have exaggerated the excitement produced by things in a lab just a bit, but it was all I had.

A few minutes later, Braden's footsteps returned, followed by the clicking of Bella's paws on the hardwood floor. His deep voice was close to my ear when he spoke, causing a chill down my spine. "You still with me?"

"Yeah. Only I'm pretty sure I've become one with this table."

He let out a low laugh. "I'll help you up." He turned me onto my back then held out his hand, which felt large and strong as I gripped it. Then he supported my neck with his other hand and pulled me up to sit.

As soon as I let go of his hand and relaxed my shoulders, a crazy thing happened. I could suddenly move my neck. I didn't have a full range of motion, but I could turn it in both directions without pain. My back felt looser too. I wiggled around and felt so much better than I had just a half hour earlier.

"This is . . . wow. I can actually move," I practically sang. It hadn't seemed possible.

"That was the goal." He crossed his arms in his Michelin Man pose, a satisfied grin on his face.

"Goal achieved! I'm healed."

"Well, you're not healed, but it's a start. Now don't do anything crazy at work today like lifting lasers or whatever."

"Aye aye, Captain. Seriously, thank you. I think you've earned yourself another dinner. If you're around later, name the dish, and I'll make it happen."

He took a step back and his jaw clenched. "I, um, have plans." He didn't look happy about it.

"Ah, like, plans to go over your tax bill with your accountant?" It was the only reason I could think of that would make a person look so miserable.

"No, like a date."

"Oh. Okay, well, cool. Good for you."

Of course, he'd have an active dating life. From the attention he'd gotten around town last night, I could imagine he had women lining up every night of the week.

"I could cancel . . . I mean, if you still can't move around, you might need some help with things . . ." He rubbed a hand over his chin and looked at the ceiling, maybe considering what would be involved in canceling his plans.

I waved my hands at him in protest. "No, no! Absolutely not. I don't want to keep you from your life. Go on all the dates. We'll do it another time. Or not. All good."

"Are you sure? Because then I'm back on a twenty-four-hour shift, so I won't be around for a while . . ."

"Absolutely. Now lemme get some real clothes on so I make a decent impression on my first day at work. Can't greet the physics community in my teddy bear pj's." Now that I could move my neck, I could see the bears clearly.

I pushed past him and made my way up the stairs. Feeling so much better than I had thirty minutes earlier, I moved in and out of the shower, gathered my hair into a knot on top of my head, slapped on some mascara and cherry red lipstick, and pulled on a navy-blue wrap dress and a tall pair of pumps.

The full-length mirror on the back of the bathroom door convinced me I looked good enough to pass muster on my first day. I didn't have much time to consider alternate outfits or better makeup application, so I grabbed my laptop case and my purse and headed back down the stairs.

Braden was waiting for me, kneeling down and having a quiet conversation with Bella. "You're gonna be a good girl, right? No digging . . . or I'll have to take away your yard privileges." Bella sat obediently in front of him, taking in every word he said, as though she knew what he expected her to do.

He rubbed her under her chin and kissed the top of her head before he noticed me standing there.

His eyes traced over me from head to toe and clouded with heat for a moment, but just as quickly, he blinked it away.

"You ready?" He turned toward the door, and I noticed his toned muscular arms stretching at the dark blue sleeves of his T-shirt.

I seriously needed to get a grip. I couldn't spend the next few months ogling my roommate, no matter how benign my interest was. He wasn't a piece of meat. I had to stop looking at him like one.

"Sure." I cringed a tiny bit as I hoisted my purse and laptop bag over my shoulder. I wasn't loose and pain-free yet.

Braden shook his head and reached for the straps, pulling them off my shoulder and hanging them on his own. "You're gonna undo all the good work we did in ten minutes. Let me carry it."

He put a hand on the small of my back and steered me toward the front door. I tried not to react to the feel of his hand, but there was no doubt he'd left a permanent heat signature burned into the fabric. Spending time with him was causing my brain cells to leach from my body.

When he dropped me at the front entrance to Lawrence Livermore Lab, I couldn't scurry away fast enough.

"Thanks! See you later. Or not. Just . . . whatever. Have a great day," I rambled. Then I hugged my stuff and bolted inside.

CHAPTER EIGHT

arah

WHEN I'D DRIVEN DOWN to meet with the physicists at Lawrence Livermore Lab, I'd been as starry-eyed as an astronomy kid who gets invited to NASA.

I'd swooned at the IMB Sequoia supercomputer. I'd gawked at the giant lasers and the areas of the lab that required top national security clearance. I'd imagined myself among kindred spirits in the physics world. But I hadn't really anticipated how it would feel to arrive on my first day.

It felt amazing. Like all the work I'd done for my entire life had paid off.

My new boss procured my badge and escorted me to my first meeting of the day. A middle-aged man with a full head of graying brown hair, Dr. George Prescott walked at a brisk clip. His rimless glasses cast orbs of light on his cheeks, and his shoulders slumped as if he'd spent many hours at a computer.

"Dr. Finley, your team is excited to meet you," he said, leading me down a long hallway. He'd learned about my research at Berkeley and invited me to apply to the program. Nervously fiddling with my badge, I craned my neck for signs of physics luminaries I might recognize.

"Oh, please, call me Sarah," I said, surprised that colleagues used such formal greetings. I'd called him George.

He grinned. "Aw, I was just teasing you. Thought it might be nice to sound official on your first day here. And rest assured, you won't be left to muddle around in the dark. If you have any questions about how things run here, we're all ready to answer."

I took in his khaki pants, brown shoes, and navy-blue button-down and felt an unexpected wave of relief wash over me. For the first time since I'd arrived in town, I didn't feel nervous, which was crazy because this job had big career implications for me. The feeling came from finally being around my people, the science goofballs who found humor in messing with each other's data, rather than people like Captain Braden with his intimidating abs and disarming smile.

Until I stood next to a man who reminded me of my fellow professors, I didn't realize how out of sorts I'd felt around Braden. I wanted to know more about him, and even though Finn had told me to ask Braden questions, I preferred to observe and intuit. So far, that hadn't gotten me very far.

What a relief to be with a man like George who wanted to answer my questions. A man who put on a nice, no-fuss work outfit that didn't emphasize his muscles because he would move mountains with his brain, not his abs.

"Dr. Finley?"

I flinched when George waved a hand in front of my face. We stood at the conference room door. "Um, yes?"

"I said your first name several times, but you were off dreaming."

"Oops. Sorry." First day and I can't focus.

"It's quite alright. Shall we?" He gestured to the door handle, and I nodded before he pulled it open.

It was a windowless room with a whiteboard on one wall, ergonomic chairs around a glass-topped conference table, and a minifridge in a corner. On the other walls, poster-sized images conveyed all science, all the time—the hadron collider, atomic lasers, and a periodic table with the element Lawrencium, named after its discovery at the lab, highlighted in yellow.

For the first time since I'd crashed into town, I felt the full impact of what I had the power to accomplish. My work here could have big real world implications.

Three people sat at the conference room table, all of them occupied on their computers and multitasking with notepads open next to them. George quickly made introductions.

Drew was a tall, lanky man with a shock of white-blond hair and a bowtie around the neck of his white shirt. He looked a few years older than me, and he let me know he had a husband of ten years, four kids, and two cats. "A lot of eyeballs at my homestead," he said.

"That must be intimidating when they're all looking at you," I said.

"You have no idea."

"Glad to have you on the team. Your research on joining methods and nuclear materials will be key to this project."

He nodded enthusiastically. "For sure. I'm excited to see where we go."

Charlotte was the eager young newbie at the lab who'd work wherever she was told and absorb whatever information we threw at her. She reminded me of myself when I'd just finished my PhD—eager to please, a little worried she'd be challenged with a question she couldn't answer, and determined to skate past the grunt work and do something meaningful. "I don't have kids, so I'll work the weird hours. I don't need to have a life." She shoved aside a tendril of her curly brown hair that had fallen out of her hairband.

"I get that. I work weird hours too sometimes, so we can compare midnight binge foods," I told her.

Then there was Keith, the oldest member of our team at fifty-six, an expert with lasers. He'd worked at a Japanese lab with the world's highest-powered laser beam and operated the solid-state lasers we'd need for our project.

Keith wore a hoodie sweatshirt with a picture of a laser on it and the quip "Do not stare into the laser beam with your remaining good eye." He wore dark-rimmed glasses and had a full head of hair and a gray goatee. "Glad to have you with us, Sarah," he said.

After some small talk and discussion of research methods, we agreed on what parts of the project we could work on independently and what we needed to do as a team. I spent two hours in meeting with them, and my mind only wandered to Braden once, wondering what he was doing. Maybe twice.

I quickly got myself back on track. "We're going to cover new ground in friction stir welding, and that excites me. I hope it excites you too." There was a smattering of agreement that we were all onboard to revolutionize the tiny area of science where physics met engineering. I loved that these humans shared my enthusiasm for something like this. I could already tell George had done great work at assembling a top-notch team.

After our meeting, I went to my new office, closed the door, and sat at my desk. I pumped my fist and let the grin spread across my face. I'd dreamed of working here since first checking the box to select a Physics major on my college application.

I took a few minutes to let it sink in that I was actually here.

Then I went and took a selfie with the world's highest-energy laser. I sent it to Finn because I knew he'd find it interesting.

He texted immediately.

Finn: Hey, nerd girl. Is that a giant laser, or is that Braden walking around naked again?

Me: Haha.

Finn: How're you doing? I heard you had a little fender bender.

Uh oh. That wasn't good. How had that news already gotten back to Finn?

Me: No big deal. Just a rear-ender.

Finn: You sure you're not downplaying? Braden was worried.

Braden reached out to Finn? Well, at least that implied there was no local news item on the girl who crashed into a firetruck. I couldn't figure out why Braden calling Finn both mortified me and warmed my heart. The guy was so stoic that it surprised me he'd given me a thought beyond our necessary interaction.

Or maybe I seemed like more of a basket case than I'd realized.

Me: I'm totally fine. Your friend has a weird machine that unlocked my muscles.

Finn: Not sure I want details on that...

Me: Not giving any, and get your mind out of the gutter.

Finn: Impossible. Oh, and hey, my apologies in advance for the skirt parade.

What was that supposed to mean? Maybe it was a quaint Carol-wood tradition I'd learn about soon.

Me: ???

Finn: Your new roommate and the lineup of women you won't be able to keep straight. He's notorious.

Me: Whatever. I can handle it.

I clicked my phone off and leaned back in my chair, trying to figure out why it bothered me to have Finn spell out what I already knew. Of course, a sexy firefighter would have a slew of attractive women on speed dial, and it wouldn't stop just because I was crashing in his spare room.

If there wasn't a pole dancing studio in town, I needed to find some new way to blow off steam and occupy whatever free time I had.

That way, I wouldn't have a free moment to think about Braden and who he was dating. Or see it in person.

CHAPTER NINE

raden

THANK FUCK.

If I'd had to spend one more minute with that woman in a pajama top that was somehow sexier than most lingerie I'd had the pleasure of stripping off a woman's body, I was going to lose my shit. As it was, I couldn't help but picture her upstairs showering, fantasizing that she'd call for me because she couldn't reach the soap.

Then when she appeared in that figure-hugging dress and sexy professor pumps, I almost lost my mind. Even Bella looked at me like I'd better hit that, and she salivates over a tennis ball.

This had never happened to me before, and by this, I mean forfeiting all control over my reactions to a woman. Sure, plenty of women had turned my head, but Sarah had turned me into a walking hard-on.

It wasn't just the way she looked, though I couldn't ignore her lips, the impossibly blue oceans of her gaze, and her long, supple limbs. She had a sweetness about her, a genuine interest in the world around her, and I still couldn't get out of my head that she cared what happened to me on the job when she barely knew me.

I didn't have much time to analyze it because my shift started in ten minutes, and I needed to make every green light to get there on time. I took a shortcut around town and pulled into the parking lot of Engine 97 nine minutes later.

On my way through the side door to the locker room, I noticed that some of the plants along the walkway needed water. "Hey, whoever's planning on washing the rig had better spray those plants out front," I yelled to no one in particular.

Someone would hear me. And if they didn't, I'd say it again.

Keeping plants alive was a pet project of mine, a hobby I'd inherited from my grandmother, who loved to garden. She made it her goal to keep vegetation alive in her front yard, and it didn't matter if she was growing weeds or strawberries—she tended to them exactly the same way.

"Beggars can't be choosers," she'd told me. "As long as it's mostly green and mostly alive, it earns a place in my yard."

In the years when my mom was holding down two jobs as a single parent, I spent a lot of time at my grandmother's. She lived between school and my house, so it made for an easy stop on my way home. My step-brothers were off doing whatever they felt like doing, and sometimes I didn't want to go straight home, even when it was late after football practice, so I'd stop at Gram's.

She took the divorces harder than I did and more or less disowned my dad. "I raised him better than that," she said.

"I'm sure you raised him fine, but he's a grownup. Whatever he does isn't on you." I felt fairly certain that it was true, though I had no proof.

"A man doesn't leave his family." She said it like a mantra, as though saying it would reverse time and make her son choose a different path.

"This one did," I reminded her when I was fourteen. My dad wasn't a sentimental man. He didn't talk about love or falling in love. That is, until the day he told us he was leaving to be with some other woman he loved, a woman who was not our mother. He also didn't tell me or my brothers that he loved us until the day he moved out, almost like a parting gift.

At age five, I was the middle child of three wild, unruly boys who tested every boundary. The full brunt of not having a male role model didn't hit me until puberty smacked me even harder. Back then, I confused being a selfish asshole to women with being cool. I followed the example of my only male role model and treated girls like they existed for my temporary pleasure.

The worst part—I didn't ever stop to examine what a dick I was because I still managed to get dates with anyone I wanted. It shouldn't have come as a shock that I entered high school with some pretty messed up ideas of what a good relationship looked like.

After high school, I never dated anyone for long, and if any of the girls I had fun with asked for a commitment, I either ran in the other direction or promised commitment and proceeded to cheat. Never cared enough to change my ways or risk my heart.

Until Ellie. She was the one woman I considered breaking all my bad habits for, and instead, she broke me.

"Morning," I said, walking into the gym, surveying the empty treadmills. Placing the patches from the stim machine on Sarah's skin and picturing what she'd look like without those ridiculous fucking bear pajamas almost did me in. Then, sitting next to her in my truck and smelling her lotion or perfume or whatever it was that smelled like honey and flowers had me fighting a semi. If we didn't get called to a fire, I needed to release my adrenaline somehow. As soon as I finished my paperwork, I planned to run.

"Morning, man." Mitch motioned me over to spot him on some bench presses. He was coming off a double shift, which I know he took to avoid problems with his girlfriend, choosing to sleep here instead of going home. We hadn't talked about it yet, but a man doesn't take extra shifts unless he needs the money or wants to avoid something at home, and Mitch didn't need the money. I'd ask him once he'd gotten some sleep.

"How was the night?" I asked instead.

"Quiet. You? All good with the roommate? She okay?" He snapped the gum he was chewing, and a couple other guys smirked.

"Yeah, a little locked up this morning, but fine." I tried not to let my mind wander to the physical therapy session.

"Oh right, I heard you got a 'roommate,'" said Sean, one of our drivers. "You losing your touch? Chicks won't let you bang them anymore unless you give 'em room and board?"

"Eh, you're a fucking riot, Sean. You taking that comedy act on the road?"

"Gotta admit, she's pretty hot, though she wasn't really at her best after slamming into the back of the engine," Mitch said.

Sean smacked a hand into his face. "Ha, how did I not lead with that? Wait, I need to understand more about this. Did she not see the truck? Oh, wait, this all makes sense. She's vision impaired. No wonder she doesn't mind seeing your ugly face every day." He erupted into hysterics. If I hadn't trained with Sean and been friends with him for a decade, I'd have popped him by now.

I let them go on. They had to get it out of their systems. There was no chance everyone at the station didn't know about the accident and my new living situation, and I was going to endure their nonsense for about five more minutes, and then I'd shut it down for good.

"Alright, alright, anyone else have anything to say? Yes, I have a roommate. She's the sister of a friend, and she's in town temporarily for work. There will be no banging. Got it?"

"Oh, well, if you don't want a piece of that, can I have her number?" Sean pulled up the Contacts app on his phone and pretended to enter her number, elbowing me with a shit-eating grin.

I smacked the back of his head. "You're cleaning bathrooms today. Just changed the chore list." I flashed a genuine smile. I had no problem sticking it to any guy who crossed a line.

"You serious?" Sean whined like he'd lost a nut.

"As a heart attack." I left them and went to the kitchen for some decent coffee. Sarah's awful brew made the watered-down excuse for coffee here taste like a dream. I'd have to give her some pointers on using the French press.

The coffee pot sat empty, and as I emptied a packet of grounds into the machine, the image of Sarah sitting stiffly on the stool in my kitchen came back into my mind. I wondered what made her so stoic about keeping her pain to herself. I'd seen how much she hated people fussing over her after her accident, but she hadn't told me why.

It wasn't until Cash walked in carrying a couple bags of groceries that I realized I'd been standing motionless holding the empty coffee pot. "Dude, you look like a statue," Cash said.

I went to the sink to fill the pot. "I was trying to decide how badly I wanted coffee," I said, covering.

"You mean, badly enough to pour water into a machine? Shit, how lazy are you?"

I'd have to work harder to teach these guys some respect. Cash was a probie, and he'd already learned from the others that he could shoot his mouth off with minimal consequences. That was what I got for trying to build camaraderie—they treated me like the older brother whose only function was to buy them beer until their party woke the neighbors and they needed someone to talk down the cops.

Yeah, I might have had some experience with my two younger brothers shoving me into that role for real. Old habits were hard to break, and I mostly liked the guys in my unit, so I ignored their wisecracks.

The coffee maker started to sputter, and I leaned against the counter while Cash emptied the groceries. "What's for dinner?" I asked.

He looked momentarily nervous. "I thought you weren't going to be here."

"I'm not. Don't look so guilty."

"Not guilty, but I shopped accordingly. I bought five steaks."

"Steaks? Nice. Way to make friends, probie."

"That was my thought."

I grabbed a package of Oreos he'd just removed from one of the grocery bags and started to tear it open. Then I thought better of it. I needed to power down a few sips of coffee, do my work, and hit the machines in the gym. It was the only way I could think of to get rid of the agitation gnawing at my gut. That, or I needed to hit the showers and rub one out, and I didn't much feel like doing that with a station full of guys walking in at any minute.

Why was I still thinking about Sarah?

It made no sense. Twenty-four hours ago, I'd never met her, and my life was fine. I felt excited about Kelsey—legs for days, long blond hair, all-up-in-my-business-hinting-at-blowjobs Kelsey.

Now I debated canceling on her tonight. Should I make sure Sarah got to her physical therapy appointment? Maybe she'd need a ride.

She's a capable thirty-three-year-old woman with an Uber account. She doesn't need you.

The really strange thing was I sort of wished she did. Having a brilliant, capable woman like Sarah rely on me to get her neck unlocked had felt good—it satisfied me in a way that one more blow job from Kelsey never would. Feeling Sarah's gratitude for skills I took for granted made me see them as valuable, and I liked it.

But the last thing I needed was to get emotionally involved again with someone who'd only want me until she realized I was punching above my weight class. I wouldn't be enough for someone like Sarah. So why was I picturing myself taking her to dinner instead of Kelsey?

I needed to get my head out of my ass and focus on my date, who wanted me for a good time and was happy when I delivered, while my roommate was busy tucking herself in at nine so she could be fresh in the morning to improve on rockets.

I admired the hell out of her, but that didn't mean we belonged together.

"Yeah, so I won't be here later. Got a date," I told him.

"Uh, o-kaay?"

I shook my head. "Never mind." I took the coffee with me and went to pound the treadmill until my lungs burned.

CHAPTER TEN

arah

AFTER MY FIRST week at the lab, my team fell into a groove. We'd drawn up enough models to know the exact results we hoped to get. Now the fun part would begin—experimenting with the lasers and recording data until we found the strongest bond—something that could withstand G-forces in space.

In the lab, Keith worked with a quadrillion-watt laser that he mysteriously referred to as Batwoman. He'd spent a decade working on different applications for its powerful beam, and he still had boundless enthusiasm for building something even more powerful.

Today, Keith wore a hoodie with a picture of a cat on a wanted poster with the tagline, "Wanted dead or alive: Schrodinger's cat." I'd never tire of physicist humor.

"I've already compressed the beam into a shorter pulse to keep the heat down, but we need it to do much better," Keith said, ruffling his hair. I stood next to him wearing protective goggles and watching him calibrate the beam.

Lasers lay far outside my field of knowledge. "I'm going to leave that to you, Keith. The heat is an issue with aluminum alloys, and that's what the space program needs."

I went back to our workroom. Sipping a green juice, Charlotte sat in an ergonomic chair and recorded our data. As the most junior member of the team, she got stuck with paperwork, but she was detail-oriented and liked that part of the job.

"Copper is the clear frontrunner," Drew said. He wore a purple bowtie with a striped shirt and jeans, his usual uniform when we weren't gowned up in clean room conditions. At the moment, we were in my office looking at spreadsheets of data from our first week of work.

"We knew copper would perform, but no one can afford to build rockets from copper," I said.

"That's why it's a problem."

"It's not a problem. Yet. We should still work with the copper and study it. Why do the electrons move faster? How do we calibrate the laser to get the same results with aluminum?"

"Oh, is that all?" I didn't mind his sarcasm. Our objective was challenging, which was why we'd allocated six months to accomplish it.

"Yes, just that." I liked Drew. So far, he and I had found a good working rhythm. He reminded me a little of my dad, and sometimes I leaned into his comforting presence. My dad had died so long ago, but never a day went by that I didn't miss him.

His death had shifted the way I dealt with my siblings in a way that was now so embedded that it impacted how I approached the world. With Finn and my oldest sister Isla away at college and my mom mentally unstable after losing her husband, I became the de facto parent to Becca, Cherry, and Tatum.

That meant I grew up fast and took on responsibilities for looking out for them and guiding them. Sometimes they resented it because I was practically their age, but I didn't care. They needed an authority figure, and I stepped into the void. It was overwhelming, so I put my life on a schedule—if I followed it to the letter, I could give my sisters what they needed and still find time for my graduate degree, the career I wanted, and eventually, I hoped, a relationship. So far, everything had gone according to my controlled plan, and I wasn't about to abandon it now.

"Hey, should I start another spreadsheet for today's results?" Charlotte asked as her phone started beeping. She had an alarm that went off every three hours to remind her to eat something, so her blood sugar didn't get too low.

We'd been going hard all day, so I hadn't realized it was already seven at night—a hazard of lab work. The lights were always on, and often we got so carried away with an experiment that we lost track of time.

"No, we should wrap up," I told them. "Come on, guys. We've been at this all day, and we'll be right back here in the morning."

Charlotte perked up. "You don't have to tell me twice. I need to eat."

"We all do. Is anyone free? Dinner on me if you show me a good dinner spot in town."

I had three takers in seconds.

Fifteen minutes after that, we had an outside table at Juicy BBQ and Dry Spirits, and each of us had a full beer in front of us.

"This is good for team building," Drew said, unwilling to loosen his bowtie after work.

"Ha. You just like that I'm paying," I joked, drawing a finger through the condensation on my glass and watching the droplets join. "But you guys are worth it. We make a good team."

Charlotte raised her glass and we all toasted. "To team spirit."

A few minutes later, a giant platter of loaded nachos landed in the center of our table, and small talk gave way to racing each other to the bottom of the plate. After a couple bites of pulled pork, cheese, and other morsels I couldn't even identify, I felt much better.

That was when I happened to glance across the street to see a familiar figure—a firefighter in low-slung dark jeans and his characteristic muscle-hugging T-shirt.

He was with a woman—a date.

That much was evident by the way he placed his hand on the small of her back. My spine tingled at the memory of him doing that with me—once—after my car accident. Then, on the morning that my neck had been locked up, he'd treated me gingerly, taking such good care to get me moving again.

But since then, he'd been busy with work, and so had I. We'd interacted like roommates, ships passing in the night. As it should be.

It had taken all week for the memory of his fingertips brushing my skin to fade a tiny bit. But his hand on his date's back brought back all the lustful feeling I'd been working hard to shove away.

I allowed myself to watch him since they were too far away for him to notice me voyeuristically tracking his every move.

His date was pretty—I could see that from far away. Petite with curves and ample breasts, she had long red hair that reminded me of my younger sister Cherry, the only redhead in our family.

I told myself that I most definitely did not have a crush on my roommate. My interest in him tipped toward the purely scientific —cataloging what a handsome firefighter did for fun, what kind of woman he found attractive.

You are so full of crap.

They entered the restaurant across the street, and I couldn't see anything else. I deflated, unable to decide if I wanted to see him lean in and kiss her neck or if that would make me throw up on the nachos.

If I saw him kiss her, my dumb brain might realize he was off limits to me. He had a life here long before I arrived, and he wouldn't abandon it to satisfy my roommate lust.

"Old laser physicists never die. They just become incoherent," Keith said to the roaring appreciative laugh of my physics friends. These were my people. Like attracted like.

Nevertheless, while my team prattled on and the jokes got even worse and therefore more hilarious, I couldn't help glancing at the door to the restaurant across the street, wondering if Braden's date was running a bare toe up his leg under the table.

Probably.

Braden struck me as someone who knew what he wanted, and she was on a date with him now. He'd given no indication that woman was me.

CHAPTER ELEVEN

arah

BETWEEN WORK and his social life, Braden kept himself pretty busy. I barely crossed paths with him after the first morning he drove me to work, other than to exchange pleasantries over coffee. And even then, he rarely lingered once I came into the kitchen. As soon as I came home, he either headed out on a date, or one of us felt tired and went up to bed.

It was fine. I didn't need a bestie. I didn't need a dinner date. I just needed a place to stay.

By the end of my second week at the lab, I'd fully immersed myself in science and successfully kept my mind focused on the unique power of lasers to soften metals at the molecular level.

Keith had given me an abbreviated download on the work he'd been doing with Batwoman, and I felt even more optimistic about the prospects of our project before we'd finetuned of our approach.

Also, thanks to a parade of friendly Uber drivers, I'd stopped thinking about my smashed-up car and my mortifying grand entrance into town. Which meant I didn't think about firetrucks or the people who drove around in them. It was mind over matter, and I had more important things to focus on than what my roommate was doing to keep his biceps in top form.

I'm not thinking about that at all.

So I was a lying liar whose mind drifted to Braden throughout the day. By five o'clock one afternoon, I'd gotten so fed up with myself and my lack of mental control, that I gave myself a stern talking to. It went a bit like this: "You are a grown woman with a doctorate who is here to do important work. You may not jeopardize it by letting your focus drift to a man. That is all."

My inner lust child may or may not have told my bossy self to shut the hell up.

Ever since I'd seen him out on his date, my diligent powers of recall had replayed every look and touch recorded in my lecherous mind. I knew it was ridiculous.

On the other hand, welding metals and recording energy transfer and temperature conditions only provided so much entertainment. My work had the potential to produce an incredible outcome, but much of lab work was the drudgery of recording data.

Of course, my attention was drifting.

Eventually, I'd get into a groove and forget Braden even existed. I hoped.

I needed to concentrate and plan for my team meeting in the morning, so I put my head down and dug into a report Keith had written and lost myself in the pages.

After work, I'd take an Uber back to the house. If I finished up early enough, I might even race over to the body shop and see if they had an updated estimate for completion.

Then I'd swing by the grocery store and stock up on some Greek yogurt, salad stuff, and baking potatoes, so I could make myself a decent dinner. I felt pretty confident Braden had a date and would go straight from work to pick her up like he'd done each time he had plans.

So it shocked me when he sent me a text.

Braden: Hey, I got done early. I'm out front if you need a ride.

Me: In front of where?

Braden: The lab... Where you work...?

Then he sent me a selfie with the main building in the background. He was squinting into the sunlight, which lit his face up in warm pinks and painted amber tones on his hair. It was official—concentration destroyed.

Me: That's so sweet. But I was going to Uber.

Braden: Well, now you don't have to. Are you finished?

Am I ever.

I was finished the moment his face reentered my brain.

Me: Yes. Be out in a sec.

Braden: Take your time.

When I exited the building, Braden was standing outside wearing aviator sunglasses and leaning against his truck. Sipping something brown through a paper straw, he blasted me with a smile I'd yet to see in full force, and the combination of his white teeth and the confident curve of his lips made me forget my train of thought.

For a second, I let myself imagine I was on a real date with Braden, the object of that charismatic smile, for reasons other than being his roommate with no car.

"Hey." He reached behind to where a second cup sat on the hood and handed it to me. "Do you like iced tea?"

I licked my lips, suddenly feeling parched by his heat. "Oh, who doesn't? Thank you."

"Lots of people, actually. Especially the super-sweet kind I like. I took a gamble."

I grinned and stirred the tea with the straw. "I have a massive sweet tooth." I took a sip. "Oh, this is heaven." Braden smiled and opened the door for me.

I hopped up the step and onto the seat before he could reach out to help me. If the mere sight of him had my internal body temperature shooting up to scorching levels, I couldn't risk what grabbing his hand might do. I busied myself pulling on my seat-belt, so he pushed the door closed and went around to the driver's side.

"How was work?" he asked, pressing the keyless ignition button and ignoring the rear camera, instead putting a hand on the headrest behind me and turning to navigate the exit from his parking spot. I caught a woodsy whiff of pine and sweat and felt myself inhaling deeper before he plucked his hand away and dropped it to his thigh. With an elbow propped on the open window ledge, he steered with one hand, piloting the massive truck away from the lab and toward town.

"So great," I said, unable to take my eyes off his hand or his leg, which flexed as he moved it from the gas pedal to the brake. His hand looked capable of things I'd never had the audacity to imagine happening to my body—soft touches in places that would make me melt and sigh and swoon.

I stifled a shudder at how quickly my mind drifted there and quickly covered with work talk. "My team's really gelling. We all complement each other well."

"Good to hear."

"How about you? Rescue any cats from trees today?"

He smirked but didn't take his eyes off the road. "Your impression of my job comes right out of a picture book, doesn't it?"

"No, but the cat thing goes along with me imaging you in scenarios that aren't dangerous. I can get pretty far denying reality and living in my head. A girl needs to sleep at night, after all." I couldn't explain it. I barely knew the man, but some part of me had felt protective of him from the moment we'd met. His gruff moments hid a softer side that I sensed had gotten bruised along the way.

He turned down a leafy street we hadn't gone down before, and he cast a glance my way. "Tell me about that. I know Finn's got a caretaking gene, but he's the oldest male, so it kind of makes sense. Where does your protectiveness come from?"

I exhaled a breath I hadn't realized I'd been holding. "Probably same place as his. I was the oldest kid in the house when my dad died and everything fell apart. I had to keep everyone on track— my sisters, even my mom. Guess the habit stuck." It was a simplified explanation, but for most people, a satisfactory one.

"And you like to be in control," he said, not looking at me. When I eyed him, I saw his smirk. "Is that why you control the narrative, make it up if you have to?"

I felt myself flinch.

I hadn't expected him to zero in on my exact psyche, at least not so quickly. I inhaled slowly to slow the panicky thumping of my pulse that resulted from having my motives laid bare. Normally, it was a side of myself I protected by deflecting or laughing off an observation.

"You got me. Probably comes from watching cancer take my dad and not being able to do anything about it. So having a plan makes me feel like I'm in control in a world where things don't make sense—probably why I chose a field where I study the laws of the universe." I shook my head at the realization. I hadn't quite put it into words before.

Braden looked into the distance and chewed his lip. "I understand that. But I hope you allow yourself to experience the magic sometimes, you know? Sometimes the unexpected yields the most beauty."

I patted his leg, ready to wrap up the navel-gazing. "That's a beautiful thought, Yoda, but not for me. I like to know what to expect. It calms me. Unforeseen dangerous situations do not make me happy. So can you please humor me and stay out of trouble?"

He nodded, the corner of his mouth ticking up. "Understood. Only cats in trees. No unnecessary risk."

"All I'm asking."

In my cartoon firefighter episode, Braden would hoist himself from a lower branch to a higher one, his biceps making the tree look like an unworthy opponent. Then he'd scoop the cat into his arms and carefully climb down without a hint of sweat from the exertion. "You have to admit, my cat-rescuing version has its perks. You could end up with a kitten playmate for Bella."

We turned down a residential street with houses like Braden's neighborhood. It felt like he was taking a longer route than usual. I didn't mind the extra time chatting in the truck.

"Bella would eat a cat."

"Oh. Okay, no cats."

He rolled his neck and tapped a finger lightly on the steering wheel. "Your version wasn't so far off from my day today. Wildfire season's just starting, so most of our calls were for pretty basic stuff."

"What's 'pretty basic' to you? Leaping from a flaming six-story building into a tiny net?"

"Funny. No, we had some small calls—smoke alarm in an office building, kitchen fire. Then we got called to a highway incident with a sixteen-wheeler that hit the center divider and flipped. That got a bit gnarly. Truck was carrying butane gas, and it started to leak, so there was an explosion risk."

"No, no, no danger." I put my hands over my ears. Then I took them off. "Okay, my curiosity won out. What did you do with a flipped truck full of gas?"

"Extracted the driver. Cleared the scene, closed down that stretch of highway, and soaked up as much of the spill as possible with peat moss, vermiculite, and clay. Then we waited for a hazmat team to deal with the larger cleanup." His voice was deep and commanding, and its powerful rumble sent a straight shot of heat between my thighs. Apparently, authority and skills turned my crank. I looked out the window so he couldn't see my lust-filled eyes. "Fortunately, it was more of a leak than a spill. When it's more than twenty-five gallons, we need to report it to the EPA, and if there's any groundwater contamination, it goes to OSHA . . . there's a protocol. But like I said, it wasn't needed."

"Wow," I exhaled, impressed. "That's a basic day? I pretty much sat at a desk."

He chuckled, and my skin heated even more. He was so serious most of the time that it felt like a huge win to elicit some laughter. "We have different jobs. Sometimes I sit at a desk, but that's when it's quiet, and I can study burn patterns and fire behavior."

I swiveled in my seat and tucked my legs under me. "Ooh, now you're talking. Hit me with some science, fireman." Anything involving new information excited me. But then I spotted something as we drove down First Street that interested me even more. "Ooh! Hold on, can we stop? Or can you drop me here? I need to get something."

He swerved the truck into a parking lot in front of a Domino's Pizza and looked around. "What's here?"

I was already opening the door and hopping out.

"Hang on. Where are you going?" he called after me, exiting the truck.

Walking a few paces ahead of him, I pointed. "Bike shop." In three strides, he caught up to me and grasped my elbow.

"You couldn't have just said that? I cut someone off back there. I thought it was an emergency or something." He waved his hand up and down my body in the universal uncomfortable male sign for feminine issues.

"Well, it kind of is. I may never drive again. I don't want to rely on Uber. I'm getting a bike."

"I can drive you where you need."

The butterflies in my heart fluttered at the idea. The past few minutes in the car was the most time we'd had together in two weeks, and I liked talking to him. I liked *him*. But I couldn't impose like that—it went against my principles of self-sufficiency.

Damn principles of self-sufficiency.

"No. It's an imposition for you to drive me around."

He reached past me and pulled the door handle of the shop open. "I don't mind driving you around."

I couldn't look at him. If my eyes took in any part of his face or body, I'd cave and hop in his car, go with him everywhere, even if it was the opposite direction of work. I walked into the shop with bikes lined up in the middle of the floor and a group hanging from the ceiling. "I'm already staying at your place. There's a limit to what you should have to endure."

"Will you stop it? I'm not enduring anything." He sounded aggravated, his tone gruff, a tiny muscle ticking in his jaw. But I was too entranced by the multi-colored bikes to worry about it.

I bypassed the section of mountain bikes and zeroed in on the pastel-colored beach cruisers. Carolwood seemed pretty flat, so maybe I could get away with a bike that didn't have gears. "Hey." Braden put a hand on my shoulder.

I wondered if there'd come a day when he could touch me and I wouldn't feel like he'd cranked the e-stim machine to a hundred. "Yeah?" I turned to see him looking concerned.

His voice was soft, careful. "Why did you said you may never drive again?" I shrugged. "C'mon, don't think like that. I know car accidents can be traumatic, but you'll get over it."

He was being so kind. But PTSD wasn't really the issue. "Right. I guess." I looked back at the bikes. "You know, I can buy one and ride back to your house. You don't have to stay."

He reached for my face and tilted my chin to look him in the eye. My breath hitched, and my insides melted like a chocolate fountain.

I couldn't look away. Why would *anyone* look away . . . ever?

"Sarah, what aren't you telling me?"

I couldn't decide whether it frustrated me that he could see through my attempts to be stoic, or whether I loved that he just knew. What a relief not to hold everything in all the time. But . . . what did I have left if I lost my ability to control what people saw?

Not all people. Braden.

I blinked away from him and let my shoulders drop. "Fine. I guess if you're going to live with me, you might as well know . . . I'll probably lose my license."

I saw the recognition on his face. "You've had other accidents?"

"A few. It's not just that. I have . . . I don't know how to describe it. My mind wanders when I drive . . . Like, a lot. It gets worse with the longer distance or when there's traffic, and I . . . "

"Crash into things?"

I nodded, ashamed that I couldn't do something as simple as drive a car. "I can calculate the annihilation rate of slow positrons, but I can't take a road trip without running into a bus. I don't know what's wrong with me."

He nodded in sudden understanding. "That's why you couldn't commute here from Berkeley."

"Not without a driverless car." I lowered my gaze to the floor. He might as well know everything.

"I wondered about that. Finn didn't say."

"Well, now you know. And even if I don't get my license suspended, my insurance rates will pound me, so I'm really going to need this bike . . ." I started to pull away, but his light touch on my skin made it impossible.

"Hey." He moved his hand from my chin to my cheek. A sweet gesture, but I knew it didn't have the same meaning for him—he was a professional lifesaver, after all. He knew how to comfort people going through trauma. "There's nothing wrong with you. So you're a distracted driver. In this day and age, join the club. At least you weren't texting."

"Because I don't have a death wish."

He smiled at that. Then I noticed the dawning of recognition on his face, and he checked the time. I'd waylaid him. "You have plans. I'm so sorry!"

"Don't worry. I can push them back."

"No, no, don't. I'll feel even worse. Please. Go enjoy your date, and I'll ride back to your house and learn my way around." I did my best to smile convincingly.

He hesitated, lines creasing his brow.

"Relax. I'm not going to call up Finn and say you abandoned me," I said.

He looked again at the time. "I'm happy to help you pick out a bike if you want to come back tomorrow. I just . . ."

"No, no. I'm good."

After another moment of indecision, he nodded. I watched his easy saunter to the door, imagining an alternate universe where he'd turn around and tell me he'd rather cancel his date to hang with me. The shop's bell jingled as he pushed it open. "Okay, just . . . text me that you made it back to my house, okay?"

I gave him a thumbs up and moved into the depths of the store, ready to find a two-wheeler that spoke to me. It didn't take long. I settled on a one-speed cruiser with a rack on the back, onto which I attached a square basket.

I calculated that the ride from Braden's house to the lab was about five flat miles. If I caught all the lights, I could make it to work in under a half hour and probably wouldn't be so sweaty that I'd need to change clothes. My new yellow bike, with its bell and brown leather seat, fit the bill perfectly.

After paying, I dropped my purse into the basket and rode to a grocery store for some dinner things. And maybe wine.

I'd been exhausted most nights after work, but my new purchase energized me. Tonight I'd have the place to myself. Time to have some fun in the kitchen while the hot roommate painted the town fire engine red.

raden

THE FEELINGS of guilt over leaving Sarah in the bike shop disappeared when my doorbell rang. I opened the door to find Kelsey standing on my doorstep in tight black jeans, a purple tank top, and no bra.

To be clear, the only reason she didn't need a bra was that she was twenty-two and her C-cup breasts still defied gravity in a way that normally made my dick hard just thinking about them. And now they were pressed to my chest as she brushed her lips against my cheek.

Kelsey's long, dark hair curled into waves around her face, and mascara made her brown eyes look even darker than usual. "Hi, hon," she said, sweeping past me with a bottle of pink wine in her hand. That was how she referred to it, "I'll take a glass of the pink."

She'd come over before each of our dates. "It's a thing. I like to meet at the man's house for safety reasons." Her cooing voice had sounded a little young, probably too young. Then, after a couple glasses of pink wine and a nice dinner, we'd gone back to her house where I enjoyed her young tits and young everything else.

I'd taken Kelsey to dinner three times. Three dinners that had led to fairly hot sex in her living room, two orgasms each for her, and a goodbye fuck against her front door before agreeing to see each other in a week or so.

It wasn't love, and it was never going to be love, but it was evolving into the perfect situation.

"Hey, hon," she hollered, and I realized I was still lingering by the front door. She'd called me 'hon' on our first date, which told me the nickname didn't mean much to her. That was fine. I'd stopped using any sort of endearments because I could never match the feelings that I thought should accompany them.

Except for calling Sarah 'Damsel.' I just couldn't break myself of that one.

"Sorry. Spaced out. I didn't get much sleep last night." I walked over to where she was rifling through my kitchen drawers looking for a corkscrew, even though she'd done the same thing twice before. "Listen, we should head out," I told her, not wanting an awkward encounter with Sarah when she got back from the bike shop.

Kelsey ignored me, and each time she opened a drawer and slammed it again, her breasts jiggled inside her tank top. Normally, that would be enough to have me hard. Instead, I found myself slightly annoyed that she was so clueless about where I'd keep utensils.

Quit thinking.

Kelsey was exactly what I needed—no complications, no heavy conversation about the future, no misunderstandings about spending the night together.

I took her hand, intending to walk her toward the front door. But she pressed into me, rubbing her hand over my cheek.

"I'm sorry you're tired." She moved her hand down to my chest, where her fingers edged lower until her acrylic nails teased my abs, and she dipped them into the waistband of my jeans. "I'll make sure you don't have trouble sleeping tonight."

I breathed in her slightly cloying flowery perfume and tried not to compare the bottled ordinary scent to Sarah's fresh citrus and flowers—every time she walked by, I had visions of a summer garden.

"Deal." I needed Kelsey to wear me out. I needed to drive into her so hard that I forced distracting thoughts about my goddamned roommate to the sidelines. It made no sense that Sarah entered my thoughts at all. She was a temporary guest, end of story.

If I needed a reason why she and I made zero sense, all I had to do was look at her, feel her goodness, listen to her brilliance. My relationship with Ellie taught me that women like that might have firefighter fantasies, but when those wear thin, they walk away.

Kelsey wouldn't do that. She loved whatever I could give her.

And yet . . . even with Kelsey's fingers massaging their way into my pants, I was distracted. It felt suddenly wrong to have her stripping my clothes off within the first five minutes of seeing me.

It felt . . . empty.

I grabbed Kelsey's wrists and extracted her hands before she could wrap them around my dick. "Dinner first? Play later?"

She pouted and turned her upside-down smile to me before kissing me on the lips. Her mouth was soft and willing, and she succeeded at shifting my focus completely to her. "As long as it's not too much later."

Kelsey was sweet. And so willing. I didn't know what the hell my problem was. I had no excuse for not enjoying my night out with her, starting right now. So I leaned in for one kiss, telling myself to enjoy the taste of her and the escape from the rest of my life. I closed my eyes and concentrated on feeling instead of thinking.

Which was maybe why I didn't hear my front door when it opened. But I heard Kelsey shriek a few seconds later. "What the hell?" She clung to me possessively, and it took me a moment to adjust my vision and figure out what had her so distressed. Then I followed her gaze to where Sarah stood a few feet away, a grocery bag and a bottle of wine in her hands.

"Oh. I'm so sorry." Sarah looked frozen, staring at us with aqua blue eyes that were wide with surprise and embarrassment. I quickly looked down to make sure no errant naked parts were exposed. Kelsey didn't move her hands from around my neck and had trouble freeing the garble of words that had collided in my throat.

"No, don't even . . . we were just . . ." What in the hell was I saying? I leaned my forehead against Kelsey's and pointed. "Roommate. Sorry, Kel . . . Sarah, I should have . . ."

Sarah waved her hands dismissively. "No, it's me. You said you had plans, I just didn't . . . never mind. I just came for a corkscrew." Her eyes darted past us and around the kitchen. If I'd been able to form words, I'd have told her where it was, but in a second, she'd opened the correct drawer and found the corkscrew.

"Gosh, I was just looking for that." Kelsey's voice was breathy.

A moment later, Sarah was gone in a blur of pink cheeks, honey hair, and the dizzying scent of lemon and flowers.

"Well, that could've been awkward," Kelsey snorted. "Good thing she didn't come home five minutes later when I had your cock in my mouth."

I shook my head, still having trouble forming words. There was no logical reason for me not to leap at the chance to have Kelsey's pretty lips all over any body part that interested her.

And yet . . . I couldn't get on board.

"Sorry about that." I finally found my voice, and it came out in a croak. I needed water,

Kelsey shrugged, arms still wrapped around my neck. "I recall exactly where we were." She pressed herself against me again. Within seconds, her lips were on mine, and my whole body went rigid. My thoughts returned to Sarah. I felt like I owed her an apology.

"Hon, you need to relax. Here let me help." Kelsey started again for my belt buckle, and I grabbed her hands to stop her.

"How about we pick this up after dinner? Maybe some Italian food, then back to your place?"

Kelsey smiled. "I like that idea."

I guided her down the driveway toward my car. She stood for a moment by the passenger door as I looked back at the house. I heard Kelsey's irritated huff as she opened the door herself and climbed in.

"Oh, shit." I'd left Bella outside because Kelsey didn't like dogs. I quickly texted Sarah and asked her to bring my dog inside, grateful that Bella liked her so much.

She wasn't the only one. And that was rapidly becoming a problem.

DINNER WAS FINE. I ate a plate of spaghetti with clams and a few bites of salad. Ordinarily, it was one of my favorite meals. Tonight, it tasted off.

Everything was off.

Kelsey told me a story about her downstairs neighbor, who was taking singing lessons and not learning very well. "She told me she wants to try out for 'The Voice' or something, and I didn't want to say anything, but hon, that's never gonna happen." She laughed, and I gave her a strained smile.

"Maybe she'll get better after a while," I mumbled, pushing the pasta around on my plate. I didn't feel hungry. Kelsey shrugged and smiled at me the way she always did, and I tried to remember what we'd talked about on the last three dates because this felt like a struggle.

It was me. I had no doubt about it.

Kelsey sipped her wine and leaned forward, giving me a view of her ample cleavage and batting her lashes. Then she leaned in to kiss me. Her lips tasted like the garlicky pesto sauce from her penne, and I felt her nails skate along the back of my neck as she rubbed her nose along my jaw.

Kelsey had no problem with PDA. I knew this from our last dinner, but that had been at a dark corner table in a brew pub. Really dark.

This was an upscale Italian place in Pleasanton. I knew people here, and I hoped to return with my dignity intact, so I put the brakes on before Kelsey decided to straddle me.

Our chairs were on adjacent sides of a small square table with a white cloth and a candle in the middle. She had her hand on my thigh and was making circles with her nails, working her way up my leg, staring into my eyes, and letting me know unequivocally what she wanted.

I should have wanted it too.

"You okay, hon?" she asked.

I felt like an asshole. "Yeah, sorry. Spacing out again. So, you were telling me about your neighbor's singing?"

"Yeah, I was . . ." She shrugged and moved her hand to my chest, massaging circles there. "There isn't that much more to tell." She looked down at our plates and swallowed down the last of her wine. "I'm pretty good to go here if you want to go back to my place. Maybe my neighbor will serenade us."

I wanted to *want* to go to her place. I tried to find enthusiasm for the plan. But even a guarantee that I'd get laid in the next thirty minutes didn't sound like an enticing option.

"You know what, I'm not at my best tonight. I apologize, Kelsey. You deserve a better date than me."

"Aw, hon, don't apologize. It happens. Life gets in the way sometimes." She took out her lipstick and dabbed a deep pink shade on her lips before rubbing them together. Then she took out her phone and started scrolling. I wondered if she was getting ready to find another man who might be more accommodating than me. The thought filled me with relief.

I felt terrible about disappointing her, but I could tell things were only going in one direction if I went back to her house. I'd either freeze up and not be able to get the job done, or I'd have sex with her and end up feeling like I'd used her, which was infinitely worse.

So I paid the check and drove her home. After walking her to her door and turning down her last-ditch offer to come inside, I left. I couldn't believe myself. I'd dated dozens of women, and never had there been an instance when I couldn't close.

Your dick has died. That's the only explanation.

There was another possible explanation, and I hated to think it involved the woman living in my house. I'd pushed thoughts of Sarah away for two solid weeks, and each day it got more difficult. I knew I couldn't date her, not if I wanted to emerge from our roommate situation with my heart intact, but I was beginning to realize that just knowing Sarah was making it impossible to date anyone else.

CHAPTER THIRTEEN

 arah

I FELT terrible for poor Bella, forced outside when she loved being around people. Braden's text didn't explain why he'd locked her out, but maybe he didn't want her jumping all over him when he had a perfectly willing woman to do that and more.

As soon as his truck pulled out of the driveway, I opened my bedroom door and went back to the kitchen. I couldn't unsee the image of Braden with his hands all over his date, and I fought off the gloomy feeling that this would be my reality for the next six months—a sideline observer of Braden's dating life.

It's fine. You have your own life, a celibate one.

Bella was overjoyed to get back into the house and showed it by jumping on me and licking my stomach.

"Oh, sweetie, I'm sorry you got banished. It's us girls now," I told her. She and I had a lot in common—both single females, hungry, and home on a Thursday night. And we both pined for the same guy. Seeing my similarity to a dog made me at least try to rein in my ridiculous, untethered feelings for my roommate. I had a tiny shred of pride. Somewhere.

Bella ran in circles around my legs before trotting off to find a ball, which she dropped at my feet.

"You want to play?" I took the ball and threw it outside, leaving the door open. As usual, she chased the ball and lay down on the grass, chomping it rather than bringing it back. The breeze from the yard felt nice as I puttered around in the kitchen.

I poured a generous glass of cabernet and admired the well-designed kitchen, modern with a white tile backsplash behind the stainless steel stove, white painted glass cabinets, a poured concrete countertop that matched the one on top of the island.

The morning Braden found me sitting there after my car accident felt like months ago instead of two weeks. If anything could put an abrupt halt to whatever niggling idea festered in my brain that Braden and I might someday date, seeing him with his hand up another woman's shirt did the trick.

I planned to bury my feelings in chocolate, right after I ate my single serving salad.

That's right. With no one here to judge my cooking skills or lack thereof, I went premade on the salad, homemade on the chocolate truffle brownies.

I gratefully unwrapped the boxed Greek salad, sprinkled dressing on top, and shook it to mix the ingredients. Done. Then I poked around the kitchen, taking out measuring cups and spoons. Everything was exactly where I'd expect it to be.

Braden's kitchen had a logic that spoke to me—cooking utensils and potholders within reach of the stove, silverware and plates near the dishwasher for easy put away. Even the wine opener was exactly where I'd have put it if this was my house.

I mixed up the brownie batter without consulting a recipe because—please—it wasn't my first chocolate rodeo. A pan of brownies was always the perfect complement to a dinner of salad and wine. And the wine was going down easily, maybe too easily.

So I poured another half a glass and cranked some music up on my phone. Who needed a pole? I could get my dance on while the oven preheated. Braden wouldn't be back for hours, and I ought to enjoy myself.

Then I added a healthy pour of bittersweet chocolate chips to the batter. They were my secret ingredient—the mixture of milk chocolate in the batter and semi-sweet chips gave the brownies just the right level of sweetness.

I'd finish them with bittersweet chocolate buttercream frosting and a sprinkling of sea salt and try not to eat the entire pan myself. But if Braden brought his handsy date back here after dinner, all bets were off.

raden

I HEARD music coming from the house when I was halfway up the front walk—dance music. It was jarringly pleasant. Sure, I listened to music in my car or on earbuds while I worked out, but I went more for motivating rap anthems or classic rock. This sounded like a Top 40s playlist at a wedding reception.

It felt like joy. It surprised me how much I liked hearing it in my own house.

When I flung the front door open, Bella scrambled to greet me, paws dancing on the hardwood floors. As I knelt down to apologize for locking her out earlier, my senses were assaulted by the warm scent of chocolate and a Taylor Swift song about not needing a man.

For two years, I'd convinced myself how much happier I was living alone, but my emotions instantly called bullshit. I liked coming home to signs of human life in my house. And my heart surged with desire to see Sarah, redoubling the feelings I'd fought all night long.

I was getting tired of fighting.

"Hey, girl. Sorry about earlier," I told Bella. She gave me the kind of stink eye a golden is capable of, which is not much. After I rubbed her under her chin, all was forgiven.

Bella followed me to the kitchen, which had to be the source of the chocolate. Whatever it was, I hoped there was enough for me too.

When I got to the kitchen, I froze.

There was Sarah, wrapped in a light blue towel, her honey-colored hair hanging down her back, leaning over the open oven door wearing two giant red oven mitts shaped like lobsters. I'd bought them at a craft fair in town a few years ago and rarely used them because they had curly feelers hanging off the ends, which got in the way.

But on her, the whole ridiculous outfit was perfect.

And hot. The unexpected sight of Sarah in bare feet and several other bare parts had my dick perking up despite myself.

Twirling to the music, Sarah brought a pan of brownies out of the oven and turned to put them on the counter. When she saw me, she screamed.

"Shit!" She nearly dropped the brownies but then righted them and held the pan, gawking at me until the heat bled through the mitts. Then she flung it to the counter and struggled to strip off the lobsters with little success.

"Great, these things are glued on." She continued to struggle, and her towel slipped a couple inches, revealing the swell of her breasts, which were milky white against the blue towel. And they were heaving.

I couldn't tear my eyes away, and as she saw where my gaze was fixed, she crossed her arms over herself and secured the towel, the floppy lobsters dangling from her hands.

A tendril of her hair dropped in front of her eyes, and I wanted to sweep it away, but I didn't dare come closer. As it was, she looked terrified at the sight of me.

"Sorry! I'm so sorry," I choked out, backing away from the kitchen until I nearly tripped over the ottoman in the den. So I sat on it and tried to seem convincingly interested in the basket of dog toys because the towel was pretty short on the bottom and was coming undone at the top.

She couldn't fix it because of the mitts, but the last thing I was going to do was get between a thin layer of towel and her breasts.

After a second, she freed her hands, resecured the towel, and grabbed her cell phone to turn down the music. "Jesus, you scared the crap out of me. I didn't think you'd be back for hours. Are you . . . with guest?" she stammered. Glancing around to check, she didn't seem immediately concerned with the fact that she was wearing only a small swatch of blue terrycloth.

I held a hand over my eyes, looking at her through the slats of my fingers. A useless effort.

"Just me. I'm so sorry. I smelled chocolate and couldn't resist."

She grinned, one hand on her hips, the other fanning over the confections like a game show host. "Brownies. I might be a little addicted to this recipe. It has coffee in it, probably why." She swayed to the side, her hip resting on the counter.

I took note of the half-finished bottle of wine on the kitchen counter. Was she tipsy? Her relaxed grin said she was, which I found unexpectedly charming for this hard-charging woman ruled by science and plans.

Sarah stayed like that for a moment, her smile warming me until she looked down at her barely-covered body and her eyebrows shot up in horror. She pulled the towel more tightly around herself and backed farther into the kitchen. I stayed on the ottoman.

"Oh gosh, you're probably wondering . . . I was . . . I took a bath while the brownies were baking and forgot about them, so I rushed to get them out."

I nodded. "I'm glad you're getting comfortable in the house."

She barked a laugh. "Um, yeah, just a little." The pink color rose in her cheeks, and seeming even more self-conscious, she stood watching me expectantly. When I didn't take the hint and leave, she moved carefully from the kitchen and past me, never turning her back, still holding onto the towel like a protective shield. "I'll, um, be back in a second."

While Sarah darted upstairs, I went to the kitchen, grabbed a beer from the refrigerator, and wiped the cold across my forehead. Jesus, I was burning up. Just glimpsing her creamy skin had heat crawling over the back of my neck and a fire building everywhere else.

I needed to get a grip. I snapped off the cap and took it back to the ottoman, using crack ninja mind control to think about anything except Sarah soaking in the bathtub upstairs.

And...epic fail. I exclusively pictured her in the tub.

After a minute, she came back, hair in a ponytail, wearing a hoodie sweatshirt and a pair of shorts that made it impossible not to admire her long, shapely legs. She was probably in such great shape from pole dancing. Great. That opened up a brand new playground for images of Sarah shimmying around a metal shaft.

Fuck me.

"So," she said, grabbing the bottle of wine and her glass from the kitchen and plopping down on the dark gray couch opposite where I sat. "How was your date? Did you have a nice time?"

Did she honestly want to know about my date? I knew she loved knowledge, but this seemed a little overboard. A grin played across her face, eyes sparkling like she cared and wanted to know. I couldn't think of anyone I'd ever met like her.

I scrubbed a hand over my chin, reminding myself I needed to shave one of these days. "It was alright."

"'Alright?' Come on, fireman, you can do better than that. Was it fun? Love connection? Or is this not a conversation you want to have with your roommate?" She poured another half a glass of wine, and I took note that very little of the wine was left in the bottle.

"I don't mind the conversation, but there's not much to tell. Tonight . . . I'd say no, not a love connection." I opted against telling her that part of the trouble was that I wished I was out with her instead.

I braced myself for her next question. She seemed infinitely curious about everything—there would be more questions.

"Sorry to hear you didn't find the magic. Assuming you're even looking for that . . . ack. There goes the patriarchy again, putting ideas into my head that relationships have to lead somewhere. Oops. Loveless fun is good . . . or . . . you know what I mean." She waved a hand in front of her face as though to fan the idea from the room.

I held up a hand. "It's fine." I sipped my beer and put thoughts of love firmly from my mind.

Her eyes gleamed, and she tucked her legs under herself on the couch, which made it easier to look at her without feeling like I was gawking. "What do you look for in a woman?" she asked. I didn't expect the question, and two weeks ago, I'd have refused to answer because I wasn't really looking for anything. Intentionally.

But now, the only thing I could say for sure was that it didn't freak me out as much to have the conversation.

I swallowed hard, understanding from her question that Finn hadn't said anything about my past. It made sense—he conveyed information on a need-to-know basis, which was partly why we'd stayed friends for so long. He respected boundaries.

And while I could tell Sarah the same lie I'd been telling people for two years, the whitewashed version that seemed fit for public consumption, I felt like she deserved the truth. She'd been honest when I'd asked her questions, and it made me want to meet her halfway.

"I guess . . . kindness would be the first thing," I said.

She laughed for a second. "Well, obviously." Then her face grew serious, and her cheeks reddened. "Sorry. I was thinking you were joking. But if you're not, then *yes*. Kindness is something you should *insist* on." She sipped her wine and stared into the glass.

"Don't apologize. I know it might seem obvious to someone who *is* kind, but yeah, I ought to look harder for it."

Her mouth tipped up on one side, and the way her gaze assessed me from head to toe was like a caress of silk against my skin. "You deserve it," she whispered.

I swallowed thickly, unsure how to respond. I wanted to deserve *her*. No way in hell I planned to tell her that. No indication she agreed.

Sarah quickly raised her glass to her lips and looked away as she took a sip. Torn between wanting to go deeper with the conversation and worrying that I wasn't ready to be so open, I defaulted to gruff guy generalities. "Anyhow, after someone being a generally nice person, I'd say I look for common interests and, you know, attraction."

Her eyes flipped to me in almost comical seriousness. "Yeah? Way to be specific. Who'd have thought to include common interests *and* attraction in a compatible female?"

"Are you giving me shit about my answer?"

She shook her head dramatically and continued in a playful voice. "Not at all, you robot. C'mon, fireman. You can do better."

If it wasn't for those sparkling sunset pools she had for eyes and the fact that she was definitely a little bit drunk, I might have taken offense at her finger wagging. But she was damn cute.

"Okay, fine. You want more?" I shifted in my seat. Sarah nodded in anticipation, her grin spreading. Bella, who'd been curled up on her bed, seemed to be siding with her, suddenly looking at me from under quirking eyebrows. "Okay, here goes . . ." I took a deep breath and prepared to bare my soul, still not completely understanding why Sarah and the way she looked at me made me want to tell her everything.

"What do I look for in a woman?" I took a deep breath and stared at the ceiling as though it contained the answers. "It would be simple if all I had to do was make a list—must love dogs, like outdoorsy stuff, career aspirations a plus. I kind of don't give a shit about any of that. Those things come. In time."

I chanced a glance at Sarah and saw her eyes locked on me, her jaw slack. Slowly, she nodded, and I felt emboldened to continue. "It's the intangible stuff that isn't part of some list. A connection —I don't know where the hell it comes from. That's the magic. The way the entire world falls away when we're in the same room. Like nothing else—*no* one else—matters. She knows me. And even though everyone else can feel her soulful inner beauty when they're around her, she burns brighter for me.

"So I guess…I want a level of understanding where I instinctively sense her missing pieces. And give her whatever she needs to shine like she deserves. So it's not about looking for a certain set of characteristics—liking the same movies or wanting to visit the same vacation spots—it's about losing myself to be a part of her. So I don't know that I'm looking for a 'love connection' as much as something that's unbreakable."

Sarah had been sitting forward, so focused that she almost spilled her wine before noticing and righting the glass. Then she slumped back against the couch with a hand on her cheek. I saw the rise and fall of her chest and realized my pulse had sped up as well.

Where the fuck did that come from?

I was not the expressive kind of guy who generally waxed poetic about love. Especially because I didn't believe it in. Not anymore.

She shook her head, eyes glistening and fixed on me. Not gonna lie—I loved the way it felt. Maybe because she had the potential to connect with me the exact way I'd just described.

Which is why you need to shut it down. Now.

She also had the power to leave me so much worse off than Ellie did if I wasn't careful.

"Braden, that's just . . . wow." She shook her head again and bit down on her lip. "I really hope you find her. And while you're at it, order me up one of her too. I don't date the ladies, but that sounds freaking amazing."

I laughed. "Yeah, well, she doesn't exist."

"Why d'you say that? C'mon, where's my optimistic fireman? You just haven't met her yet."

I ran a hand over my scruff, which was a nervous habit. "I did meet her. Or at least I thought I did. I was engaged . . . previously. To a woman—Ellie was her name—who I thought was at least some of those things. Or if not, she fell pretty damn close."

Sarah put her wine glass down and leaned forward, resting her chin on her hands. "What happened?" she asked softly, her forehead creased with worry. "Did she die?"

I couldn't help my smile at her earnest concern. "No. Nothing like that. She's alive. But she's with a different guy. She met someone else two months before the wedding, moved to New York to live with some brilliant hotshot lawyer she met on a business trip." I waited for her to digest that information.

Sarah blinked a couple times and squinted as though what I said didn't make sense. To me, truthfully, it still didn't.

"Yeah, at first it was phone sex, then he started flying out to see her. They were screwing in the spare bedroom right up until two weeks before the wedding when she dumped me officially. In a text. Said I wasn't enough for her. She needed someone more educated, with more depth."

"*Depth?*" She spat the word out. "Screw her, Braden. What a horrible thing to say."

"She didn't mean it the way it sounds."

As usual, I was defending her. I'd been doing it since the day she left, not to make her look less cruel but to make myself feel less fucked over. If her reasons sounded valid, it was objective, not personal.

Sarah scooted closer and put a hand on my knee. The heat spread like a late summer brush fire consuming dry leaves.

"Braden. You *are* educated. Your job is selfless and admirable. And you have more depth than most people I've met. I'm sorry she said that." Her scowl and the crease in her brow underscored her words. She closed her eyes, then leveled me with their expressive sea of blue. "Wait, did you also just say she told you all this in a text?"

"Well, not all of it. She started with the 'I can't marry you,' and that dovetailed into a screaming match in person."

"Good. She deserved some screaming at."

I appreciated that she wanted to take my side, but if she'd met Ellie, she'd see that I was outclassed. No doubt, everyone saw it. Except me.

"Maybe in the moment, but it wasn't meant to be. She grew up in downtown Chicago, loved big cities. She was never going to be happy here. She was too good for me. I was just too dumb to see it until it was way too late. Willful blindness."

She picked up a pillow from the couch and threw it at me. Her aim was decent. If I hadn't ducked, she'd have beaned me in the face. "Hey."

"You're an idiot. Albeit one with fast reflexes."

"Why, because I don't understand particle physics?"

She rolled her eyes. "First of all, no one *really* understands it. That's why we call everything a theory. We're just really convincing when we talk about shit we can't see."

"Okay . . ." I wasn't sure where this was headed.

"You're an idiot because you think she was too good for you. That's absurd."

"If you met her, you'd know."

She shook her head. "You're wrong. She just wasn't the right one. And I'm sure it felt awful, but she did you a favor. I know it hurt, but seriously, good riddance. She didn't deserve *you*." People had said that to me before, but hearing her say it felt different because I cared what she thought. And it triggered a movement—a shaking off of rust and stubborn atrophy—in a deep part of my heart that had been dead for a long time.

"It's fine. I'm over it. It's been two years," I lied. Like I always did.

It felt like an iron cage was squeezing my chest. I didn't want to lie to Sarah. But I'd already opened up more than I'd planned. Time to lock everything back down.

"Anyhow, that's the deal, and that's why I know now that the perfect relationship doesn't exist. But hey, we can fantasize, right?" That's all it was—a fantasy.

Sarah nodded and flopped against the back of the couch. She looked defeated, leaning her arm against her forehead, or maybe that was just how I felt.

"So . . . now it's your turn." Desperate to shift the conversation away from my morose self, I got up and pantomimed a spotlight shifting to her. She put her hand up in mock blocking of the glare.

"You can ask, but no promises I'll bare my soul," she laughed.

"Oh, come on. I gave you complete honesty. I expect no less."

"Fine." She shrugged.

Rubbing my hands together like I was hatching an evil plan, I got another beer from the fridge. "Let's see, where shall I begin?" When I saw the tray of brownies on the counter, I couldn't resist. "I think this inquisition calls for some chocolate."

She jumped from the couch. "No, no, you can't eat them yet. They need frosting, but they're still too hot."

"I'm sure they taste great without frosting." I pulled a knife from the block on the counter and bounced my eyebrows to see if she'd agree to my plan.

But she took the knife from my hand, and when she did, the brush of her fingers against mine was red hot fire. The barest graze sent a thrill of electricity along my skin.

Was it possible that she didn't feel it too?

She gave no indication as she put the knife on the counter and looked at me like she was reprimanding a toddler. "Fifteen minutes. I promise you'll like them better once they're frosted. You can't eat naked brownies."

In my mind, she was telling me we should eat brownies naked, and I immediately pictured her lying on the floor with a brownie covering each breast, and I was fine with that.

I tried to shake that thought from my head by looking around the kitchen. "Am I crazy? I don't see any frosting."

"I have to make it. So ask me your questions, and I'll make the buttercream."

I took a slug of my beer and leaned on the counter, studying her while she measured powdered sugar and put the remainder in the cupboard with my other sugar. "How'd you know where I keep the sugar?"

She looked at me like it was obvious. Maybe she'd already gone through all the cupboards and drawers and figured out where I kept stuff. "I went to where I'd put sugar, and it turned out that's where you have yours. In the logical place."

"Is that how you knew where to find the corkscrew?"

"Huh?"

"Earlier. You went to the right drawer the first time."

She shrugged. "I guess."

"Okay, forget about that. Let's talk about your ideal man. Spill."

She didn't say anything for a moment, and I started to think she might not answer. For all I knew, she was dating someone back in Berkeley, and he was her ideal man.

"Actually, you don't have to answer that. It's none of my business."

Quirking an eyebrow, she smiled. "Just like it was none of my business when I asked you? Come on, we're roommates and we never see each other. This is a chance to get to know each other. I'm not passing that up."

I shrugged, glad that she was game. "Okay, then. Tell me. If your perfect man walked through the door right now, what would he be like?"

She started unwrapping sticks of butter. "He can't walk through the door right now. I need to focus on work. The perfect man doesn't fit with that. But I guess someday I'd like to meet someone who makes me *feel*, you know? I spend most of my time thinking and analyzing and *controlling*." She winked at me, and it was all I could do not to wrap her in my arms.

"Someone who could share that burden without making me feel like I'm a nut job for being the way I am, that would be magical. I've never experienced that kind of support—I always feel a little apologetic for being myself. Oh, and I want mind-boggling sex, like orgasms so intense the neighbors feel aftershocks. Like, earth-shattering, screaming, rollicking orgasms . . . not that I've even come close to experiencing that, but I have a feeling it's out there. With the right guy. You know?"

Do I know? Not sure. Because I'm pretty sure I just died.

CHAPTER FIFTEEN

arah

MAYBE I SAID TOO MUCH. I definitely said too much.

I blamed the wine.

And the guy. It was impossible to have Braden Michaels standing in front of me in all his abdominal splendor and not wax rhapsodic about the kind of orgasms I'd only read about in romance novels.

From the way Braden was looking at me, I had the sense I'd freaked him out with my candor, or maybe it was just that he didn't really want to know all the details. Either way, I watched as he made a herculean effort to close his mouth and blink back the shock from his eyes.

"I'm not saying it has to be all those things, but if we're talking about the ideal, then I stand by what I said . . . within reason. I'm a scientist, after all. It's only possible to have what exists in the real world."

I looked at Braden, a little alarmed that he still stood frozen with his arms crossed in front of him. Was he ever going to move, or had I turned him to stone?

"Anyway . . ." I turned the mixer on and used the noise to fill the dead air. I loved watching the butter mix with the sugar into a perfect buttercream frosting. I dribbled a little vanilla in, along with some chocolate I'd melted earlier—it was still soft enough to blend well into the frosting, and the dark, rich color took over.

A moment later, I felt the warmth of Braden's body next to mine as he peered into the bowl of the mixer. For a chocolate lover, it was hard to stay away. "That looks pretty good," his voice rumbled near my ear. I tried to fight back the shivers it caused.

"It's sinfully good." Once it was perfectly mixed, I tipped the whisk attachment out of the bowl and scraped down the sides with a spatula. "Can you grab the tray of brownies? You can have the honor of frosting them since you were patient enough to wait."

Holding out the bowl of the mixer, I waited until he moved the brownies to the counter in front of us. Then I handed him the spatula. When he took it, I felt like his hand lingered on mine longer than it needed to, the touch of his fingers sending heat through my veins that hadn't happened with a man since . . . ever.

I took it as scientific evidence that Braden Michaels had raw animal magnetism that other men didn't have. Fascinating.

Even if I only experienced it through the occasional brush of fingers, I had no doubt he was turning my very core molten like the velvety melted chocolate. And it felt so good I found myself looking for more ways to innocently touch him.

"How should I do this?" he asked.

"Exactly the way you are . . ."

"Huh?"

Huh?

Nope, he wasn't asking how he should touch every inch of my remaining skin. He'd brushed past me by accident.

"Um, I meant, hold the spatula like you are, then spread it in one even layer. If you spread it in too many small strokes, you might tear the tops of the brownies."

"Fine, if I can eat my mistakes."

"Nope, you can eat them when they're perfect."

He cast me a side-eye and his lips twisted into a smirk. "Has anyone ever accused you of being bossy?"

"Only my sisters. It's kind of my role to be the responsible backbone, in other words, bossy. I may or may not have a history of making sweeping decisions on their behalf. Just ask my sister, Becca. Story for another time. Anyway . . ." I grabbed the green and white box of sea salt and got ready to sprinkle the tops.

"What's that?" He raised an eyebrow suspiciously.

"The secret ingredient. Well, one of them. Sea salt brings out the chocolate flavor. I promise you'll approve when you taste them."

"Don't make promises lightly. I'll hold you to them," he smirked.

"I'd expect nothing less." He finished spreading and I finished salting and we looked at each other. "Moment of truth." I took the knife and sliced through to make sixteen squares in the pan.

I wasn't worried. Despite a litany of botched recipes I laid claim to, this one never disappointed.

"What do I get if these brownies don't live up to your promises?" He leaned against the counter with one hip, his snug dark jeans highlighting the taut muscles in his legs and his tight black long-sleeved shirt leaving no ridge of his six-pack to the imagination.

The smirk on his face threw me. Was he just toying with me because I'd audaciously promised he'd like them? Or did he want something? Was he . . . flirting?

Well, that's just plain crazy talk.

Guys like Braden—beautiful larger than life heroes with medical smarts who put their lives on the line to save people—didn't flirt with their normal scientist roommates in the kitchen. They had no shortage of excessively hot women to fill their every sexual want or need, women like Kelsey. If voluptuous, young women were his type, I was not.

Nevertheless, I didn't shy away from a dare, so I tipped up my chin and challenged him.

"Well . . . what do you want?"

"Hmmm . . ." He pretended to be considering the question, but I knew he had something in mind. He grabbed a spatula from a ceramic jar of utensils and began spinning it in his hand. "If I find that your brownies fall even a little bit short of your lofty promises, you have to agree that I will drive you to and from work every day unless our schedules don't match. "

That made no sense. "So you're going to add insult to injury if you don't like my brownies by adding chauffeur to the already-long list of favors you're doing me?"

He shrugged. "It's my compensation if these things are anything short of fantastic."

"I think you've got it backwards—I should owe *you* something if I lose."

"Those are my terms."

"Fine. It probably won't come to that. I feel pretty confident in my brownies." I pulled a couple sheets from the paper towel dispenser and laid them on the countertop. I nodded to Braden, and he carefully lifted one square onto each paper towel.

"How about you?" he asked, eyes still flashing.

"How about me, what?"

"Is there something you want if I decide your brownies *do* live up to the hype?" He winked. The damn fireman was flirting.

I narrowed my eyes at him. "What's your game, mister? You're the one who's in charge here. You get to lay down a verdict once you taste these things," I said, pointing to the squares in front of us. "You want me to wager something, just so you can find a tiny bit of fault with my recipe and assure I don't get it?"

He took a step closer to me, and I could feel the heat radiating from his large, muscular body. Maybe that was his intention, to throw me off. It was working. My heart started beating so fast I could feel it in my throat.

Two could play at that game. I took a step closer to him, so we were almost touching. I had to tilt my head back to look him in the eye, which emphasized how tall he was, easily over six feet.

"I'd never do something so underhanded." His eyes met mine and moved briefly to my lips before returning to stare me down. His closeness made my body ache with desire, a warm flush spreading under his gaze.

Maybe that's why I blurted out the first thing that came into my head. "Fine. If the brownies are as good as I say, you have to kiss me."

I saw the surprise register in his eyes for a split second before he recovered. His shock was nothing compared to my own.

Where the hell had that come from? I swallowed hard and steadied my gaze at him, unwilling to back down.

His smirk returned, and he nodded at me, taking one step back.

"Fine. Deal."

We shook on it.

I immediately wanted to take back my wager. Not that I didn't want him to kiss me, but I was a person who clung fast to my plans so I could feel in control. As I veered off course from putting all kissing on hold until after I'd gotten tenure, all my life goals felt endangered.

"Actually . . ." I started to backpedal, but Braden held up a hand. He picked up the paper towels with the brownies and handed one to me. He even went so far as to clink brownies in a chocolate toast.

"Best of luck to you." He paused to take a whiff of the brownie, blinking hard. Then he took a generous bite. I was so fixated on watching his straight teeth bite through the chocolate and his lips wrap around the bite he'd just taken that I forgot I held one of my favorite desserts in my hand.

The planet may have stopped spinning in real time and begun moving in slow motion, just so I could see the muscle in Braden's jaw pop as he chewed the bite, and his stormy gray eyes fix on mine until he finally closed them.

When he swallowed and licked his bottom lip, it was almost like he'd licked me. I went limp. "Oh my God," he moaned, eyes rolling back.

I barely heard his words amid the whole-body orgasm I was having. But something about the heated look gave me told me I'd succeeded in wooing his tastebuds. "Verdict?"

He took another bite and threw up his hands. "I concede," he said around a mouthful of brownie. "You win. These are amazing."

I felt pretty solid in my brownie-making skills, and I liked the affirmation. But then . . . oh shit. I didn't want him to feel obligated to kiss me. It was like something out of a high-school spin the bottle party. I felt ridiculous.

I started waving my hands. "But forget about the whole wager thing. That was just a joke. You don't have to—"

"Yes, I do." His eyes clouded with heat, the barest smile on his lips replaced with serious intention. "A bet's a bet."

His hands cupped my face as he leaned in closer, and I felt the air leave my lungs in a whoosh. I inhaled roughly, taking in the scent of woodsy aftershave and fresh soap, watching the fire in his eyes until they blurred in my vision.

The heat from his hands and the way he brushed the pad of his thumb over my cheek caused my eyes to drift closed. His lips brushed softly against mine, like a whisper. My breath hitched, his fingertips licking my skin like flames from a torch.

The first graze of his lips was just an exploration, light and slow and tender.

I wanted more, but I didn't want to rush. If I was getting one kiss, I wanted it to be everything. Sliding my hands up the hard planes of his chest, I rested them on his shoulders and leaned into his body. His lean muscles seemed to absorb my softer curves like they were meant to meld with them.

He tilted my head to a new angle and covered my mouth with his, still gentle, dragging lips over every inch of mine and setting every nerve ending on fire. So much better than I'd ever imagined in the idle moments when my gaze fell on his lips, and I wondered how they would taste.

They tasted like sweet sin and chocolate decadence that had nothing to do with the brownies. When he tugged my bottom lip with his teeth, I went limp like a noodle.

His hand went to the band holding my hair and pulled until the strands came loose, dancing over my shoulders. He ran his hands through them before wrapping the strands around his fist, tipping my head back, and groaning into the kiss.

I couldn't have pulled away if I wanted to, entirely dragged under by the current of his lips and his body pressed against mine. I wanted to drown in it. Every kiss delved deeper and unearthed new levels of pleasure rippling beneath my skin until my entire body was on fire.

Opening against his mouth, I felt the glorious sweep of his tongue against mine. With languid intensity, my body begged me to say yes to everything and anything he wanted.

Each time his lips, his hands, his body shifted, I fell deeper under his spell. I couldn't push away the intensity of desire I had for him. More, just . . . more.

I wanted it and he kept giving.

Our mouths fused perfectly. To hell with the plate of brownies—I could live on his kiss for a century.

As he moved his hands along the ridge of my jaw, butterflies exploded within my chest at the unexpected delight of his calloused fingers moving along my skin. I wanted hours, days of this, and I tried to give him every indication of that by matching his tongue stroke for stroke and curling my fingers around his neck.

Spinning to push me against the refrigerator, he pressed harder against me. His kiss tore through my body like lightning as his mouth ravaged mine, taking and giving and delighting me with every brush of his tongue.

I felt no inhibitions. It was crazy—just one kiss, and I couldn't get enough. I tightened my grip on his neck, digging my nails into his skin. He groaned against my mouth.

When his lips traveled over my cheek, and I felt his breath on the skin below my ear, a moan escaped my lips. "Sarah . . ." he growled, sending a quiver over my neck and through my core.

His mouth returned to mine, and I pressed into him, feeling his arousal hard against me. It was crazy how good he felt. Crazy how powerless I felt to stop.

When he pulled away, I felt the loss like an epic black hole in the universe. Our eyes met, and I saw the hazy agreement that neither of us had expected a kiss to feel like that. We were both breathless.

But we'd agreed to one kiss.

One very long, very intense, everything kiss.

"You really know how to pay a debt," I gasped, slumping against him. Braden held me up and gently guided me to the couch I'd been sitting on before. He took the seat across from me, clearly putting distance between us, which was the only thing that prevented me from jumping him.

"It was hardly a sacrifice." He smiled. I liked how it looked on him.

"Nor for me."

He ran a hand over his face. "But . . . it can't happen again."

The words tore through me like a sharp blade. I tried to control the muscles in my face, but I knew I couldn't hide the hurt and disappointment. And he saw it. "Right. Of course," I agreed.

I'd asked for a kiss and he'd obliged, but he couldn't be clearer about where we stood. He was paying back a bet.

No need to tell me twice.

I had more pride and self-control than to force myself on him if he didn't want me. I'd been with enough guys to know that sometimes the chemistry isn't right. Or the timing. Or . . . whatever. He'd been kind enough to play my little game and indulge my request, but clearly, he wasn't interested in me beyond an obligation.

It was fine.

"Anyway, I should get to bed. Big day ahead of me in the morning." I stood and headed upstairs without eating a brownie. My mind was a mess of conflicting emotions—lust and pain and rejection and desire. And before I got halfway to my room, I started to get mad. Really, really mad.

He said he didn't do relationships, but I never asked for that. If he could kiss Kelsey or whatever the hell other women he had non-relationships with, why couldn't he kiss me?

I'd just thrown my 'no dates, no kissing' plan to the wind, and I sure as heck didn't want to be dismissed and shut down when he didn't even give me a good reason.

If I wasn't his type or he didn't want to complicate things with his roommate, he could have the balls to say it. And no matter how mindlessly or expertly he could kiss, I felt pretty certain he wasn't going through the motions when he kissed me. He was as into it as I was. So what the hell?

I turned around and marched back to the kitchen.

CHAPTER SIXTEEN

arah

BRADEN WAS mid-brownie when I spun back into the room like the Tasmanian Devil fueled by blood lust. Or, in my case, just regular lust. I strode toward him, balling my fists as though prepping for a fight.

"I need a better explanation." I threw my hands on my hips and glared. He slowly chewed and swallowed the bite in his mouth and drank a sip of water. Maybe he was using the time to figure out why I was so worked up because he looked wide-eyed and clueless.

And a little scared. He took a few steps back from me, effectively pinning himself between me and the sink.

"Okay," he exhaled. "What do you want to know? Why I ate a second brownie? They were damn good." He folded his arms across his chest, and the bulge of his biceps momentarily distracted me. I found that annoying. And entrancing.

"What exactly was wrong with that kiss?" I hissed like a petulant child.

He cocked his head to the side the same way Bella did when she was listening but not understanding a word.

"You want a critique?" He had the sexiest and most aggravating smirk on his face. "Are you gathering data? I know you're a scientist and all."

I couldn't believe him. "Yes, Braden. I'm all about the scientific method when it comes to kissing," I spat out with a scowl.

He waited for more, but instead of explaining, I grabbed his face in both hands and crushed my mouth to his. At first, he froze. Then he relented, melting into my lips like I'd lit a match.

A guttural moan escaped him as I held his face close and pressed in deeper, sucking on his bottom lip the way I wanted to, biting down on it and challenging him to meet me there.

He responded with his entire body, cupping the back of my head in his hand as our mouths moved against each other in perfect rhythm. Leaning against the sink, he pulled me in hard, lifting my hips to his waist. I wrapped my legs around him and pressed closer, challenging his tongue to dance with mine, drinking him in because it made me feel alive.

Maybe he'd tell me again that it couldn't happen. Maybe he'd reject me twice in one night.

I don't care.

I just needed an explanation if he insisted it was wrong.

I pulled away and leaned my forehead on his. "That. What was wrong with that?"

His jaw ticked as he swallowed hard. Our eyes locked, and the heated look in his told me I was right—nothing was wrong with the way it felt. But . . .

"Fuck it." His mouth crashed against mine, taking everything I would give and returning it in equal measure. The stroking, tasting, exploring, devouring.

After a frenzied few minutes, he slowed the pace of the kiss to a languid dance, brushing his lips across my jaw and sending shivers down my neck. He worked his way along my jaw with light kisses until I folded into his embrace.

Wordlessly, his mouth angled against mine, and he drew out a slow, seductive kiss, sucking my bottom lip until I sighed against him.

His tongue licked the seam of my lips until I opened for him, desperate to feel the sweep of his tongue while his hands tangled in my hair.

There was nothing wrong with kissing him like that. I felt breathless and dizzy and I wanted more. How breathless and dizzy could he make me? I wanted to reach the edge where I was barely hanging on.

Our tongues swirled, his wrapping around mine in a lazy seduction until I was quivering.

We kissed until both of us were sweating, panting, and inches from ripping each other's clothes off.

And I felt a little proud of myself. I wasn't an experienced seductress but any stretch, but I'd come downstairs on adrenaline, and I didn't wait for permission. I took what I wanted and didn't apologize.

Except . . .

"We can't do this," he huffed again, sounding as frustrated as I felt.

Braden pulled away and rubbed a hand over his face. He looked like the grim reaper had just paraded through the kitchen with his name at the top of the list.

I gaped at him, still breathless, "Why the hell not?" My voice sounded high-pitched and frantic.

"Because. I'm the wrong guy for you."

"Isn't that my decision to make?" My anger started to build all over again. It felt like a polite way of saying I wasn't the right woman for him.

"Not necessarily," he said quietly.

My face fell, and I pressed my lips together to stanch the nauseating sting of rejection. Here I was, aching with need, still tipsy, and practically throwing myself at him. And he was turning me down.

I'd never been one to beg. If he wasn't into it, fine. But the hard-on in his pants told a different story, so I needed him to say the words. "I just thought . . . It seems like . . . okay. If you feel no attraction here, then just say so. I don't need your pity."

His eyes went as wide as dinner plates, and his jaw dropped. "Pity? Are you kidding? It's taking every bit of mental strength I have not to carry you to that couch and fuck you until you come six times, screaming my name. No attraction? One kiss, and I want to kiss you for five hours."

"Oh. Um, okay." I stumbled over my words, trying to mesh the warmth humming in my veins at his words with the confusion I still felt about his reasoning. I squinted at him questioningly. "So, not the chemistry."

He threw up his hands and groaned, "All I've done since I met you is try to stop thinking about all the ways I want to kiss you. All the things I want to do to that body of yours. Chemistry is not the goddamn problem."

I went limp against the kitchen counter, my hands curling around the drawer pulls to hold myself up. My panties felt damp, and my heart rattled in my chest.

"So, what's the problem?" I barely choked out the words. If we both felt the same searing chemistry, what could possibly be not right about it? "Is it because of your ex?"

His laugh came out like a bark and he shook his head. "No. Definitely not my ex. In fact, since you crashed into my life, it's the first time in two years that I haven't given a shit about my ex.

"So . . ." I still wasn't understanding.

"You. This is about you. You have a plan and a schedule and a relationship goal. And I'm not that guy. I'm who women come to for a good time. I don't do relationships."

I huffed out a frustrated breath. "Again, not for you to decide. Sure, I have plans, but they're *my* plans. Who's to say I can't have a good time while I'm here? Why can't I kiss you without you telling me it can't happen every five minutes?"

He ran a hand over his scruff, then over his eyes. "You shouldn't change your plans for me. For this. You're a nice person, Sarah. You deserve a good guy who wants a relationship, not a player like me."

Braden had no way of knowing it, but he'd just poked the bear. Being called nice was a slap in the face. I wasn't just a nice girl who studied hard and baked brownies. I was a multifaceted woman who could make plans and change them when she felt like it. I wasn't the workaholic, responsible drone my family expected me to be. I had cravings and desires, and one of them was standing in front of me, acting like he knew everything. I wanted to punch him. Then kiss him for a long, long time.

"You don't dictate what I deserve. Or what I want." I spoke quietly and folded my arms.

His face reddened, and he scrubbed a hand over his features again, exasperated. "Jesus, woman, do you really disagree with me, or do you just like to argue?"

I licked my lips. "I do like to argue. But I don't want to argue about this."

His eyes heated, pupils dilating. I watched them lazily roam over me.

"What do you want, Sarah?" His voice was low and husky. It was a white flag surrender.

What do you want?

I wanted Braden unleashed and uncensored. I wanted him charged with lust. I wanted him to make my body feel things it had never felt before and would probably never feel again. The scientist in me was curious. The woman was desperate and impetuous.

I had a choice. I could accept his analysis, revert to being the rational planner I'd spent a lifetime perfecting, and go upstairs and dig out my vibrator like a nice, acquiescent roommate. Or I could ask for what I wanted.

Braden waited, and I could see his pulse throb in a vein of his neck. He was trying to do the right thing, whatever he thought it should be. It was on me to tell him what it was.

"What if I want the player?" I stepped closer to him. Our bodies were almost touching, and I could feel the tension in the air like electricity before a summer storm. Only we were the brewing storm, and all it would take was one errant spark to burn the house to the ground.

"I don't want a plan for the future." I whispered, locking eyes with his. I saw the Adam's apple in his throat bob as he swallowed hard. "I want right now. And I want to know what happens after a kiss like we just had." My voice was quiet and soft, but my eyes communicated my seriousness.

He leaned closer, his voice a rough breath against my ear. "Damsel, I'm more than happy to show you."

As soon as the words were out, his mouth swept across my neck, leaving tremors in its wake. His lips were on mine in a slow, deep kiss. His hands pushed into my hair.

It was a different kiss than the one from earlier. It was furious, desperate, consuming.

His tongue wrapped around mine and stroked, taking what he wanted. His hands cupped the back of my head and held me at the perfect angle for our mouths to find each other and mesh in a collision of lust and heat.

There was no going back. Every nerve ending in my body was begging for more, urging me forward.

I wanted to feel every sensation, every quivering breath, every blur of my edges he could find in me. This was about me obeying what my body needed. It was about pent-up desire that had been building for two weeks that felt like two months.

It was about finding a piece of myself that had been buried for years while I held firm to my responsible role in the family, the one everyone could rely on, the one who planned everything out all the time. I wanted to try something unplanned and unexpected that belonged just to me.

Even if for only one night.

CHAPTER SEVENTEEN

raden

EACH WAKING hour that I'd spent thinking about my mouth roaming over every damn inch of Sarah's skin felt like a fever dream leading to this. To her.

Our mouths fused, and our tongues tangled and roamed, but I needed more. I wanted to consume her, to own her.

We should slow down.

My brain tried to play referee between my body and hers, but it might as well have tried to stop an eighteen-wheeler rolling downhill with no brakes. If I couldn't be the good guy I knew I should be, I'd be the good time she asked for. I wanted to take her with abandon and rock her world until the feel of my body was tattooed on her skin, until she was ruined for every man who came after me.

It was wrong to want to possess her like that, but she already had a hold on me that was impossible to resist.

Slow the fuck down.

We'd already kissed, so we could do that some more without me feeling like I'd crossed more lines, but I should draw a firm line after that. Or . . . I could let her make the rules and treat her like anyone else I'd enjoy for one night. But she wasn't anyone else. She was quickly becoming an obsession because she was so much more than one night's enjoyment. I didn't want to treat her that way. So we'd just kiss some more, and then I'd stop us.

But the frantic way her nails grazed the back of my neck and then dug in with abandon assured me she did want more. She wasn't my friend's sister and my temporary roommate. She was mine. And she wanted everything that came with it.

"Don't stop," she pleaded, giving me all the reason I needed to grab her ass so hard it would probably leave a mark. I bit her earlobe and exhaled a breath against her neck the way I already knew would make her moan. "Finn didn't mention these skills when he pitched you as a roommate."

"It would help if you didn't mention your brother's name." I licked a trail down the side of her neck to her collarbone, where the soft skin smelled like citrus and flowers I'd already come to associate with her. She tipped her head back to give me better access. My cock was throbbing in my pants, and all I wanted was to bend her over the back of my couch and fuck her until she saw stars.

"Done." Her voice was sultry as she lifted off my shirt. "I'll only mention your name. And then it will be loud. When you make me come."

She said she wanted a player, which made me want to give it to her. "There's nothing hotter than you talking about me making you come." I ran a hand along her stomach, gliding carefully over the skin and feeling it pebble under my touch.

We were still in first-base territory, and I could still stop things before they got way out of control.

I should stop things.

"If we're going to do this, there should be rules," I rumbled, having no idea what the rules would or should be. It just seemed like a good idea since I already knew I'd have no self-control when it came to her.

"Okay, rules are good. Do you have any in mind?" she breathed, pushing my shirt up and running her nails over my abs.

Then her tongue.

I couldn't form a sentence at that point, let alone a coherent set of rules.

I answered by lifting her hoodie over her head. She wasn't wearing a bra, and seeing the creamy white skin of her supple breasts with their hard nipples pushed me over the edge.

There would be no more discussion of rules. Just be me with my hands on every inch of her body, absorbing every sound she made and working to elicit more, worshipping every curve of her neck and the heat of her skin until she screamed my name.

I moved us into the den and sat on the couch, positioning Sarah so she straddled my lap. "The whole time I was on my date, I was thinking about this. With you. Even though I knew it was impossible," I whispered near her ear before licking a path down her neck and sucking on the tender skin at the curve. "I couldn't even kiss her. That's why I was home so early."

"I admit I felt a little jealous of her." Sarah ran her fingers over my jaw, planting a row of kisses in their wake. "Because she had you."

She ground her hips against my rock-hard cock, and her breath caressed my neck until I groaned. Stopping things was no longer an option.

CHAPTER EIGHTEEN

arah

KARMA WAS DOING ME A SOLID. Whatever nice things I'd done in a prior life, consider the debt paid in full.

"God, you're beautiful," he whispered, nuzzling my ear. "So beautiful," Braden whispered, lifting me up and rearranging us on the couch so I was leaning back against and he was on the floor in front of me. He slid my shorts down my legs and tossed them aside.

I wriggled to the edge of the couch to make it easier for Braden and his expert hands. My eyes may have gone a little wide when he lifted one of my legs onto his shoulder and gazed at me, his eyelids heavy. The storm in his eyes had turned them a darker gray, and right now, they blazed with intensity as they roamed over my naked body.

"Yeah, this is happening," he promised, running one finger up the inside of my thigh until I moaned with pleasure. He bit down on his bottom lip and shook his head. "Just watching you enjoy this is going to ruin me."

Unable to articulate more than a sigh, I relaxed into the couch and pushed my hands into Braden's hair while the light dance of his fingers made me insane.

I watched his face as he licked his bottom lip, almost like he was anticipating how much fun he was about to have. The possessive look was so damn hot that an unexpected gasp fluttered from my lips. Searing heat burned through my core and the nerve endings along every inch of my skin sang like a church choir.

His finger circled my entrance, swirling in the wetness I knew was there for him, before sliding inside and circling there.

Then I felt his tongue. Hot and wet against me, that tongue made slow passes that were relentless in the most amazing of ways.

Braden was an expert. A gold medal winner.

He licked in light strokes, getting firmer and more intense as he teased the beginnings of an orgasm from my body.

Then his tongue circled my clit and sucked, separating my mind from my body and making me quiver with every single pass. It was almost too much to bear. Almost. But then I wanted more, arching my hips toward him and begging for him to send me farther. The strokes of his tongue came slowly, luxuriously, until I responded with moans and sighs that barely described my utter bliss.

He was watching me, waiting for my response to each touch, then giving me more. Even when my eyes rolled shut, I could feel the heat of his gaze. When I started to lose control, his quiet moan told me he loved what he was doing to me.

Inside, he added a second finger, curling them as he moved and hitting the perfect spot that had me arching against his mouth and hand.

"Come for me, Damsel," he said, breathy and sexy. It was a command, a necessity. My body answered with its own plea.

The painful pleasure he built exploded in rolling waves that built until they crashed on the shore. I moaned his name and fisted his hair to ground me.

When he moved slowly up my body, kissing his way over the skin, I brushed my hands through his hair and pulled his face to mine.

Kissing him with the taste of me on his lips made me feel sexy in a way I'd never experienced. The smoking hot, sexy firefighter had just pushed me to a point that defied all comparison. And judging by his satisfied groans and the heat in his eyes, he enjoyed it as much as I did.

Lifting his head, Braden kissed my neck again before moving down to one breast and sucking hard.

Then he bit my nipple. The shock of the painful sensation shot a new wave of desire through my body. Soothing it with a swipe of his tongue, Braden smiled at me.

"I'm not nearly done with you," he growled and dug his fingers into my skin like he couldn't stop if he tried. That thought was like a drug—the idea that he was so turned on and wanted me as much as I wanted him. "I want you in my bed."

Braden lifted me up, and I wrapped my legs around him so he could carry me up the stairs to his bedroom. The mystery chamber . . . I'd never been inside.

"You skipped this room on the tour, fireman. I was wondering if I'd ever get a peek," I teased, covering for the fact that I suddenly felt nervous. It was crazy, I knew, but being in his bedroom seemed significant after two weeks of imagining the sex den that lay behind the doors.

He laughed. "I was afraid if I brought you in here, I wouldn't be able to keep my hands off you."

It was an ordinary bedroom with a large king-sized bed with a puffy gray duvet and pillows with pictures of Bella on them. I relaxed and pulled Braden's mouth to mine for a searing kiss that I hoped would communicate how much I wanted him. "Put your hands on me, please," I panted.

In answer, he laid me on the bed and hovered over my body, devouring my mouth until my lips ached and my chin burned from his scruff. Kissing him was so intense, so good, I almost didn't need to do anything else.

Almost.

Reaching for his zipper, I quickly freed him of his jeans and boxers. My eyes felt greedy at the sight of him, and I reached to stroke his hard length while I took in every muscled plane of his body and let my gaze rest on how beautiful he looked in my hand.

"What you do to me . . ." He watched me stroke him and shook his head, eyes ablaze and clouded with lust. "It's fucking insane."

He worked his fingers inside me again until I was throbbing again with need. A second later, I heard the tear of a condom wrapper. He rolled it on and worked his way slowly inside me. Taking his time, he let me feel every inch of him until he filled me.

"Damsel…" His breath was ragged near my ear, and a shiver of pleasure tore through me. "So good." He moved, and my body responded. Our hips rolled and circled, pleasure building and building.

He was addictive.

He was perfect.

He was going to keep me up all night.

When he flipped us over so I was riding him, I watched the smile glide over his features. It didn't matter which way I was facing or how Braden touched me. He had an expert ability to elicit orgasms on demand. When I started to tremble with new waves of pleasure, he was right with me, soaring over a cliff without fear of falling.

Panting, glistening with sweat, and momentarily sated, we collapsed next to each other.

"Okay, that was . . ." I made a gesture near my head with my fingers. "Brain cells—gone."

He gave me a wicked grin. "Gonna take that as a compliment."

"You should." I curled my body against his side, and he wrapped his arms around me. He didn't strike me as a guy who liked to snuggle, but he was a big muscular cage of warmth that made me worry I'd never be able to fall asleep any other way again.

The thought of sleep caused the wheels to churn in my brain again, and I started to think I should leave his room before I outstayed my welcome. I shifted in his arms and turned to see his face. "Maybe I should let you get some sleep." It was my chicken-shit way of asking if he was antsy for me to go back to my room.

He shook his head and held me tighter. "No chance, Damsel. You're sleeping here with me tonight." He stated the words, but I caught the hint of a question in his voice and caught him glance away for a second. I lay my head on his chest and stroked the hard ridges of his abdomen.

"Okay. I'm sleeping here with you," I assured him, feeling contentment I almost didn't recognize because it was so new—I was going off script and having a fling with my roommate—and I'd never been happier.

P.S. We didn't actually sleep.

raden

MORNING SMACKED me in the head like a third-grade teacher who'd caught her star student reading porn.

Not enough coffee in the world could make up for how exhausted I was, but I awoke with a smile on my face and an anvil of guilt on my chest.

I should probably have had my head examined. Not probably. Definitely.

No question, I enjoyed last night. I more than enjoyed it, and that felt like a problem. Of course, I knew Sarah was an adult capable of making her own decisions about when and with whom she wanted to hook up. The problem was me.

For two years, I'd intentionally dated women where there was no potential of more than a few nights of fun. Easy, uncomplicated. Sarah was the polar opposite—complex, intelligent, beautiful, witty—everything I wanted in a relationship that I'd spent two years convincing myself I didn't want.

Nothing permanent could ever develop between us. She had five and a half more months in town and had outright called us a fling. Whatever fun we had or continued to have was temporary, but I already knew that the more time I spent with her, the harder it would be to let her go.

I would. I'd have to. No sense worrying about that today.

Last night I'd curled my body around her and fallen into a deeper and more relaxed sleep than any time in memory. Watching her sleep next to me in the morning, her honey brown hair streaking the white pillowcase with light, I felt content.

It had been a long time since I'd woken up feeling happy and hopeful about something other than the adrenaline rush of a fire. All my habits—speeding down the open highway on my bike, working out until I ached, doing emergency rescue and fighting blazes—made my pulse race without risking my emotions. Now, after one night, I found myself wanting to risk it all.

She will leave. Everyone leaves.

That sobering thought shot the wind from my sails. Messing around with Sarah would never end well. Better to call it a one-time indulgence and not let it happen again—if I could hold myself to it. Problem was, I didn't want to, not at all.

I raked both hands through my hair.

I'd never been so grateful for a twenty-four-hour shift. I needed time away from the house, away from Sarah. I needed to cool the fuck off and spend my time with dirt and dudes who'd distract me from everything at home. The firehouse had always reliably filled that role in my life, especially for the past two years.

Why did I feel like everything was different? It couldn't be. Not just after one night.

If I were honest, I'd have to admit it wasn't just one night. Sarah had slid effortlessly beneath my skin the moment I saw her on the ground outside her car. The two weeks since then had been a prison of my own making. Last night, she set me free.

When I sent her off this morning on her new bike, she looked like a spring daisy, glossy hair pulled back into a low ponytail, her sensible black pants creased down the front, her short-sleeved pink sweater hugging her gentle curves. She had her laptop in the basket of her bike, along with her purse, and she'd gathered one pant leg using a rubber band so it wouldn't get caught in the gears.

She was an adorably sexy, brilliant nerd who'd let me do crazy-hot things to her body all night long.

And the problem was I didn't *want* to block out last night and be her roommate again for the next five months and fifteen days.

I wanted more of her.

Dude, you've really fucked yourself.

Fortunately, I was saved from the hamster wheel of thoughts when I arrived at the station to find Mitch in the middle of telling a joke. ". . .one was going, but the other was definitely coming."

"And that's what *she* said!" Duke, one of our new engineers, high-fived Mitch. I'd heard the joke twice before and didn't need a repeat. Duke had his ankle wrapped in an ace bandage, which I might not have noticed, except that his foot sat on the kitchen table while he powered down a bowl of Cocoa Krispies.

"Hey, not super sanitary." I pointed to his smelly foot a few inches from his breakfast. "What's up with the foot?"

"Morning, bro." Mitch rolled his eyes and got up to dump the milk from his cereal bowl.

I intended to pull him aside to ask him if everything was okay with his girlfriend, but I wouldn't talk to him about it in front of Duke. "Morning," I grunted. "We should chat later."

Mitch waved a hand. "No need. All lady problems solved for now." I cocked my head and studied him, trying to figure out if he was telling the truth or blowing me off. He winked and poured the last bit from the coffee pot into his cup and pointed at Duke before heading out. "You need to hear this one. See you guys on dailies."

I went to the fridge, but it looked more barren than the one in my kitchen. I arched an eyebrow at Duke and pointed at his foot. "So what happened?"

He scooped a mouthful of cereal and hung his head, shaking it back and forth. "I know, I know."

"No. Tell me you didn't!" His guilty look said he did. "Damn. After I warned you?"

We had problems every time guys rotated in from a station with a longer fire pole. They weren't used to the shorter distance to the bottom and fucked up their landings. Every time. Lots of broken ankles. Many newer stations didn't even have poles, but ours still had the original one, and most of the guys still liked to use it.

Duke would be lucky if all he had was a sprain.

"I know. I practiced a bunch of times, but I woke up from a deep sleep and rushed out on autopilot. Hit the ground hard."

"Aw man, that sucks. Sorry."

He shrugged. "It doesn't hurt that bad. But I'm probably benched a couple days 'til it heals."

"I'm betting a week at least, but I hope you're right."

"Thanks. I'll be cooking for you all, I guess. Speaking of, you want some waffles? There's extra." He pointed to a stack I hadn't noticed.

I helped myself to two and poured on some syrup. Sarah and I had both overslept, but while she'd managed to seem perky, I felt spacey and was jonesing for any breakfast I could find. "These are good. You make these?"

"Eggo made 'em. But I'll hit the store later, and tomorrow I'll get some hash browns going and omelets. Or, I dunno . . ." Poor guy, he looked miserable, his mouth pulled down into a scowl, body fidgety without exercise.

"Chin up, Duke. This too will pass. Maybe don't use the pole anymore. Only saves about four seconds," I chuckled. Firefighters were a stubborn bunch. We tended to learn things the hard way.

"One thing you can do is make sure we've always got two fresh pots of coffee," I said, noticing that both of the pots were down to the dregs. I got the impression Duke hadn't done much kitchen duty at his old engine company. The coffee job was as basic as it came.

"Sure thing." He hobbled to the counter and started measuring beans. I took my waffles into the truck bay to get started on the day's schedule.

Cash was out there polishing the ladder truck and flashed me a knowing grin. I hadn't worked with him since Sarah's collision with the rig, and of course, he'd be itching to give me shit. I could see in his cocky face that we weren't going to make it through the day without some comment.

"Hey, we're going to flow water through the hydrants today, make sure they're not broken. Head out in ten." I told him, glancing at the clock on the wall.

He nodded and kept working. "How's the new roommate?"

"Nerdy and annoying, thanks for asking. Now we're heading out in nine." I could be an authoritative asshole when I wanted to be.

"Looked pretty hot to me. You think she wants to socialize?"

"Not with you. Eight minutes."

And there it went. No chance of getting through my shift without thinking about her. Not that I really had a chance at blocking her out. I liked the thought of her too much.

We each had a busy week at work, and I needed to pull two twenty-four-hour shifts in three days, so we could each cool down in our respective corners. There would be no repeat of last night.

For now.

CHAPTER TWENTY

*S*arah

I SPENT the beginning of my week sort of paying attention at work and sort of lost in an elated dream state—Braden's hot mouth and hands all over me, all the time. I barely saw him, but the memory of the night we spent together eclipsed other thoughts.

Metals and their atomic structure could wait.

Eventually, my attention turned back to physics, and strangely, I felt more focused and invigorated than I had since I'd arrived. That ticked one more box in the column of reasons to deviate occasionally from science and well-thought-out plans.

My team and I were already making progress calibrating the lasers to work on several types of metals that we'd never had success welding before—iron ore, aluminum, and steel. I couldn't have asked for better results after such a short time.

Everything was on track to progress toward all the milestones we'd devised at the outset, and for only a couple weeks' worth of work, we'd done better than expected.

By Friday, I was thrilled about the work but barely standing from exhaustion. I'd put in three twelve-hour days over the week. The one thing that still had me going was a text Braden had sent me a couple hours earlier.

Braden: Meet me in front of the lab at 7, Damsel.

Me: Done.

When I emerged from the double doors to see Braden leaning against his truck, his muscled arms crossed in front of him, I couldn't stop the giant smile of anticipation from spreading across my face.

I'd missed seeing him all week, and this time I felt no guilt whatsoever about him going out of his way to pick me up. Seeing him standing there—the highlights in his hair kissed by the sun, his gorgeous smile aimed at me—reminded me of the end of the movie *Sixteen Candles* which my sisters and I watched on repeat when we were young.

"Are you by any chance a John Hughes fan?" I asked, wondering if tough guy firefighters watched those kinds of movies at the station.

He cocked his head. "You mean the movies?"

"Yeah. Have you seen *Sixteen Candles?*"

He looked down at himself and up at me. "You're suggesting I'm channeling Jake Ryan?"

I flew at him. "You do know! Have you been doing that on purpose, the whole car leaning thing?"

He smiled. "I admit nothing. And his car was red." He stared at the secretive campus just beyond the gate I'd exited and looked a little wistful.

It gave me an idea. "Have you ever gone on a tour of the lab?" I asked.

"Never. Lived here a long time, but I've never been inside. I guess I wasn't that curious before."

"And now?"

"Everything you've told me about what you're doing sounds fascinating. So now I'm curious."

I nodded at him. I could do something about that.

Twenty minutes later, Braden had received clearance to come inside. I could only show him the parts of the lab that were open to visitors, but there were tours of the National Ignition Facility several times a week, and I knew the drill. I'd taken a tour the first time I'd been here after my interview.

"Are you sure this is allowed? Aren't there nuclear secrets at this place that I need some kind of top government clearance for?" Braden hesitated in the lobby of the lab, where I got him a visitor badge. "Or genius physicists who are very protective of their patented inventions?"

"Not where we're going. Don't worry."

Still, his eyes darted around and he crossed his arms as we walked. Here was this six-foot-two-inch tall man with enough brains to reimagine fire shed areas and enough muscle tone to defy gravity, and he looked nervous walking into a building filled with what were essentially really well-funded science experiments. Yes, some were used for national defense, but still, science projects.

"Did your school have a science fair?" I asked him.

"Um, yeah. I made a solar oven out of tin foil. It took twelve hours to dry out a slice of white bread."

"But you learned something, right?"

He folded his arms across his chest. "Sure, I learned not to enter the science fair again."

I smacked him. "No. You learned something about tin foil and the sun and heat and what it takes to make a slice of toast."

"Sure. I learned I was glad we had a toaster."

"Fine. Well, that's all anyone's doing here—trying stuff out and refining it until it works. And I'll tell you, a lot of the time, it doesn't."

We stood outside a 3D printing lab where several monitors displayed images of rocket parts being made in the printers. He looked from the models to the screen, skeptical. "So, what's your point?"

"My point is that yes, there are parts of the lab that require high-level security clearance, but we're not going there. I can still show you some pretty cool stuff." I took his hand and started walking him down the hallway toward the National Ignition Facility. "This is where the first sustained, controlled nuclear fusion reaction was created."

We walked into the room, which contained giant laser bays and a massive target capsule. I watched the expression on Braden's face change from interest to obsession. His eyes got wide, and his mouth fell open.

Expectations exceeded—goal achieved.

"I'm not certified to conduct an official tour. But we can go inside the target bay."

The room looked like the inner workings of a futuristic computer, all gears and clean metals housings for wires, ladders, and circuit boards. The floor shone spotlessly and reflected everything in the room. "This is where it all happens. Pressures so extreme that the laser can compress something to one hundred times the density of lead. In some cases, it reaches a temperature of a hundred million degrees."

"Holy fuck," Braden gasped, shaking his head. "I have no concept of what that means, and I work with fire for a living."

"Pretty much. The laser in here releases fusion energy, kind of the holy grail of nuclear science."

"In regular person terms, *por favor* . . ."

"The idea is to generate a greater amount of energy from fusion than the amount of energy that was there at the outset."

He bit his lip and blinked, thinking. "You know, there are some parallels to fire science and how energy is created. There's no fusion involved, but some of the energy concepts sound similar." His smile broadened.

I nodded. "I had a feeling you might find something here you could chew on." And I wanted him to understand a little bit of why I found the field so interesting.

We toured around for another half hour, and I made sure to show him the IBM supercomputer and the lab where our welding was taking place. Keith was still at work, geared up in a mask and goggles and working with an experimental laser.

Braden and I watched through the one-way glass. "So this is what you do all day?" He observed Keith, and I pointed at how he was aiming the laser's beam at two squares of aluminum alloy and trying to get them to fuse. It still wasn't holding the way we needed it to.

"Pretty much. We're at the point where we know the lasers can accomplish part of what we need—getting the atoms moving fast enough that they begin to join. And what they're doing is better than the friction tool that's conventionally used. What we haven't done yet is make that happen at the right temperature and at a cost that makes it viable."

"But you're making progress?"

"Yup. I feel confident, and we still have two months to get a prototype that a space exploration company could use. Obviously, it needs to be incredibly strong to withstand the G-forces of a rocket."

He nodded, his mouth hitching up on one side. Then he leaned close to my ear. "Do you have any idea how much your brilliant brain turns me on?" His voice was a barely audible growl, but it ignited a delicious heat between my legs, and my heart started hammering.

I turned to him, not entirely sure if he was propositioning me or just trying to throw me off.

"Is that so?" I teased. I'd spent a good part of my week thinking that I'd like another night between the sheets with my roommate and his impeccably beautiful, hard body.

"It is so." His whisper turned into a soft breath of a kiss beneath my ear, and I turned into a puddle of jelly.

Braden's lips skimmed my neck lightly, sending tendrils of heat along the surface of my skin. A wisp of his breath made me gasp, turning my head to the side to give him better access. He didn't dive in. His movements were luxurious and slow, taking me by the hand and turning me, so my back was against the wall in the empty hallway.

I knew there was a chance someone might walk by at any moment, but my body had gone limp, unable to harness the muscle strength to pull away from him. His lips met mine, still gentle and caressing.

I immediately calculated the shortest distance to my office, which had a door that locked. In my mind, I was already splayed out on top of the research reports on my desk.

I'd never felt nearly enough passion with men I'd dated to consider having sex in my office—or any office. I'd never fantasized about being taken on my metal university-issued desk on campus, let alone acted on it. But there was a first for everything.

"This is my office. Normal, regular, plain. No window. Don't care. It has files and a computer and a desk and a chair, as you can see. The best thing is it has a door we can close," I yammered in a desperate spree of words while I pulled him toward me and fused our mouths together.

His mouth was hot, desperate. And I wanted to feel his lips work their magic on every part of me.

"You give a good tour, beautiful." His voice was rough but sweet.

Braden lifted me like I weighed nothing, and I wrapped my legs around his waist, right at the level where his hard length found the perfect spot. He spun us around and perched me against my desk.

He dragged his lips against mine until I wanted to beg for more. "Braden . . ."

His hands teased the skin at my waist, pushing my sensible blue sweater up and out of the way. Unwinding my arms from his neck, I leaned back on the desk, pulling him with me.

Braden pushed my sweater higher as he hovered over me, his mouth closing on one of my breasts, kissing it and working the nipple through the silk fabric of my bra. I heard myself moan and worked my hands down his sculpted abs until I reached the waistband of his jeans.

I undid the belt and the top button before he unzipped himself the rest of the way until his erection sprang free, ready for my greedy hand. I ran my fingers lightly over the head and wrapped my hand around the length, starting to stroke as he groaned through his kisses.

"You're going to kill me with those hands." He threw his head back and closed his eyes.

Good.

I wanted him to feel the same loss of control I did when he grazed my skin.

Then his mouth was on mine again, and our kisses felt bottom-less. He was right there with me, his tongue sliding along my jaw and nipping at the skin before trailing a row of kisses down my bare stomach.

My body shivered as he moved lower, sliding my pants over my hips. I'd worn a pair of black skinny jeans, and there was enough give in the fabric that he didn't need to unbutton them.

I swear, it never crossed my mind how grateful I'd be to stretchy fibers.

Braden reached for the wallet in his back pocket and pulled out a condom. He tore at the wrapper and rolled it over his thick length before teasing my entrance.

"Fuck, I want to spend an hour making you ache for me . . ."

"You're doing that already . . ." I was panting, so ready.

He smirked. "I can do better . . ." He teased me with light brushes that made me ache for him. "Patience . . ."

He enjoyed torturing me a little too much.

I decided to turn the tables. I leaned toward his ear and whispered. "You know, a place like this has security cameras everywhere. Even in here."

His eyes widened and he froze. "Shit."

"What, not an exhibitionist?" I teased, batting my lashes at him. He cast me a side-eye, and I winked so he'd know I was messing with him.

"You will pay for that," he warned, his smirk returning.

I nodded. "Quit torturing me and give it to me, fireman."

I didn't have to tell him twice. On one glorious thrust, he filled me. On the next one, he went deeper, and my toes curled.

This was what I'd been craving all week long. Everything about our bodies together just worked. His hips circled, and mine responded.

Wrapping my legs around his back, I pulled him closer, feeling every thrust and wanting more.

His kisses melted my lips with their heat. He shivered as my hands slid luxuriously over his abs, and I scraped lightly with my nails.

Then my back began to arch as I felt the build between my legs. I wanted to hold onto the feeling, savor it, but there was no controlling anything anymore. As pulses of light built and burst, blinding my body with their explosion, I felt Braden riding his own wave over the crest and heard him whisper my name on a curse.

My hand clamped over his mouth before someone at the lab thought our nuclear secrets were under attack and shot Braden on sight.

But, wow.

That was . . . wow.

When he pulled back, he nodded his head, looking smug. "Nuclear fusion's got nothing on us." He crossed his arms. Yep, he looked damned smug.

I huffed a laugh. "I'm going to have to agree." Then I sighed because I caught a faraway look in his eyes and had a feeling about what was coming next.

He pressed a thumb against the creases in my forehead. "Hey, what's wrong?"

"I was sensing dissent in your brain. Is this where you say it can't happen again?" I braced myself. "Come on, lemme have it. Let's bring on the reality check."

He shook his head slowly and leaned down to press his forehead against mine. "Is that what you want?"

"No," I sighed.

"No," he confirmed, taking my face in both hands. "Damsel, it won't be the last time."

My heart lurched in my chest, and I had to insist that it chill.

Down, girl. We're agreeing to more sex. Not a relationship.

Even if it felt like the beginning of something.

Knowing I'd only be in town for a limited time and Braden wasn't a relationship guy, my logical mind launched into protective mode. We needed to be on the same page from the get-go.

"Rules! We never came up with our rules."

"What kind of rules? Sex rules?"

"Yes. No. Sort of. Just rules about how we're going to do this." I waved my hands between us as Braden buckled his pants. Meanwhile, I was still bare-assed on the desk with my pants around one ankle and my sweater pushed up. "Just rules so we have the same expectations."

"Got it. You're a rules girl."

"Rules, laws, inconvertible truths. . . "

"Let's just start with rules."

"Fine. Rule one . . . Finn. This is none of his damn business." I said. "I know he's your friend, but my family has boundary issues. I don't need their commentary."

He put a hand on his chest and feigned a heart attack. "Keeping things from my childhood friend? You're leading me to the dark side, woman."

I patted his hand. "Relax, it's comfy here. And speaking of comfy, since we're roommates and all, living in close quarters, it's hard not to be in each other's business, but . . . if you're with other women, I don't need to see it."

Better yet, no other women, but I could hardly ask for that.

He frowned, and his head jerked back as though he was surprised at the suggestion, but please—one look at him and it was clear he could have dates every night of the week. I needed boundaries.

"Fair enough, and right back atcha. But if we want to hang out with each other—and do this—we need to be forthright. Ask for what we want." His face was serious, and he sought my eyes in agreement.

"I like that. For example, I want you. Again. Tonight. Good?"

"Yes. Way to make use of an example. I don't want to wait until tonight." He leaned in and gave me a deep, thorough kiss I felt in my wobbly knees.

"And we don't lie to each other," he said solemnly. "If this gets uncomfortable, we need to be honest."

"Agreed." I shook my head. "Oh, and obviously, no falling in love." I mainly said it for myself, so I could hear it. I needed to remember to keep emotions out of our white-hot sex situation. I'd only be in town for a short time, and guys like Braden weren't for keeps. There would be plenty of time in my future for a relationship with a nice quiet professor.

Braden let out a bark of a laugh. "Correct. No. Never." The fact that he agreed so readily affirmed that I was right to caution my heart at the outset. Whatever happened between us was purely for fun.

Temporary. Meaningless.

"Okay, sounds like we're in agreement. Let's seal it properly." I extended my hand to shake on it.

Braden laughed, shaking his head. "No way. We can do better than that. We can do much better," he said on a low growl near my ear.

He pushed me backward on the desk and leaned over me, pressing his whole body into mine again. The heat in his eyes told me he was as insatiable as I felt.

It was like looking at a decadent dessert menu and not having to choose chocolate over key lime pie. I could have both and more.

I loved our rules.

CHAPTER TWENTY-ONE

arah

WEEKS TURNED INTO MONTHS, and after a while, I didn't even think about riding my bike home. I knew that unless Braden was working a twenty-four-hour shift, he'd be waiting outside the lab each day to pick me up.

He always stood there in his aviators, leaning against his truck. And I always loved seeing him there. We loaded my bike into the back, and he shut the hatch on the back.

"Do you have anything going on this weekend?" Braden asked, opening the passenger door and taking my bag off my shoulder. He dropped it behind the seat and waited for my answer before he closed the door.

Casting a glance at the lab where my team was still working, I felt a little bit guilty about leaving so early, but we'd all made it clear at the outset that we knew our objectives, and everyone worked at their own pace. "I should probably come in at least one day to record some of our data."

"Could that day be Sunday?" He didn't wait for my answer before closing the door and going to his side.

He hopped in and looked over at me. I shrugged. "Sure. Sunday's fine. Why? Do you have a house project for us to do this weekend? Are we building the fire pit?"

"Not this weekend, no." He started the engine and pulled onto the road. "I had something I thought you might like to see, but it's kind of an overnight thing, so you'd need to be free tomorrow." He looked almost embarrassed when he said it, as though it was a big ask.

I put my hand on his leg and turned to face him, overly serious. "Braden. Are you asking me for a sleepover?"

His lips crooked up. "You already have sleepovers every night. This one is just in a different location."

"I'm not going to say no to a sleepover. I'll even bring my good pajamas."

He drove us down a road we didn't usually take, but I could still tell we were headed back to his house. "Define 'good pajamas.' I've seen your pajamas. Are they the ones with bears or the other ones?"

"Well, fireman, I just may have a pair you haven't seen." I quirked an eyebrow. When I'd packed one set of pink lace lingerie, I didn't expect to need it, but it's always a good idea to be prepared. "Are you going to tell me where we're going? Road trip?"

He shook his head. "Nope. But I will tell you this—it's less about the journey and all about the destination."

"Sure you don't have your Zen backwards? Life's supposed to be all about the journey, not the destination."

"Not in this case. The journey happens once we get there."

"Interesting." So far, he hadn't steered me wrong, so I decided to go with whatever guiding principle he felt like using.

We pulled into the driveway of Braden's house, and he walked to the front door with me, but once he opened it, he wrapped an arm around me and pulled me tight against him, folding me into the hard, sexy ridges of his chest and crushing my lips with his. "Mmmm . . . Been waiting to do that all day."

"Well, we could always forget about the road trip and just stay here for more of that." I leaned my head against his chest and sank into the feeling of total contentment. "I'm not picky."

He kissed me again, slower this time, with deep, slow strokes of his tongue as his hand caressed the side of my face and ran through my hair.

Every damn kiss was like that, giving me everything I wanted to feel in my heart and soul. Then I'd get some bonus feels I never imagined possible that blossomed with heat over every inch of my skin.

I melted into him as his teeth grazed my bottom lip, and his lips roamed down my cheek to where he nipped at my jaw. Lazily, my hands roamed over his chest and encircled his neck. Then I moaned at the absence of him as he pulled away.

"I know." He kissed my lips once more. And again. "It's hard to stop. But we have to."

"Do we?" It seemed like a random parameter he'd pulled off a dusty shelf when he could go with the flow, and we could happily spend the rest of the weekend in his bed.

He looked at the time on his phone. "I'm afraid so. We're on a schedule. Go upstairs and pack a bag and meet me down here when you're ready, k?"

Giving him a salute, I headed into the house, but not before he smacked my ass and looked at me like he'd like to take a bite out of it. That idea tempted me. So did going off for the weekend without knowing the plan.

It felt freeing to give up the tight control I normally sought in order to avoid uncomfortable surprises. I trusted Braden enough not to need a plan.

My heart raced with a tiny bit of panic at that realization. Our temporary just-for-fun arrangement wasn't supposed to engender things like trust and actual feelings.

And yet, there they were.

For now, I resigned myself to enjoying the present and whatever road trip Braden had in mind. I'd get a firm grip on my feelings when we got back. I'd have to.

I took the stairs two at a time and threw together a combination of clothes that could work for a variety of settings since I didn't know where we were going.

That meant I'd stuffed my overnight bag to the gills, shoving in a dress, heels, shorts, a hoodie, jeans, and whatever else I might possibly need in the next twenty-four hours. Then I threw in an extra pair of heels, my favorite pair of red stilettos with a bow on the back, the pink lingerie, and a bikini because you never know.

In ten minutes, I was back downstairs, where Braden was waiting with two iced teas. He handed me one and kissed me once more before escorting me back to the truck. Before he closed the front door of the house, he called to Bella, who came barreling outside and leaped into the backseat.

"Ooh, it's dog friendly?" I rubbed Bella behind the ears as she wagged her tail so hard the truck shook.

"Oh yeah. She'll probably have more fun than we will." His mood was lighter than I'd seen it over the past few weeks, which made me all the more intrigued about where we were headed. I imagined a beach or a hiking trail where Bella could run free, and I mentally checked that I'd packed a pair of running shoes that would work for a hike.

"Is she always this happy to go in the truck, or does she know where we're going?" Braden saw through my not-so-subtle attempts to gather clues about our destination and gave nothing away.

"Not telling you, control freak," he sang.

"Fine. I'll live in suspense," I grumbled. I'd come a long way in two months, but my love for controlling outcomes was deeply rooted. I couldn't just become fancy-free and comfortable without having a plan just because I'd discovered great sex.

And that's what it was. Great sex with a great guy.

Sure, it was just sex. I had no illusions that I was anything more to him than the rest of the women he dated, but for now, my body was thrilled to be on his current shortlist. I'd return to Berkeley after six months and begin dating again in earnest. For now, I'd have my fellowship at the lab accompanied by a side of phenomenal sex.

So why did something about the arrangement feel wrong to me?

Maybe because you're lying to yourself. You don't do non-relationships.

"Hey, where'd you go?" Braden asked.

"Huh?" I hadn't realized I'd spaced out while I sorted through the angst in my head.

"I said I doubt Bella has any idea where we're headed. She just likes the truck. And most of the time, it works out well for her and we end up someplace fun. Once in a while, it's the vet and I get the stink-eye."

We pulled onto the highway, with Bella sprawled on the backseat, ball in her mouth like she knew we were headed someplace where she could fetch it. "Did you plan on getting a dog before she fell into your life?" I turned in my seat to scratch Bella between the ears. She stood up and started to climb into the front seat.

Braden laughed and gave her a gentle nudge. "Bella, sit." She obediently resumed her position behind us. "Yeah. It was something my ex and I couldn't agree on. She wanted a labradoodle from a breeder, so it wouldn't shed, which I was totally against at the time because I wanted a rescue. A big dog like a Bernese or a Newfie. But when I saw this girl, it was a love match. She was this happy, scrappy thing, probably the runt of the litter, but I could tell she was feisty."

"She still is feisty."

"Yup. People said she'd either settle down when she was two or five. It's looking like five."

"And your ex? How'd she feel about the shedding?"

He chuckled, and it was the first time I hadn't sensed a dark cloud descending when he talked about her. "She hated it. Maybe that's why Bella was always so possessive of me—she knew I loved her, furball or not. She never got that love from my ex." His smile dimmed.

"I don't know how a person could meet her and not fall in love," I said, resting a hand on his leg. Braden looked at Bella in the rearview mirror and nodded. Then his gaze shifted to me and lingered before moving back to the road.

I didn't have time to analyze it because he started peppering me with questions. "Have you had pets? Plants? Goldfish? I'd kind of peg you as a cat person."

Looking at him warily, I gave him a playful punch. "Why, because I'm single? Sad cat lady?"

"Hardly. Cats are smart. They don't do anything without thinking it through. Unlike dogs, who will chase after anything you throw for them and bound around looking for love, cats are particular. Discerning."

"Now you're saying I am a cat?"

He shrugged, laughing again. "I have no idea what I'm saying. I'm saying I like that you put thought into everything. I like that you're discerning."

"You just like that I seduce you with brownies and let you eat them off my body."

"Trust me, that's not all I like." He smirked. "So tell me, is that a thing with you, the brownie seduction?"

"Ha. It is now."

"For the record, I approve." He reached out and slowly brushed his fingers up my thigh, which unleashed a jolt of desire at my core. I put my hand on his to still it. He looked at me and raised an eyebrow. "You worried I can't multitask? I assure you I can drive and make you come in a blinding cascade of stars at the same time."

"I have no doubt. But I can't keep a thought in my head if you're gonna do that. Just warning you, in case you thought we were having a conversation." He started moving his hand again, and conversation of any sort seemed irrelevant. Having fully given myself over to however Braden wanted to ravish my body, I was fine with either.

His eyes met mine, and the smolder I saw gave me no doubt about which one he preferred.

"I can't be held responsible for whatever car accident you're about to get into. The blinding cascade can wait. Let's talk." I placed his hand back on his own leg and looked at his profile, noticing the angular blade of his nose and his high cheekbones. His face was beautiful, and when he smiled at me, I couldn't look away.

"What do you want to talk about?" He slid his hand back up the bare skin of my leg, edging higher this time. He kept his eyes on the road, so I did nothing to dissuade him. Yet. Someone had to be the adult in the truck, and I prepared myself for the role of spoiler.

"Tell me about your brothers. Are they all firefighters like Mitch? Is that a thing—does it tend to run in families?"

He shrugged and shifted slightly, so he sat a little closer to me on his seat. Eyes still facing forward. But now, his hand moved up the inside of my thigh until his fingers brushed against my panties, which— let's be honest—were damp with arousal the second I saw the heat in his eyes. He grinned like a naughty kid but said nothing, moving the tiny wisp of fabric aside and stroking straight up my center.

I sucked in a breath and slid lower in the seat, leaning my head back.

"My older brother Devon coaches football at the high school in Pleasanton. Sean, the youngest of our band of misfits, is a medic.

Then there's Mitch, who you know—he's my half-brother from my dad's second marriage. And his younger brother Sinclair who's between jobs. But he has a law degree and helps me with projects from time to time."

I sighed and tried to hold back the orgasm already unspooling where Braden's two fingers had been driving me insane while he spoke. "Sorry, I didn't hear any of that." I thought I was speaking, but apparently, I was just panting with words.

"Unimportant trivia. Focus on this." He bent his fingers to expertly hit my g-spot while circling my clit with his thumb. How he managed to do that while driving baffled me.

"Holy fucking moly."

He chuckled and never took his eyes off the road. But I stopped watching his driving because the heat in my core was building, and without any self-control, I moved against his fingers. Then I was telling myself to breathe as I fell hard and fast, pleasure exploding like pinpricks of light piercing a blackout.

There was no chance to feel self-conscious about my raw, unchecked reaction to him. It felt too good.

Braden's expert fingers had drawn out one of the best orgasms I'd ever had in my life, and he'd done it while cruising down the highway like he was innocently on his way to a church picnic.

Mentally, I bowed down in complete awe.

When I was finally able to articulate words, I opened my eyes to find Braden driving with a smile plastered on his face.

"See, now I find this unfair. You can drive and do *that* without so much as leaving your lane, and I let my mind wander to my grocery list and end up crashing into things."

"We all have our skills, Damsel. This is one of mine." The muscle in his jaw jumped as he controlled his smug grin.

He was so sure of himself.

So cocky.

And I loved it.

CHAPTER TWENTY-TWO

raden

WEATHER IN CAROLWOOD and the surrounding areas was perfect for growing wine grapes, which had resulted in a slew of amateur winemakers buying property, planting varietals, and establishing small labels. Many did it purely as hobbyists, producing a few dozen bottles a year to drink or give to their friends.

But some of them went on to be more prominent winemakers with tasting rooms and tours. They supplied local wine shops and restaurants and maybe even competed with wine produced in the much larger Napa Valley region.

I was a minor player who'd lucked into a fertile plot of land that allowed my winemaking operation to grow quickly into something I never imagined when I bought some cuttings from a local winemaker and started growing my own varietals. That was over a decade ago, and even though the operation was still tiny, now I made more money from the winery than I did at my job.

All in all, I had ten acres of vines and a small tasting room that was on a winetasting route which pretty much guaranteed a steady flow of visitors. I'd hired a part-time employee to run the tasting room and a couple of guys to tend to the vines a few times a month. The rest of it was automated—drip irrigation and some sprinkler watering on timers.

In the two years since Ellie moved out, I'd never taken another woman to the winery. There were too many memories of us wrapped up in the place, and if I'm honest, I wasn't ready or willing to replace them with thoughts of someone else.

Sarah was different.

She made me want to share this part of myself with her because I knew she'd appreciate the work that went into every part of the process. She wouldn't just look at the winery as an opportunity to get drunk on free wine, which, unfortunately, was what a couple of my dates had proposed after I mentioned my wine-making hobby.

So I'd stopped mentioning it.

"Oh my God, I love this place," Sarah purred after she'd finished running down one of the lanes in the vineyard with Bella. After less than an hour, Bella was yelping like she'd been cooped up for a month, racing through the fields. Her ball was lost somewhere among the vines. Maybe we'd find it later. Maybe not. There were probably a dozen lost balls out there. "When did you get into winemaking?"

"About ten years. You probably noticed there are vineyards everywhere. So it's not an obscure hobby. I had to wait until I had a little time and money to spare before I bought the property and worked out how many of the existing vines to keep and how to introduce new ones. I'm still learning about viniculture, but each year's crop teaches me something new. It's like a living laboratory."

She smiled at me and nodded. "See, you pretend to be this gruff, burly fireman guy who carries hundreds of pounds of equipment into burning forests, but underneath all that, you're a scientist." She bounced on her toes, excited.

"I never said I wasn't interested in the science. I told you I study burn patterns and fire behavior. That ain't fingerpainting."

She held up a finger. "Yes, but on top of that, in your spare time, you're geeking out over grapes and the way different soil makes the wine taste. You're a science nerd, Braden. You just happen to be a nerd in a smoking hot body with a face that should be on a billboard. Frankly, it's a little unnerving."

She was too much. If I wasn't careful, I would break all of our rules and have fun doing it.

Danger. Do not do that.

"Talk science to me, fireman. Tell me about viniculture." Her voice was a throaty whisper near my ear. It would have taken zero effort to pick her up and take her any which way I wanted, and I knew she wouldn't complain. But she deserved a tour and a whole lotta science talk if she wanted it, and I intended to deliver.

"Let's walk." I reached for her hand. Her fingers twined with mine, and we strolled down one of the vineyard lanes under a sunset sky, the weather gods doing us a favor with the pink and rose-colored clouds hanging in the distance.

"This area is pretty close to the Mediterranean climate you'd find in big wine-producing regions like Italy and France. Hot days, cool nights, coarse soil with gravel for good filtration, and enough rain to satisfy deep the roots of older vines."

"How old *are* these old vines?"

"Some are pretty darn old, planted by Robert Carolwood himself."

She stopped walking. "Wait, there's a Robert Carolwood? How did I not know this?" She poked me in the chest like I'd been holding out on her with crucial information.

I shrugged. "You're not from here, for one thing. The town was named after a British guy who jumped off a ship and ended up here, married a Mexican citizen and inherited a ranch, and started planting vines instead of olives and fruit orchards like most people were doing."

"Cool info, Braden. You impress me constantly." The warm sun bathed her face in pink light as she smiled at me, and I felt like I'd saved an entire town from burning to the ground.

I felt myself losing the battle against more than temporary feelings for her, and it scared the shit out of me.

"I might be able to impress you a bit more," I said, leaning to whisper into her ear. "I know someone with a property that has some of the vines Carolwood planted in the mid-eighteen hundreds."

Her eyes shot to mine. "Seriously?"

"Yes, and the wine's incredible. I may have a bottle at the house you can try."

"Awesome. But tell me more about this place. Where are your vines from?"

I plucked a bunch of purple grapes from one of the vines, pulled a few of the grapes into my hand, and held them out for Sarah to taste. She grabbed two, and I tossed the rest in my mouth.

"Mmm, these are delicious." It warmed my entire body to hear her moan with delight.

"These vines descended from a crop that came from France originally—from cuttings taken from a pretty prestigious vineyard at a chateau there. I got lucky. That's probably why I've been able to turn this hobby into more of a side business. The wine is crazy good."

I led her to another row of vines with white grapes and we sampled them.

She pointed to the vine. "The grapes taste good, but I guess I don't have a very fine palate. How do you distinguish a grape that's going to make crazy good wine?"

"Time, practice, trial and error, luck . . . then so much of it is the process, the enzymes, the temperature regulation and the fermentation time. Again, trial and error, a lot of luck, a lot of tasting and spitting out bad wine." I couldn't pretend to know everything. "I'm still learning about this stuff, batch by batch, tweaking things, trying new things."

She nodded. "That's exactly what I do every day in the lab. My welding project isn't going to produce something that tastes as good as wine, and I sure need a lot of luck, but . . ." For the first time, I saw the concern in her face that maybe she wouldn't make her milestones or get the outcome she hoped for.

That vulnerability tugged at a part of me that desperately wanted to help her get there, even if I knew nothing about friction stir welding. "How about we go grab dinner and talk it through? I've been meaning to ask where you are with the project. You haven't talked about it."

"Only because my head's stuck in the middle of it. But sure, I'd love to tell you."

"Do you like Italian?" I figured the odds were good—who didn't like Italian?

"Love it. But don't think I'm leaving here before I taste some wine from your fancy French grape children."

"I wouldn't let you." I pointed to the small stone building near the entrance to the vineyard. "The property owner used to live in the loft of the tasting room, and it makes for a pretty cozy sleepover. I already stocked it with several types of wine we can have after dinner."

Sarah wrapped her arms around my waist and leaned her head on my chest. "We're sleeping in a loft? I love that." Stroking her hair, I leaned down and rested my cheek on the top of her head.

There was nothing about this moment I didn't love. It was going to get me in trouble—I could just feel it.

arah

I INHALED the scent of garlic and meatballs in the tiny Italian restaurant, noticing that every table for two was filled.

We stood at the front of a dark room painted to look like an outdoor street in Venice, with frescoes on facing walls painted to look like two-story homes. The faux windows had real windowsills with potted ivy spilling out, and lanterns hung like streetlamps. There were even clotheslines with laundry strung from one balcony to another and a starry night sky painted on the ceiling.

While we waited, I watched two different servers bustle by with plates of pasta with clams and shrimp scampi that smelled amazing. The growl of my stomach reminded me I hadn't eaten much for lunch.

"This place is popular." I wrapped my arms around Braden's waist, bracing myself for the host to tell us they had no space for two people who had the poor judgement to show up without a reservation. Wearing a body-hugging black sweater and rubbing a hand over his dark goatee, the host was on the phone, telling someone there was no chance of getting a table.

"The food's decent," Braden said, loudly enough for the host to overhear when he hung up the phone. He pinned Braden with a scowling stare, and I expected him to snub us after that review.

Instead, he cocked his head at us before yanking Braden in for a hug, clapping him on the back. "Bastard, what's it take to get you in here more regularly? It's been like six months, you jerk."

Braden laughed and apologized. "I worked a bunch of overtime this year . . . you know how it is, shit gets in the way . . . but I'm here now, and I brought a friend, so you need to behave. Alex, this is Sarah."

He greeted me with the same hug as he gave Braden without the clap on the back. Instead, he kissed my cheek. "Pleasure, Sarah. Welcome to my gin joint, though I don't sell gin—just pasta. And Braden's wine. Which I get at a deep discount."

"Funny. Price just went up for you."

Alex showed us to an empty table I hadn't noticed in a nook at the back. He promptly dropped a bottle of red wine on our table and handed Braden a wine opener. "I'd do the whole sommelier thing, but I know you don't need me to tell you about your own wine."

"Dude, it's your restaurant. You could at least open the bottle. I am a paying customer."

"Since when?"

Their banter continued as Alex opened the bottle, and Braden rolled the cork through his fingers while waiting for Alex to pour a taste into a glass. "I assume you'd like the lady to do the tasting since you don't know shit about wine," Alex laughed, sliding the glass over to me.

Braden rolled his eyes. "She should taste it, and you should go fuck yourself."

Not knowing much about wine myself, I tasted and nodded that it met with my approval, but as soon as Alex left us alone, I admitted I was out of my depth. "Gotta be honest here, pretty much all I know about wine is that it tastes good."

Braden lifted his glass, and the muscles in his forearm flexed. That was enough to distract me from anything he might want to tell me about wine. "You don't need to know much more than that. It's all about the taste, whether you get all artsy and describe cherry overtones and floral notes and oak from the barrel or you just say you like it—same difference."

"Awesome. I'm relieved to know I don't need to acquire any knowledge to enjoy it. And I *am* enjoying it, by the way. It's delish."

"That doesn't sound at all like you. You're a knowledge sponge."

"I know. I like that it doesn't annoy you that I'm always asking questions."

"Annoy me? I'm into it. Genuine curiosity is a turn-on." He grabbed my hand under the table and gave it a squeeze before excusing himself to go to the bathroom.

While he was gone, I leaned back in my chair and sipped some wine from my glass, trying to suss out hints of fruity something or other and failing. I must have been concentrating pretty hard because Alex looked at me and laughed on his way out of the kitchen.

"You look like you're working hard at something," he said, patting my arm.

"Trying to taste overtones or whatever in the wine. I'm still just tasting grapes."

Alex grabbed the bottle from our table and examined the label. Then he pulled out his phone and tapped and swiped a few times. "Okay, here. Tell Braden you taste currant, clove, and coffee. You'll blow his mind."

I laughed. "Thank you. Will do." I took another sip, concentrating on the new flavor suggestions, swirling the wine on my tongue.

Alex waited for me to assess it. "Well?"

I shook my head. "It's hopeless. I still taste grapes. But it's good to know what I'm supposed to be tasting. Thanks for the tip."

"Don't mention it." He lingered, his head tilted to the side like he was deciding whether or not to say what was on his mind. "He's a good guy. So how long have you two been together?"

I'd never been short on things to say. Teaching gave me the ability to think on my feet. But Alex's question made me stammer. "Oh, we're . . . it's just . . . we're friends."

Alex huffed a laugh. "You sure you don't want to phone a friend on that one? Final answer?"

"Yeah. I'm sure. We're roommates."

Alex shook his head. "Oh. Okay, well, good on you. That sounds like a nice arrangement for you both." He looked at me again with his head to the side, so I waited for the rest. "Just as long as you're aware your roommate is completely in love with you, then great."

"He's not—"

"Are you harassing my dinner companion?" Braden clapped Alex on the shoulder and slipped back into his seat.

Alex shrugged. "Naw, just talking to your roommate about wine."

I didn't hear their small talk after that because my brain was still back on Alex's assertion that Braden was in love with me. Which was *not* true. Alex had misinterpreted. Braden was no more in love with me than I was with him, and given my short stint in Carolwood and my career objectives back in Berkeley, Braden and I were a temporary amusement. No emotions allowed.

And yet, I couldn't help trying the love concept on for size. Okay, not love, not yet. But maybe Braden did feel something for me. And maybe, if I was honest with myself, I felt more than something for him.

The idea both excited and terrified me. I did have a relationship plan, and it didn't make sense to start something now. Or here.

"Well, thanks for keeping her company. Now go bother someone else so I can have her to myself." He picked up my hand again, this time lacing our fingers together and resting them on the tablecloth. Leaning in, he fixed me with his eyes, burning and possessive, melding with mine like we shared a single thought.

I pushed my worrisome thoughts away for now. Braden reached for my chin with his other hand and kissed me softly. Then more deeply.

By the time our entrees came, I wasn't sure if we were roommates or something else entirely. Maybe Alex was right. Or maybe I just wanted him to be.

Feeling something for a commitment-phobic man scared me more than the idea that aluminum might not be the optimal material for welding with lasers.

CHAPTER TWENTY-FOUR

raden

THE LOFT above the tasting room was basically a single room with a slanted ceiling, stone walls, and a king-sized bed. I hadn't slept at the vineyard since Ellie and I were together, and even then, we only made it out there a couple of times. So the loft had sat unused.

I'd had the forethought to have Janet, who ran the tasting room, give the place a quick cleaning before we arrived. So the sheets were clean, pillows fluffed, and windows cracked to let in the yellow afternoon sun.

Now the sun had long since set, and we sat cross-legged on the bed with four open bottles of wine and shot glasses for tasting. We also had a viciously competitive game of Chutes and Ladders underway.

Sarah wasn't kidding about liking to win. And although she inherently understood that the game involved no skill whatsoever, it frustrated the hell out of her that she couldn't use her mental fortitude to change the outcome of a spin of the wheel.

"You can't stand that you can't come up with some kind of theory of the universe that explains why you just fell down a chute." I taunted her only because I was finally in the lead for the first time.

"It's called gravity and bad luck. That's the theory." Her sulking amused me to no end.

"Speaking of theories, tell me about friction stir welding. You changed the subject at dinner."

"I seem to recall that you kissed me senseless. There was going to be no physics lesson after that."

"So tell me now. How does it work?"

Sarah looked up at the ceiling, something I noticed she did when she wanted to think something through. She never spoke until she knew exactly what she intended to say. Finally, she nodded. "Okay, imagine two blocks of metal sitting next to each other—copper or aluminum—hard metals. Then imagine a small vibrating needle moving in the space between them. It moves so fast that the friction stirs up the atoms in both pieces of metal, gets them moving until they start exchanging materials with each other. And with enough friction, they start to meld into one."

I nodded, my eyes fixed on her face, willing her not to look down at the tent in my boxers. But there was no putting one over on her. "Does physics get you hot, fireman?"

"Maybe it's all the talk about vibrating needles. I couldn't help thinking the whole friction thing was a metaphor for the things you want me to do to you." I leaned forward and raked my lips along her neck until they were right below her ear. "And you know how sexy I find your brain."

Her voice dropped to a sultry whisper. "Well then, I should probably tell you about our powerful lasers. They work to get the atoms moving even faster."

A second later, I had her on her back, my face inches from her, my hard cock leaving no question about where this was headed. "I want to hear more . . ."

"The lasers are powerful—we're using them on metals we've never been able to fuse before, and stronger, lighter rockets will be shot into space as a result. The end," she blurted quickly, wrapping her arms around my neck and pulling my face to hers. "Kiss me . . . then make love to me," she begged.

It was different this time—not the quick wild frenzy of two people who couldn't get enough—we were slower, more luxurious. This was love making.

It felt real.

And instead of scaring the shit out of me, I let it have me.

I slowly walked myself one step away from the fears that had defined my relationships with other people since the day my dad left us. Slowly. It would take a while. But I knew I wanted to be with her more than I wanted to protect myself.

I wanted her even if it hurt me later.

WE STILL HADN'T GONE to sleep, and given that it was four in the morning, we probably wouldn't, which suited me just fine. Staying up all night giving Sarah orgasms was followed by long conversations about why I should be baking my own dog biscuits and how she planned to train Bella to retrieve the newspaper every morning.

If anything, letting Bella roam the vineyards while we were at dinner did not bode well for future training. My dog was a free spirit.

"So tell me more about your ex," Sarah said, rolling onto her side to face me and hooking a leg over my hip.

I couldn't have heard her right. There was no way that after what had just happened between us, she was asking about my former fiancée.

"Sorry?" I tucked a fallen strand of hair behind her ear, readying myself to hear what she'd really asked me.

"Ellie. What was she like?"

"You want to talk about her now?"

Sarah sat up and pulled the sheet up to her chin, effectively cutting off any distractions. I guess she did want to talk. I ran a hand over my face, not particularly wanting to think about Ellie at all, but my affection for Sarah trumped my disgust for Ellie. It trumped everything.

"Okay, well, I guess what I fell for initially was her spirit. She was . . . she always saw the better side of a situation, always looked for the best in people."

Sarah said nothing at first, and I wondered if she regretted asking the question. She leaned toward me, cradling the side of my face with one of her palms. "Go on." Her voice was gentle, mimicking the stroke of her hand. "How'd you meet?"

"We met at a bar one night. She'd moved here temporarily to take care of her friend Jane who had breast cancer. Lived in the apartment with her, took her to all her chemo appointments, ran all her errands. Jane was a teacher at the elementary school, so she had lots of people who cared about her but no family to take care of her."

"Ellie was her person."

"Yeah. And you know from your dad, chemo wipes you out, so Jane had crashed, and Ellie was climbing the walls. She ended up at the bar near their apartment where I happened to be with a couple guys from work." I thought back on the memory of that night. It seemed like so much longer than three years ago. And Ellie . . . the Ellie from that night felt like a ghost of someone who'd never really existed.

"We drank too much, talked a lot. I thought we had a connection but looking back . . . maybe it was just the stress she was under looking after Jane and the fact that she didn't know anyone here." I hated to think about it now. "Maybe I was the only one invested. Like I said, it was her strength in dealing with a difficult situation and maintaining a positive outlook that attracted me. Probably the same reason she was the right person to help her friend deal with cancer."

Sarah hadn't moved, hadn't shifted her gaze away from me, not for a second. I don't think she blinked. "What happened with her friend, with cancer?"

This was Sarah, the woman who didn't want anything bad to happen to anyone. Of course she cared about my ex-fiancée's friend, who she didn't know.

I nodded and gently took one of Sarah's hands that were holding down the sheet and interlaced our fingers. "She's in remission. We're still friends. But . . . why do you want to know all this?"

She stared at me like it was obvious. "I just do. It's your life. I want to know you."

215

Shrugging, I continued, telling her how once Jane recovered, Ellie didn't have as much reason to be here, other than me. "By then, we'd gotten engaged, and maybe she felt trapped. I never thought of it that way at the time, but maybe . . . I don't know if getting engaged was maybe a way to try and hold onto something that wasn't mine to begin with."

Sarah reached and put a hand on mine. "You couldn't know. Someone like that, I know the type. Lightning in a bottle, or that's what they make you think. I have a younger sister like that —Tatum, she shines like the sun, blond hair and all. She was born looking like an angel—and it took me that longest time to realize she wasn't perfect. She knew it, but I couldn't see it. So she pushed me away, so I never would. And you know what? Once I realized she had flaws, it made me love her so much more."

As I heard her say the words, all I could think was that Ellie hadn't been that kind of person at all. Everything I'd thought to be true about her was my wishful thinking. She'd never pretended to be as interested in me as I hoped she'd be. She was only with me until she found something better. Looking back, I supposed there were signs, but I chose not to see them. I was blinded by who I thought she was.

But Sarah . . . she really was lightning in a bottle. The irony in the way she described her sister was that she didn't seem to realize that her sister probably pushed her away in order not to be outshone.

"I guess wanting something doesn't always make it the right choice. She sounds like she had a lot of good qualities." She rubbed a hand in circles on my back.

Nothing compared to you.

"I guess not," I agreed. And that was the problem. The more time I spent with Sarah, the more I wanted her.

I admired her modesty. I admired a lot about her. And despite the rules we'd laid down and the damned good job we'd done so far at keeping to them, I couldn't help feeling a tugging in my heart. It wanted more.

I had to shut that shit down before someone got hurt. It wasn't going to be me, not again. And I didn't want it to be Sarah—she had a life to go back to in Berkeley in a couple months. So there we were.

So far, all the lines had been crossed, but no rules had been broken.

No falling in love.

I needed to make sure I kept it that way.

CHAPTER TWENTY-FIVE

Sarah

WE'D ALREADY HAD the conversation several times, but hanging out in Braden's front yard pulling weeds felt like a great time to discuss the topic again.

"Okay, you're sure you're cool having everyone here? They're hellions."

"You remember, I know your family. Or at least I did when you were kids."

"Exactly. When you and Finn hung out, we were practically still in diapers. Harmless. Now my sisters are all grown up and vicious."

Since my car had been at the repair shop for months, I'd begged off the family dinners in Berkeley, but this week my siblings wanted to move the dinner to Braden's house so we could catch up.

He smirked at me. "It's hard to imagine, frankly. But if they're the troublemakers you say they are, even more reason why I want them all here. We could use some action in this town." Then, as though noticing me for the first time, he poked me in the ribs. "Hey, where'd you find my favorite hoodie?"

It was a worn gray sweatshirt with frayed sleeves, and it was maybe the softest article of clothing I'd ever worn. I raised my finger to my lips. "Shh, don't tell the fireman, but sometimes when he's not here, I sleep in this."

"Well, that's going to make my dreams of you sleeping in my bed even sweeter, especially when I imagine taking this off your body with my teeth." He leaned over, grabbed the hem in his teeth, and lifted it off my midriff. He kissed me there and raked the skin with his stubble until I sighed.

"Sorry I took it without asking," I apologized, feeling a tiny bit guilty, but my happiness in the worn fleece outweighed it.

"Damsel, what's mine is yours. I'd give you the clothes off my back." For as strong and sexy as Braden was, his soft side was sweet duck fluff.

I wracked my brain for any excuse I could come up with to keep my family away. Finding none, I relented. "Okay then, sisters are coming. Bring on the savages. Just trust me and know that we need a united front before they get here. I'll show you how to avoid their questions. Always keep moving." I pantomimed jabbing and ducking like a boxer until Braden pulled me in and planted a kiss that knocked all the fight out of me.

"What's the big deal with these family dinners, anyway?"

I shrugged. It was hard to explain our unique bond to anyone who wasn't from a family of six siblings.

Scratch that.

It was hard to explain to anyone who came from a family not filled with meddling intrusive sisters and a brother who thought he knew more than anyone. Losing our dad when we were young made us overlook rivalries or personality differences because we knew how it felt to lose one of our own.

I loved them all so much.

"I've missed too many family dinners, and they're giving me shit." At first, I'd enjoyed the break from everything—my teaching job and even seeing my siblings, not that I didn't love them. But I liked my adventure in this new town, and I wasn't ready to share it with them. More than that, I was afraid I'd revert to being the person they expected me to be.

The longer I stayed away, the more I could let myself believe that my temporary reality was a real one. I could pretend that my life consisted of coming home to dinner with Braden each night, huddling on his deck, spending hours wrapped in phenomenal sex positions with the best-looking guy I'd ever met. I could pretend I didn't live strictly according to science and plans. I could fall for my roommate. I could pretend it didn't have to end.

But I knew it did, which was partly why I was regretting agreeing to have my whole family drive down for dinner. At first, it seemed easier to drive myself to Berkeley to see them. One person in the car, one headache if there was traffic.

But Braden wouldn't have it. "Not on my watch."

"What's that supposed to mean? Do you have a shift at the station that night?"

He laughed. "No. Not that. I'm not putting you in my car to drive for an hour when the last time you did that, you ended up with a face full of airbag, and my guys spent a week buffing out the rear bumper of our truck." Not to mention that I still hadn't figured out whether my insurance company was dropping me.

"Why do I get the feeling you enjoy telling that story?"

"Because I do." His kiss was gentle. Then not. Then hot and seductive.

I tore my lips away from his before we got too sidetracked from the conversation. Or the weeds.

We were crouched down in his front yard pulling crabgrass out of his flowerbeds. If someone had told me a few months earlier that I was going to be harvesting weeds with the world's sexiest gardener, I'd have asked for a tab of that hallucinogen. Not really. But I'd have let out a cackle at the ludicrous suggestion.

I was sitting cross-legged in front of a planter box filled with sweet peas that were trailing all over the path toward the front door. Braden sat next to me working on a second planter box where he'd planted basil and mint, but that too had gone crazy after a late spring rain.

Every so often, he'd stop gardening and pull me in and drop a sweet kiss on my lips, almost like his body was on a timer. Like there was a certain amount of skin-on-skin contact and me melting into a puddle against him that needed to be fulfilled before he could continue on the yard. I couldn't argue with the logic of his horticultural protocols.

After he'd kissed me so thoroughly and so exquisitely that I felt dizzy, he plucked a handful of mint from the ground and rubbed a sprig between his fingers. "This will make for some good mojitos later."

I leaned down to inhale the aromatic scent and realized how good it felt to have my hands in real dirt. "You know, I have a small yard at my house, and I haven't done anything with it except grow grass. And if I'm honest, it's not grass. It's weeds that look like grass from a vast distance because they're green."

"Weeds are nice," he said kindly. "Better than dirt."

I shook my head and punched him in the arm. "You're such a liar. You told me this morning you hate weeds. We've spent an hour pulling the weeds out of your perfect plants. You're quietly judging me for my weeds."

He shrugged. "I'm not one to judge. I know you've got a busy life. And what with all your teaching and the pole dancing I don't believe you really do, who has time for gardening?"

Now I punched him harder, and he tackled me. Somehow my assault ended with me on my back and him hovering over me. "How did I end up on the bottom in this attack?"

He grinned and traced my lips with his finger. Then his hand trailed down my neck to where he rested it on one of my breasts. I felt my nipple harden immediately at his touch. He had the ability to work my body into a storm with a single touch. He bent to kiss my neck, sucking on a sensitive spot beneath my ear until my whole body hummed with desire for more.

"It's called a sneak attack. You thought you had the upper hand, which allowed you to relax enough to hand it over to me."

I was delirious with desire. "I hear you talking, but I have no idea what you're saying." My voice sounded sultry and wild for him. I'd been getting to know this version of Sarah over the past few months, and I liked her. She'd found beauty in the unexpected. "And I don't even care. Just kiss me more."

He laughed. "I could kiss you all day." He lowered his lips slowly to mine. Something was different in the way we'd been with each other since our overnight at the vineyard. Instead of feeling like roommates who were having great sex, we were acting more like a couple—pulling weeds, hosting dinners.

I liked it. It didn't necessarily mean our rules were changing. But for the first time, I was starting to hope they could.

raden

I LEANED against the passenger door of my truck, as had become my habit at the end of every workday. Maybe my life had become too much of a grind without enough surprises. Maybe I'd forgotten that it was possible to be happy.

But since Sarah had moved in with me, happiness seemed within reach.

And it freaks you the hell out, admit it.

For the first few weeks, I wasn't sure what to make of any of it. I just reveled in the fact that I could feel again for the first time in two years.

Then I started to crave the feeling like an addict.

For weeks it was easy to live in the present like we'd agreed upon when we made our rules. Six months felt like an eternity. There was no reason to think ahead. Six months of fun and great sex would surely satisfy my needs, and there was no need to think about what my life would be like when she moved back to Berkeley.

But I was starting to think. Then I was doing my damnedest not to think because it didn't get me anywhere. The whole point of us was to live in the present and not think.

Sure, just keep telling yourself that.

All I knew was that standing outside the lab each afternoon had become a highlight of my day. Every time Sarah walked through the double doors at the entrance, my heart swelled to the point that the ache was almost painful. I marveled at how much I liked this woman, how much I wanted her, how much I . . . could not fall for her.

Except that I already had.

Today, Sarah wasn't alone when she came through the doors. Walking next to her was a man, slightly older but easily the silver fox type who probably had his pick of women. He had a full head of white hair and a solid build, no middle-aged paunch or sag about him. He was laughing at something Sarah said, and his perfect teeth glinted in the sunlight.

When they got to the driveway, Sarah turned and hugged him. For a little too long, if I'm honest. Then he kissed her on the cheek and went back into the building. She bounded over to me and her lips sunk into mine. I almost forgot about the silver fox. Almost.

"Hi! I'm very excited about our field trip." She wrapped her arms around my waist and looked up at me, eyes sparkling.

I'd forgotten that I'd couched my plan in the form of a field trip. At the time, I'd thought it sounded bookish and scientific. Now, my eyes still saw the silhouette of the silver fox when I looked at Sarah.

"Who was he?" I made no pretense of my distaste for the man she'd hugged, even though I knew it was irrational. For months, she'd spent almost every night with me. It wasn't physically possible for her to be dating other people—there was no time in the day.

Except that there was time. Every day. How did I know what—or who—she did at work all day long?

This is crazy. Irrational. Get a grip.

Sarah was looking at me like I'd grown an extra set of arms and was using them to signal alien aircraft. "He? You mean Earl?"

Earl? What kind of a name was that? Was he an actual earl? "I dunno. The guy you walked out with. I've never seen you with any of your colleagues."

"Oh, yeah. He wanted to keep talking, and I didn't want you to be waiting out here forever, so he walked me out." She didn't want to keep me waiting. The jealous guy she was sleeping with. I needed to chill.

"Got it. So how was your day?"

A grin spread over her face. "Great, thanks for asking."

I opened her door and waited until she hopped in. She'd given me enough grief over the past few months that I'd finally decided to dispense with grabbing her hand and helping her in. But she hesitated, turning her aqua eyes up to me. "I know, I know. You're a capable woman. I'm not trying to help you into the truck," I grumbled.

Pressing her lips together, she couldn't suppress her smile. "I guess I . . . I kind of got used to it."

"Does that mean my self-sufficient damsel likes a helping hand?" It was hard to hide my smirk.

"I guess I like your helping hand."

"Then Damsel, I'm at your service." With a slight bow, I helped her into the truck, loving that I'd bent her to my will a tiny bit. There was no doubt in my mind she could climb into the truck. It was never about that. I liked the formality of chivalry, almost like a courtship dance, and I liked having her as my partner.

After I'd pulled away from the lab, Sarah turned to me. "Hey, how come you never pick me up on the motorcycle? That could be fun."

"No way. Not happening," I said.

She cocked her head. "Why not?"

"It's dangerous. I'm not putting you on a bike. Not ever."

She parked her hand on my thigh and leaned in. "Because you think I'm accident-prone?"

"No. Like I said, bikes are dangerous. The same way you feel about me going into a fire scene, that's how I'd feel about you on a bike."

"And yet you still ride."

She had me there. "I ride less than I used to."

"Uh huh. Hypocrite." She had me there too.

A few minutes later, we pulled up to the firehouse of Engine 97. Sarah raised an eyebrow. "Did you forget something at work?"

I shook my head, feeling a little smug about my plan. "Nope."

"Okaaay . . . am I coming in or should I wait in the truck?"

I slipped out of my seat and went around to her side. She smiled when I opened the door and extended a hand. "You're coming in."

She looked at me quizzically but matched me stride for stride up the walkway to the station. "Am I getting a tour?"

"You are." I felt my body hum with anticipation.

"Seriously? I've always wanted a tour of the fire department."

I wished I could have captured her look of delight and bottled it for posterity. "You could have asked me weeks ago."

"I know, but I didn't want to seem like a firefighter groupie."

"Firefighter? I thought I was a fireman."

"You're *my* fireman. That's different. All the rest of these guys are firefighters. Not that I want them to get hurt either. You know."

I did know. I also knew how to give a good tour of the firehouse. Over the years, we'd had school groups, church groups, and potential recruits come through for tours, but I'd never felt prouder to show the place off. Sarah bounced on her toes, so giddy that I felt more fissures form in the carefully erected walls around my heart.

And as much as I couldn't let anyone break down those walls entirely, it felt good to let Sarah swing at them for all they were worth. Because maybe they weren't worth shit.

"What do you want to see first?" I spread my arms wide.

She didn't even hesitate. "The kitchen. Natch."

"Why?"

"Because I want you to cook me something. I skipped lunch because Earl and I spent like six hours working with the lasers, and I'm starved." Earl again. I tried not to think about what she and the silver fox were doing with such intensity that it would make Sarah skip a meal. That was unlike her.

I pushed through the swinging kitchen door to the room I'd never bothered to show anyone except probies. It had a metal table with six metal chairs in the middle of the room and white painted cabinets. It was about as nondescript as a kitchen could be, unless someone was cooking, in which case there would be ingredients spread out everywhere and a mess of pots and pans.

I leaned against the sink while Sarah walked around the room, peeking inside cupboards and opening drawers. Her curiosity amused me. Her hugging colleague still did not.

"What were you and Earl working on?" I tried to keep my voice casual and curious. Not jealous.

"Oh! This is so great. We figured out a way to use the same lasers we earmarked for the project, but we made an adjustment that increased their power by tenfold. Which means we can solder the metals more quickly to prevent any melting. The whole thing I've been stressing about for weeks, I think we nailed it!"

I wanted to share her excitement even though about half of what she was telling me about lasers was lost on me. But I couldn't get the niggling image of Earl kissing her on the cheek out of my head. "Do you and Earl work together daily? Is he a big part of your team?"

She stopped moving around the room and looked at me. Then she walked over to where I stood, wrapped her arms around me, and laid her head on my chest. She didn't tell me about Earl or explain that the sixty-year-old physicist wasn't any kind of threat. She didn't need to.

I stroked her hair, and inhaled a calming breath. To hell with Earl. I had everything I needed.

Lifting her face from my chest, I brushed a gentle kiss against her lips and reached for her hand. I opened the fridge to check the inventory of leftovers and catalog whether we had any decent ingredients. "How about a grilled cheese?"

Sarah licked her lips. "Perfect."

A few minutes later, I'd hustled up two sandwiches and a couple cans of sweetened iced tea, and we continued our tour of the place.

"Where is everyone?" Sarah looked around the bay, craning her neck to check the corners where she must have thought the guys were hiding.

"Out on a call. Downed power pole, so they need to be onsite in case the wires spark up during removal. They were heading out when I left to get you." I hesitated, knowing she got nervous at the thought of me being in danger, but I had to tell her. There was a good chance that tonight's shit would get real.

She studied me. "What aren't you telling me?" I recalled asking her the same thing when we were at the bike shop, and I saw the depths of concern in her eyes about losing her license. Apparently, she'd learned to read me too. I liked it. A lot.

"There's a decent chance we'll get called out tonight on something bigger. Grisley Fire. It's burning out in Mount Diablo."

Her eyes grew wide. "Oh, yeah. I heard about that. Is it bad?"

I wanted to lie and allay her fears, but the fire was zero percent contained, and we were heading into a potentially rough night. "It's not great. Already burned over ten thousand acres. So far, we haven't been called for backup, but we're standing by. The real danger is tonight if the wind doesn't do what we're expecting."

"What are you expecting?" She took a step closer to me, protectively. I wasn't too worried about the fire, but I loved knowing she cared.

"Well, the weather report shows easterly wind in the evening, which would be great because it would force the fire back over the area that's already burned. So that'll give us time to regroup and get a handle on it."

Sarah exhaled a breath she'd been holding, and her shoulders dropped. She blinked up at me and nodded. "Oh. Okay, well, that sounds good. I feel better knowing that."

I knew she was nervous, but I didn't want to sugarcoat things so much that it was as good as a lie.

"Yeah, it's just . . . fires are weird because fires create their own wind, so even when we think we know what the weather is going to do, the fire can do something else. That's when things happen, like when the whole town of Paradise burned to the ground. It happened too fast for anyone to predict it. The fire burned four football fields worth of brush a second."

"Jesus." She was silent after that, and I knew her mind was racing with the implications. And I knew the question that would be on her mind next. "You think you'll get called tonight?"

I nodded. I couldn't lie to her. Didn't want to. "It's likely."

She took a deep breath and squared her shoulders like she was getting ready for battle. "Okay then, let's tour this place and hope for easterly winds."

EVERYONE HAS their favorite part of the station, and I was no different. I leaned into the history.

Knowing Sarah, there was a decent chance she'd done her research and already knew about the odd artifact I wanted to show her, but I held out hope it might still surprise her.

We walked into the front gallery, where I guided her to what looked pretty much like an ordinary lightbulb. Encased in a wooden display box, it burned dimly. "It's called the Millennium Light. And it holds a world record." I pointed at the barely shining bulb, which glowed like the dying light of a ten-year-old flashlight. The thing wouldn't impress a soul without a history lesson.

"Really? For what? I feel like I should have heard of this."

"Nah, not unless you live around here. You can see it's not super bright, just four watts, but this thing has been burning for over one hundred and ten years."

"Wait, what?"

"Yup. It's in the Guinness Book."

Dude, you're showing her a geriatric lightbulb.

Did she even care? What was I doing?

Her bright eyes told me she did. "Well, that's something to crow about. Go, little light bulb." She smiled, but when her eyes drifted over my face without looking me in the eye, I knew her mind was churning.

"And . . . she's gone. Lemme have it, Damsel, what's going through your head?"

She shrugged. "I'm just trying to figure out how it's possible. I mean, the thing should burn out like any other bulb. So what's the angle?"

"I don't know, but it was hand-blown and has a carbon filament, so maybe that's the secret sauce." I read from the plaque on the front of the case. "Originally installed by Oscar Damascus Walton, it's been maintained for generations. I think it was disconnected a few times to move to other stations, and there've been some power failures, so I guess the world record thing takes that into account."

"Very cool, fireman. And the carbon filament part is super interesting. I guess they don't make them like they used to, huh?" She nudged me with an elbow and grinned. The simple gesture made my heart do a backflip.

I had it bad for her. It was getting harder to talk myself out of that fact.

It was also becoming worrisome because we were way past the halfway mark of her time here, and I knew I'd feel a huge void when she left.

Everyone leaves.

We went upstairs to see the bunks where we all slept on overnight shifts. Boots lined the wall with our pantlegs draped over them so we could throw them on and go. "I feel like I've seen this setup in movies, but I guess they're based on fact. You really do hop into your boots. Do you slide down a pole too?"

Gesturing behind her, I indicated said pole. "You want to take it for a test drive? I'm not gonna lie—ever since you told me you were a pole dancer, I've been fantasizing about seeing you wrap your legs around this thing." It had been my ulterior motive when I'd concocted this little field trip.

The wicked gleam in her eye told me everything I needed to know. "I wouldn't exactly call myself a pole dancer. I do it as a workout."

"Semantics."

She grinned. "I think I can make use of this." And without hesitation, she leaped forward and slid down the pole. When she was free and clear at the bottom, I followed and moved to the side.

With her hand on the pole, Sarah walked around it in a circle, assessing the feel of it and the obvious weight of my stare on her. Would she dance? Or was the whole idea of me ogling her going to make her uncomfortable? I didn't dare say a word, lest I discourage her.

She tipped her head back and jumped onto the pole, spinning around it easily once before dismounting and nodding at me. "Yeah. This could work." The sight of her fingering the pole and winding her legs around it got me hot in an instant.

"Oh baby, it's already working." The instantaneous throb in my pants confirmed it.

Sarah stared down at her creased black pants, considering. "There's really no one here? You promise?"

"Couple guys are out back, but unless they want to be looking for a job tomorrow, they're not coming in. It's just us, Damsel."

"Okay, then." Peeling off the conservative work pants, she revealed a hot pink pair of cheekies. "I need a little more freedom of movement." My greedy eyes fixated on her fingers deftly undoing the buttons of her light pink cardigan sweater, revealing a ribbed tank top that fit her like a second skin. The delight in her eyes when she gazed at the pole made me certain my gamble had paid off—she was into my idea.

Grabbing her phone from inside her purse, Sarah shuffled through her playlists until she found one she liked. The first notes from "Blow Me a Kiss" by Pink danced from her phone, and Sarah jumped onto the pole again.

I had no idea what to expect. Admittedly, my experience with pole dancing came from a few guys' bachelor parties that landed us at strip clubs. I stood slumped against the ladder truck with my jaw hanging open while she amazed me with the strength of her abs and her legs, which were flexing and gripping the pole as she hooked a leg around the metal and spun in a circle.

She was no longer the pragmatic scientist who weighed every decision and chose based on the best outcome. She danced without a care or a plan, letting the music guide her body slower as she flipped upside down and spread her legs into a V and back upright as she gripped the pole with her thighs and leaned back for a luxurious spin.

She took my breath away with her inhibition and her grace. Curling her bare foot around the pole, she held on with one hand and leaned away, twirling slowly until she came around to where I stood. Leaning as close to me as possible, she smiled. "Thank you for letting me do this. I've missed it."

I was the one filled with gratitude.

And also some prominent wood.

"I love this side of you." I kissed her lips before she wound her legs around the pole again and moved faster with the music. A sheen of sweat gathered on her skin, tempting me to lick it off. But I didn't dare move.

"Most of the time, I'm focused on the workout." She wrapped her legs around the pole so she could flip upside down again. Tendrils of hair fell out of the clip at the back and landed around her face, framing her soulful eyes. "But right now, I'm focused on you."

"Is it a distraction?" Much as I enjoyed watching her, this was about her. I'd leave the room if it would help her loosen up and get the workout she wanted.

She wrapped one knee around the pole and swung in another circle. "Yes . . . a good one." That was all I needed to hear, and as she dropped down to the floor and readied herself to leap on the pole again, I stood agog, mesmerized, and impressed.

After twenty minutes or so, Sarah lowered herself to the ground and mopped the sweat from her brow with the back of an arm. The look of satisfaction on her face was everything I wanted for her. It wasn't just her skin that glowed. The relaxed, contented expression on her face rivaled the way she looked when she rode my cock.

But not quite.

"That was so. Goddamn. Sexy," I growled. How had it taken me this long to come up with the pole idea?

A shadow of her more self-conscious side emerged. "That was amazing. I didn't realize how much I missed it," she said, still breathless from the exertion.

I tapped the pole. "I'm . . . never going to look at this fucking thing the same way again."

"Good," she laughed. Wrapping her arms around my neck, she leaned in for a sweaty kiss, and I took the opportunity to lick the salt from her neck. Her body gave an involuntary shiver as I ran my tongue down to the curve of her shoulder.

"Are you cold?" It was always freezing in the station.

"A bit."

I grabbed my fire jacket off the hook and wrapped it around her. The thing fit her like a tent, but with her long, bare legs and wild hair, I'd never seen anyone look so gorgeous.

The next song on her playlist was something sexy by Bruno Mars. "Wanna dance?" She tipped her face up to mine.

I put a hand on the small of her back and pulled her in close. "This would kill my man cred if anyone saw us."

"Don't do a lot of dancing at the fire station?" She rested her cheek against my chest, and I inhaled the lavender scent of her shampoo.

"Nope." My dick was still rock hard, but I wanted to dance with her more than I wanted to push her against the hook and ladder truck and have my way with her. I wanted to romance her, which meant I'd fallen so far over the edge for her already that I might as well give in.

She seemed to agree, pressing tighter against me. "I've never danced in front of anyone before. But it got me kind of hot."

"Kind of?"

"Okay, very."

"That's easily remedied." I moved us across the floor until her back was up against the wall and lifted her so she could wrap her legs around my waist.

"Yes, please. You. Now." Her voice came out in that raspy, needy tone I loved.

But then . . .

The station siren went off in an angry blare, and we had the misfortune of standing right beneath it. Sarah clung to me in shocked fear until she realized what it meant. Her look turned to dread.

"You think it's the Grisley Fire?"

I nodded and gently lowered Sarah to the ground, kissing her on the cheek seconds before the incoming dispatch crackled with what was needed and where. She shimmied back into her clothes —I'd never seen anyone move so quickly, and I worked with guys trained in suiting up on a dime.

Guys who'd been hanging in the backhouse flooded in, jumping into their boots and throwing their arms into the sleeves of their coats.

"Pleasanton got called a couple hours ago. Everyone's getting overtime," I told Mitch when he came in with his jacket already on and his helmet in his hand. It was his habit to take it wherever he went instead of leaving it with his pants and boots. All the guys had their own quirks, and that was his.

Sarah saw the grim look on my face when I assessed the incoming messages. "I'm sorry, Damsel. I've gotta go." She nodded, and I could tell she had questions and worries, but there was no time to answer them. I grabbed my keys from my pocket and handed them to her. "Here. Take my truck back to the house, and I'll call you as soon as I can with a status report."

"Okay. Be careful, fireman." She tried to smile, but her face was too clouded with concern to be convincing. It broke my heart to leave her like that, which was a whole other problem I had no time to deal with.

I kissed her on the cheek. "Don't worry."

With that, she took the keys and headed for the side entrance where we'd come in. There was a faster way out, but I had to turn my back and get our guys into the rig and out the door. She'd find her way out.

From that second, I was on autopilot, running through the mental checklist of everything we needed to fight a brushfire and pinging the on-call guys to let them know they'd probably be needed. If we were getting the call before the weather patterns had shifted, it meant things were already looking bad.

Sarah didn't need to know that.

And I couldn't help feeling guilty about the fact that rushing into a danger zone still filled me with an adrenaline rush like no other. As soon as she was out of sight, my head cleared of all distractions, and I went through the checklist for the rig before we headed out. There was a reason I chose this profession, and so far, nothing else had provided the same high.

Well, until I met Sarah.

CHAPTER TWENTY-SEVEN

 arah

I COULDN'T SLEEP. There was no way.

Just knowing that a fire was blazing and people were risking their lives to put it out chilled me to the bone. But knowing that Braden was one of those people had my heart pounding like I'd thrown down six cups of coffee.

At ten, I took Bella for a walk around the neighborhood. Even though the fire was thirty miles away, the winds had shifted, and the smell of smoke served as a constant reminder of where Braden was.

She seemed aware that something wasn't right. She kept turning her head to look at me—or to look for him.

"I know, girl. I wish he was here too."

As we walked along, I noticed a fine layer of ash on all the cars. My one hope was that the wind behaved the way everyone hoped it would. If it shifted and blew back in the direction where the mountains had already burned, the crew had a good chance of containing it.

If it shifted the other way, however, it could wipe out miles of forest overnight. I didn't want to think about the realities of fire-fighting—the heat, the smoke, the danger . . .

But I couldn't think about anything else.

I knew that Braden had gone out on calls on many of the nights he'd been on shift at the station. The difference was that I hadn't known about the potential danger until the next day when he'd tell me about his night. No matter how perilous he made it sound, I already knew his stories ended well because he'd come back to tell them.

Tonight, I had no such assurances.

When Bella and I had walked the same few blocks at least five times, she started pulling me back toward the house. I realized we'd been walking for over an hour.

At least the movement dissipated some of my stress, but once we got back, I needed another outlet. Incessantly checking the news for updates about the fire would get me nowhere fast.

So I turned to the only thing that had a fighting chance of calming my nerves—*The Great British Bakeoff*. I'd already seen every episode, but it didn't matter. Watching the contestants create their showstoppers would allow me to get lost for at least a little while, and as long as I could watch other people bake things, I figured I might as well join them.

While Bella curled up on her bed in the next room, I took out all the baking ingredients I had, along with all the bowls and measuring utensils I'd need. Positioning everything on the counter facing the giant TV, I turned on the show and got to work.

Within forty-five minutes, Paul Hollywood was critiquing a gingerbread British pub, complete with a sticky toffee floor, and I had two cakes and a batch of cookies in the oven.

I checked the time again. I hadn't worried about Braden for a whole five minutes.

IT WAS strange that the smokey smell from outside was now inside. It was also strange that I could smell it amid the overwhelming scent of baked goods.

Then there was the matter of fingers pressing into the side of my face. Oh right, I was leaning on my hand, with my elbow on the counter.

But what about the fingers caressing the other side of my face? Whose were those?

"Damsel . . . Hey, sleepy."

My eyes shot open. Why had they been closed? And why did I think I heard Braden's voice?

Then I felt it again, his hand on my face, and I clasped it in both hands and turned around to face him. "Oh my god, it's you. I'm so glad you're okay." He looked exhausted, with soot outlining the shape of the mask he'd worn and lines creasing his skin from sweat and exertion.

He smiled. "I knew you'd be worried. I'd normally shower at the station, but . . ."

"Thank you for coming back. And not showering so you could come back sooner."

I threw my arms around him and held him tight.

"Have you been in here all night?" His voice sounded raspy and tired. The TV still squawked with a *Bakeoff* contestant explaining why she'd used chopped cherries in her traybake. I grabbed the remote and turned it off.

"Stress baking," I said, dazed.

"I'd say so." Braden took in the six different platefuls of cookies, the frosted two-layer cake, a tray of blueberry muffins, and a no-yeast bread loaf and smiled, leaning his forehead against mine. "I'm sorry I worried you. It's my job, but I told you I'm always careful."

"I know. Thank you for being careful. And thank you for coming back." I kissed him deeply, lovingly, almost like I could pour everything I felt about him into a kiss. And what I felt was unmistakable. It was love.

He scooped me up in his arms and carried me up the stairs, nuzzling my neck as he walked. "I still need that shower, and I'm bringing you with me. And then we're both going to get some sleep."

Cradled in his arms, I had no doubt about my feelings.

I love him.

I couldn't tell him—it broke every rule we had—but at least I could be honest with myself. And tomorrow, I'd do everything in my power to make those feelings go away. They didn't fit into our scenario. We were a good time, living in the present. We weren't forever. If I told myself that enough times, I'd have no choice but to accept it.

But for now, I could wrap myself in his warmth, grateful he'd come back alive.

"There was no way I wasn't coming back here to you." He turned on the shower and tipped his forehead against mine. "You're what kept me going while I was out there tonight. The thought of feeling you wrapped around me like this."

The heat in his eyes was almost feral. Fighting fires—facing the nearness of death—brought out a hunger in him I hadn't seen before. Pure physical need.

And here I was, having feelings.

This was why I avoided situations with unexpected outcomes. I wasn't equipped to deal with them.

CHAPTER TWENTY-EIGHT

raden

LIVING in the present had its merits. Sarah and I never talked about the future because we'd agreed there wouldn't be one, at least not for us as a couple. That took away any pressure I might have felt with a woman after a few dates—or in our case, a few months.

Except that everything had changed for me.

The more time that went by, the more I realized I wanted a future or at least the discussion of one. But I told myself to learn from the past and kill the urge to bring it up. Why mess with a situation that was working?

We both knew where we stood. We'd been honest at the outset. We were enjoying our temporary time together.

Only an idiot would try to change things up.

I couldn't afford to be an idiot.

Sarah had finally gotten her car back from the repair shop, and her insurance company seemed to be forgiving enough—this one last time. Even though I told her I'd be happy to keep carpooling —I cited the negative environmental impact of taking two cars, playing to her scientific mind—she insisted that she didn't want to burden me with driving her around anymore.

"I don't mind," I insisted. I liked driving her. But I respected her need for independence if she wanted it. Maybe it would help get it through my thick skull that we were *not* a couple, linked at the hip.

"Trust me, you'll be much happier to see me when you don't feel like my personal Uber."

"I never felt like that. And I'm always happy to see you," I said, spooning scrambled eggs onto two plates while Sarah browned a side of bacon on the stove.

She dropped the spatula in the pan, came over to me, and craned her neck to kiss me. "I'm always happy to see you too. But I think I need to embrace driving on my own a little bit, or I'll never be able to pilot that beast back up to Berkeley when my stint at the lab is over."

She went back to the bacon, flipping the strips in the pan and pouring off the grease.

But I couldn't move, suddenly stuck by a tightness in my chest that hadn't been there a minute ago. Before Sarah referred to moving back to Berkeley.

It wasn't like this was news to me. But hearing her talk about leaving without even a trace of regret brought back all the feelings I'd had two years earlier when Ellie told me she was moving out and moving on. No hesitation. No regrets.

Same as when my dad told us he'd bought a new house to live in with his new wife. He never looked back.

Everyone leaves.

The sooner I stopped fighting that, the healthier I'd be.

Sarah brought the bacon over and put two slices on each of our plates, smiling at me as she grabbed a piece and held it out for Bella, who'd been following the bacon pan with her eyes. "Good girl, Bella. Can you sit?" Bella obeyed. She held bacon in the highest esteem. Sarah backed away, holding her hand out. "Stay. Stay." When she'd moved halfway across the kitchen, she looked at Bella. "Come and get it, girl." Bella galloped at her and closed the distance between them in two giant steps.

"You've got her wrapped around your finger." I smiled through the residual tightness in my chest. I hated this feeling and had no idea what would make it dissipate.

Ask Sarah to stay after her fellowship is over.

But I couldn't do that. She had a life in Berkeley and a plan for how she wanted that life to go. It didn't fit in with any of the rules we'd set up, and nothing Sarah had done or said in the past couple months had given me any indication she'd changed her mind about where she stood.

"You okay?" She put her plate down and rested her hands on my chest. Sarah looked into my eyes, and I wanted to sail away in hers.

"Yeah. Sure." I pulled her closer, and her hands slid up my chest and over my shoulders. Her lips fit perfectly with mine, and as soon as I laid claim to them, the tightness in my chest dissipated.

I dragged my hands through her hair and held the back of her head, unwilling to give her any space to negotiate a different angle. I wanted her exactly where she was, or closer if it was humanly possible.

Our mouths fused, lips grinding, teeth nipping, and tongues thrashing as we moved from zero to a million in seconds.

Moving my hands down her back and under her gorgeous ass, I lifted her up, and she wrapped her legs around my waist. Without breaking the kiss, I spun her around and pushed her onto the counter, my erection hard and desperate, finding her center like a homing beacon.

"Braden . . ." Her voice was raspy and as desperate as I felt. I couldn't get close enough. I couldn't find enough ways to take her over. And I wouldn't stop trying.

"Tell me." I wanted her to say the words, tell me she felt as frantic for me as I did in this moment," I growled. "What do you want."

"You," she said, breathless. "Sorry, I can't be more specific than that."

Her teeth clamped down on my neck, biting the skin and using her tongue to soothe the pain.

"So hot. You're exactly what I need," I said through gritted teeth. "More. You're so much more."

"You make me this way," she panted, her lips running the length of my neck before landing on mine. Our tongues dueled, each refusing to relent before taking everything and giving it back in equal measure.

It was dizzying, gorgeous, and feral.

I worked her yoga pants down her legs, pulling them over her feet and tossing them to the side. Underneath, she wore a tiny lace thong which would have been a hindrance if the sight of it hadn't been so damn hot.

This wasn't a courtship. I wasn't asking her for a waltz around the ballroom. This was unapologetic sex without boundaries or limitations. I needed to let that be enough.

I needed to stop thinking.

I pushed the lace of her panties aside and stroked her opening. "You're so wet for me. I can't stand it."

"For you," she moaned as I plunged a finger inside her and curled it to hit the spot I knew she loved. "And if you do that, I'm gonna lose my mind."

She reached down and cupped my cock in her hand while she ground her hips on my finger. "Jesus, I'm gonna need to keep condoms in every room of the house," I groaned, amused that I hadn't thought of that yet and grateful that I'd shoved one in the pocket of my sweats before I left the bedroom.

Sarah rolled the condom on, then wrapped her hand around my cock and stroked. I was a goner. So ready. So desperate to be buried deep inside her.

I knew she felt it too by the way she lifted her hips to meet me and then stilled, letting me fill her inch by snug inch until her wet heat enveloped me, and I heard her sigh.

Way too good, the feeling of her muscles clenching around me in tiny pulses. Then she started to move, circling her hips, slowly, luxuriously. And I lost my mind.

With all my pent-up feelings mixed with desire, I wouldn't last long.

"I wanted you from the moment you told me you were worried about me in a fire," I rasped, wanting her to understand she had me in ways that went beyond physical lust.

"I wanted you then too, but I want you even more now."

Sarah started to moan my name, and I was right with her, cresting the wave and combusting like a ten-alarm fire that no one could extinguish.

I pushed all my thoughts about the future aside. There was too much good between us in the present to get all wrapped up in what ifs.

We were okay. I'd be okay.

CHAPTER TWENTY-NINE

arah

LEFT TO HIS OWN DEVICES, Braden kept a relatively clean house, and my attempts at straightening gave it a helpful boost. Tonight, it was spotless. I'd been stress cleaning all day.

Once I'd cleaned the kitchen, the den, the entire outdoor space where we'd set up two long folding tables and chairs Braden had borrowed from who knows where, I found a recipe I'd seen one night on the Food Network. Then I bought the ingredients to chicken piccata, garlic bread, heirloom tomato and burrata salad with basil, and a giant casserole of baked ziti.

And I'd yet to cook anything.

"Why are you so wound up?" Braden came up behind me and dropped his hands on my shoulders as I stood arranging hot pink peonies in a vase on the table I'd set for eleven on the patio outside. Then rearranging them.

"I'm not," I said, not even reacting when he dropped a kiss in the crook of my neck. That didn't go over well.

Braden spun me around to face him. "Talk to me, Sarah."

"My family stresses me out."

"But they're your family. You've known them your entire life, and they still like you."

I turned back toward the flowers and pulled a few unruly leaves from the stems, and moved the blooms around again.

"Hey." Braden took my hands in his to still them. "The flowers are fine. You are not. What's up?"

"I'm different around my family than I am with you," I admitted. I told him a little more about how my siblings saw me a certain way, and even though we were all adults, we reverted to old habits. My family expected me to be the responsible, unfun one who kept everyone in line.

"I don't see you that way at all." Braden observed me as though looking for my other side.

I leaned into him, grateful. "Thank you. That's why being here has been so good for me. It pushed me to see myself differently. I guess I'm worried about slipping back into old habits, being who they expect me to be."

His arms encircled me. "I'm here. I've got your back. This is going to be fine." He sounded so calm, it made me almost feel that way too. But not quite.

"My sisters meddle. And they're observant. They'll know something's going on between us."

"Would that be terrible?"

"I don't know," I huffed. A part of me wanted it to be evident that there was something between us, so evident that Braden would dazzle them with his arresting smile and tell him he was crazy about me.

Except I was the one who was crazy.

Crazy for fantasizing. That had become an unavoidable given. But also crazy for agreeing to have my entire band of sibling misfits and their boyfriends and fiancés drive out and join us for dinner.

Not just crazy—insane.

First, let's be honest. I am a dedicated and experienced watcher of *Top Chef*. But am I a chef? Not so much.

However, I was a determined non-chef, and in most areas of my life thus far, determination had been enough.

"What the hell was I thinking?!" I spun around and walked back inside. I knew I needed to do something useful in the kitchen, so I turned on the oven and the stove. I also opened a bunch of cabinets but took nothing out. I'd locked poor Bella outside so I wouldn't abandon my menu plans and feed her all the ingredients.

He looked around, and I saw the combination of shock and fear in his eyes. He put an arm around me and backed me away from the stove after turning off all six burners that I had flaming without a single pot to put on them.

Obviously a fire hazard.

"Sarah, what's the plan here?" he asked quietly, rubbing my shoulders. From where we stood just outside the kitchen, I caught a glimpse of what he'd seen when he walked into the room. There was flour in a shallow bowl and also near the bowl and on the floor. The countertops were covered with tomatoes, some in a partial state of being sliced or diced.

Three loaves of French bread sat in their sleeves amid several heads of garlic and a pound of butter, as though they were going to jump up and magically turn themselves into garlic bread.

Fifteen raw chicken breasts were on the floor in zippered bags beside a can of corn I'd been using to pound them flat because Braden didn't own a meat mallet, and I couldn't find a hammer.

Basil pulled from its stems was strewn everywhere. An untouched can of sweet iced tea sat on the windowsill, condensation dripping down its sides.

I closed my eyes and started to laugh. Braden's grip tightened, probably because he wasn't sure whether or not I was losing it. Then he reached for the can of tea and pulled the tab before handing it to me.

I took a shaky sip, and he folded me into an embrace. We stood there for a minute or more while his unspoken words told me I'd be able to get this dinner on the table somehow because he was here for me.

When I calmed down and opened my eyes, I shook my head. "I have no clue what I'm doing. When I said I like to cook for other people, I meant one other person. Like you. I'd cook for you. But eleven people—"

He nodded and took a step closer to the mess in the kitchen. "I used to cook for everyone at the station. I can do quantity. Let me help you."

My heart swelled at those words. "Please. I'd love the help." The fight for self-sufficiency left me and I acquiesced.

"The only way out is through. You know that expression?"

"No, but I like it."

We spent the next two hours paging through the recipes, figuring out what still needed chopping and arranging, and pounding the chicken breasts into submission. That felt good.

Working together, it didn't feel like work at all. Braden fired up two sauté pans on the stove and swirled a pour of olive oil with some butter while I patted the chicken with a flour, salt, and pepper mixture.

Ten minutes later, we had fifteen beautifully browned, thinly pounded pieces of chicken simmering in a lemon-butter sauce with capers.

From there, the salad was easy, and buttering the garlic bread led to Braden buttering parts of me. For the first time in my life, I felt the ease of working with a partner. I mean, sure, I experienced that at work because people came in with different skill sets. The parts became a better whole.

But I'd never experienced that with another person in my life, partly because that phase of my life wasn't supposed to start until I got tenure and was ready to find a relationship.

Life doesn't work that way.

Braden was right about beauty in the unexpected. By trying to keep my life under tight restraints, I'd cut myself off from parts of my life I knew I wanted to experience. The unexpected moments I'd had with Braden had brought out the best version of myself.

"I think everything's good to go. I'm gonna head upstairs and shower," Braden said. "And in case it wasn't clear, that was an invitation."

He brushed a light kiss against my lips and set me free to continue puttering with the peonies. Or join him upstairs.

arah

AND . . . the savages descended.

I loved my family, but collectively, they were a piece of work.

Before they arrived, I made a sweep of the house, making sure there was no evidence of sex. I did find one lace thong inside one of the living room sconces—don't ask—but I reasoned that even if something like that were discovered, most savvy adults would assume it belonged to one of Braden's bed buddies, not me.

It wasn't like I'd have to scurry around the house and create a charade that Braden and I were just roommates. All my clothes were still hanging in the spare room that I'd barely slept in. My toiletries were still in the bathroom, and other than sexy showers together, I didn't use Braden's bathroom. I got ready for work in my own quarters.

"I can't believe you cooked!" Cherry yelled as she came through the door with two bottles of red wine.

"Why can't you believe it?" I'd have felt offended if the comment wasn't coming from Cherry, my second-to-youngest sister who most definitely did not cook. "I can follow a recipe like the next person."

"Well, yes, but I thought you were smart like me and let everyone believe you can't do it, so they do all the cooking. Ever notice how it's always Finn or Isla who has us all over? By design!" She raised her hand to give me a high five.

I laughed and hugged her tight. Despite my nerves and grumbling, I missed her. I missed all my siblings, who'd come down in two separate cars because no one had a car big enough for everyone.

Cherry drove from San Francisco with my oldest sister Isla and her fiancé Owen and my mom, who only came to our sibling dinners about half the time. She claimed it gave her a headache when we all talked over each other.

"Mom, I'm so glad you came. Yay!" I was happy to see her. We were similar, and I understood why she avoided our chaos much of the time. It grated on me too. But I'd been missing her since I'd been away for so long.

"Oh honey, I wasn't going to pass up a chance to see my brilliant daughter and the troublemaker who threw up on my lawn," she said, reaching to pull Braden into a hug. "It tickles me that you two are roommates. Who'd have thought?"

"Not me," I said, trying to recall Braden as the teenage troublemaker my mom must have sort of loved. The memories were only vague.

Braden could not have been a more gracious and inviting host. "Mrs. Finley, it's been way too long."

My mom swiftly smacked him. "Stop it with the 'Mrs. Finley' nonsense. And thank you for giving Sarah a place to stay so she can protect our national security."

"Um, not why I'm here." I rolled my eyes. My mom gave me an extra squeeze and went over to check out the cheese plate.

Owen and Isla came armed with bread from Isla's bakeries and a few bottles of white wine from Owen's most recent trip to Napa, where he owned several hotels.

"That should go on the table outside, and we'll serve it with dinner. Good?" I pointed and gestured like I was directing traffic, and given the size of my family, I kind of was.

Isla kissed me on the cheek and did as I asked, but not before leaning in and whispering, "I know you're stressed about hosting, but it'll be fine. And also, your roommate is a hottie."

"I'm not admitting to either of those things." I scowled, hoping Braden hadn't overheard her.

"Nice to see you again, Braden. Been a long time," she said as Owen moved her along. Owen was a good guy, and as the most recent inductee into our family craziness, the most sympathetic. Which meant he'd make small talk and not rock any boats.

"I'm going to start pouring the wine," he told me with a wink.

We herded everyone through the house, where they commented on Braden's excellent taste and my good fortune at finding such a nice roommate. Once they were outside and plied with drinks, I started to relax.

For a moment.

Braden cornered me in the kitchen while Owen opened the wine outside and started pouring. "You okay?" he asked, leaning in and giving my hip a squeeze, out of view of everyone else.

I nodded. "They make me nuts, but I love them. Thanks for letting me bring their crazy here."

He glanced outside and seemed assured that everyone was distracted and busy—which seemed clear from their loud voices and laughter—then he pushed his hand into my hair and brought an electrifying kiss to my lips.

"Mmm, on second thought, can we send them all away and just do that?" I whined.

"Later," he whispered. "But not soon enough."

Then the other carload arrived, and I freaked out all over again.

That group drove from Berkeley—Finn and his fiancée, Annie, my middle sister Becca and her fiancé Blake, and Tatum, the youngest, who'd invited herself to stay in my house.

"Hey, you probably don't remember, but I'm Becca, the middle sister. Also known as the best sister," Becca said to Braden, pulling him in for a hug. She introduced Blake, a chef who owned several restaurants, and made sure to tell me he'd be judging my cooking.

"Don't make me regret inviting you," I threatened, pointing them to go over and get drunk with Isla.

"Oh sweetie, you know I'm kidding. I'm the only one who'll be judging you." Becca and I had an on-again, off-again relationship. Of all my siblings, she and I could be the closest and the most at each other's throats. It had always been that way.

Finn pulled Braden into a bro hug and clapped him on the back before introducing him to Annie. "I heard you made Finn look like an angel. But I want the real stories," Annie told him.

"I will make good on that." Braden winked and waggled his eyebrows.

"And you will die if you do," Finn told him with a menacing grimace.

"Finn, stop threatening him," Annie said, playfully punching his arm. Finn kissed her cheek, then shrugged.

"Whatever, he knows where he stands." He started talking Braden up about some brand of Scotch he liked, and they went outside.

I ignored Finn and put an arm around Tatum to show her the house. Becca and Blake went outside to join the others. Not that I'd ever tell the rest of them, but Tatum was my favorite sister. Maybe it was because she was nerdy like me, or maybe it was because she was the youngest and, therefore, the least annoying.

"So . . . tell me everything. How's work?" Tatum asked while I pointed out the still-unused living room.

"So good." I exhaled and smiled, thinking about the lab.

"Specifics, please." Her eyes flashed and urged me forward with her hands. Just like me, she knew that work was the most important reason to be here in Carolwood.

"It's been going really well. If we stay on the path we're on, there's a good chance we'll hit our goal before six months." I took her upstairs and showed her the gym. Unlike me, she enjoyed working out.

Her eyes popped at the variety of weights and machines. "Wow, nice setup. And you've got a hunk to keep your fitness up at night as well."

"You're hilarious," I said, walking down the hall to show her the guest bedroom. "Here's my room."

She laughed. Actually laughed.

"Um, try again."

"What?"

"You're totally sleeping with him." I looked around the room, panicked and struggling to see what would give her that idea. The bed was made, but so what? I always made my bed.

"Come on, let's go downstairs before I get worried you've lost your mind."

She followed me. "Fine, if you don't want to talk about it, I'll let it go. For now."

"Thank you."

But it was killing me.

My sisters and I didn't keep secrets like this. If there was someone important in my life, I wanted them to know. Especially when I was going to leave in just over a month. I'd need them to tell me it was okay to be second-guessing whether I really wanted to leave. But I wasn't ready to share the side of me I'd been exploring while I'd been away, so I kept quiet.

Tatum picked up a throw pillow from the bed that had been sitting in the same spot for weeks. Even when Braden spent the night at the station, I slept in his room. The pillowcases smelled like him, and he said it made him happy to think of me there.

"Anyhow, we should probably go downstairs. I only used the excuse of showing you around so I could get away from everyone for a few minutes," I said, feeling the exhaustion from cooking.

"I know you did. Well, we can hang up here a little longer, or we can go downstairs where there's wine."

Before I could answer, the door flung open, and three more sisters were standing there. "We brought the wine to you." Isla handed me a glass of cabernet.

Sweeping into the room and plopping on the bed, Becca grinned. "Yes, this is the wine welcoming committee. Here to talk about your hot, sexy boyfriend who you haven't told anyone about. Why?"

I opened my mouth, hoping something intelligent and halfway believable would come out, but after the cooking and cleaning, I was too exhausted to get creative. I slumped against the bureau of drawers and took a sip of wine.

My sisters took that as confirmation.

Cherry ran up and hugged me. "Sweetie, he's darling. And he's crazy about you."

Isla piped in, "He was always gorgeous. Don't you guys remember when Finn was in high school, and Braden used to come over?" Most of us shrugged. "Maybe you were too young, but I had a serious crush on him."

I waved my hands at them. "Okay, hold the parade. He's my roommate. And, it's been . . . fun while I've been here, but that's all it is. Temporary fun. But seriously, what did I do that made you all so sure I'm having sex with him?"

My sisters looked at each other, and I watched them exchange glances for a moment before they all burst into hysterics. I looked at Tatum, my one voice of reason in the bunch, for help. She put a hand on my shoulder. "You didn't do anything. You just seem really happy, and he looks at you like you hung the stars. That's it."

"But I'm a generally happy person. I like my job. I have a good life. What's different now?" I still wasn't seeing what they were seeing.

"Love. That's a different kind of happiness," Becca said. "And it's plain as day with you two."

"It's not love. We're just having fun," I said. I'd been saying it in my head for months, and it rolled out automatically now.

"Okay, well, fun is good too. Here's to fun with a hot firefighter," Cherry said, raising her glass. There was the clinking of glasses and discussion of firefighters, and someone may have even mentioned a firefighter calendar.

But I was still stuck in my head.

My sisters were right. It wasn't just fun—I did love Braden. And instead of having the guts to tell him, I let him believe I was still fine with our arrangement of sex with no strings. But the more I thought about it, the more I realized I wasn't fine at all.

I'd promised not to lie to him—that was one of our rules at the outset.

Then I'd fallen for him and broken that rule too.

CHAPTER THIRTY-ONE

raden

THE JUDGES on *Top Chef* would have bowed down and given Sarah a goddamned medal. Sure, I helped her push the ball over the goal line, but it was only an assist. She was as accomplished at hosting as she was at everything else she did.

Which was why it was getting harder and harder to deny what I knew in my heart—I fucking loved her.

I'm in love with her.

What to do about it was a different matter entirely.

The selfish part of me wanted to ask her to stay. She could get a job at the lab and do world-changing work. We could be happy. We could be more than temporary.

After her family left, I'd tell her how I felt. I had to let her know.

Meanwhile, Finn had some questions about the materials used for the deck off my bedroom, so we went upstairs to check it out. He was building something four times the size at his house, and I knew he had a slew of designers and expert builders weighing in, so the exact shade of the redwood seemed like a pretext for something else. I had a feeling I knew what it was.

"So. You and my sister." He crossed his arms over his chest, but his stern look quickly dissolved to a grin, and I saw the gleam of amusement flicker in his eyes. He didn't look like a guy about to pound his friend into the pavement.

No, he was going to sit there and enjoy watching me squirm. Finn swirled his Scotch in the glass. It had been stupid to come up here without anything stronger than red wine.

"I know what you said, and I . . ." What? What had I done? Had I resisted? Had I tried to keep my hands off her?

Yeah, for two weeks. And even then, I didn't try that hard.

Plopping down into one of the blue Adirondack chairs, I leaned my elbows on my knees and bent my forehead into one hand. He could give me shit—that I could handle—but beyond that, none of it was any of his business.

While I continued staring at the floor, trying to come up with the words to explain that Sarah wasn't another of the many women he'd seen me notch on my belt, a weird sound erupted from my oldest friend. At first, it sounded like he was choking, and my head shot up in fear.

I needn't have worried for his health.

Finn was laughing his ass off. I stared at him blankly, still unsure he wasn't having a mental breakdown.

He stopped laughing, took a leisurely sip of his drink, and pointed at me. "You're so screwed. Does she know?"

"Does she know what?" I wasn't sure *I* knew.

I must have looked as lost as I felt because Finn stopped laughing and leveled me with an expression of pure amusement. "Does she know you're in love with her?"

"I don't . . . I'm not . . . that's not what I'm saying." No time like the present to finish the rest of the wine in my glass. I could hear laughter coming from down below, and I peered over the rail to make sure no one had decided to come outside. The last thing I needed was for someone to overhear our conversation.

Bella dashed into the yard chasing a ball and promptly laid herself down on the grass, mouthing it and rolling onto her back. Someone must have opened the door because the cacophony of voices drifted up to where we sat, but there were too many conversations going on at once for anyone to focus on us.

Finn leaned back in his chair, sipping his Scotch with an amused expression that made it seem like he was enjoying a rollicking good romcom playing somewhere out of sight. "I know. I'm saying it. You're in love with her. I assume *you're* aware of that."

"I'm just . . . fuck." What was the point of denying it, especially to a guy who knew me well enough to call bullshit? "Okay, Yes, I love her. And not in a smarmy best-sex-I-ever-had way. The way I feel about her . . . it's not temporary."

"It doesn't look temporary." He studied me for a moment. "And by the way, please don't talk about sex and my sister in the same sentence. Even if you do love her."

"Sure. Yeah."

"Seriously. Or I will kill you."

I believed him. "Done. And I need another drink."

"Yeah, you look a little dehydrated," Finn said, smirking at the liberal sheen of sweat I now needed to wipe from my brow.

"It's a warm night."

Finn coughed "bullshit" into his hand and slapped me on the back.

I pointed to the railings that framed out the deck, running my hand over the smooth wood. "What can I tell you about the materials? Are you thinking redwood?" Anything to shift the conversation someplace else.

Shaking his head, Finn rose to his feet. "I've already ordered a cord of maple for my deck, and the design is nearly done. I just wanted to get away from my sisters and the jackasses they're engaged to so we could talk."

He started to walk back through the bedroom, but I felt like there was more to say. "Hey. Thanks for being cool about . . . things. I swear, I didn't mean to fall for her—"

"Dude, Please. You have my blessing. Just keep on making her happy, and it's all good."

AN HOUR LATER, the long table Sarah had painstakingly set was a demolished mess of half-full wine glasses, plates with scraps of chicken piccata, and four different kinds of sourdough sliced up for dipping in olive oil.

No one could eat another bite, and even the peonies looked limp and exhausted. But not Sarah's family. They were primed and ready for a raucous game of running charades.

"Okay, okay, let me explain," Sarah said, standing at the head of the table. "It's like regular charades where you have to act out a TV show or movie or book or whatever, except we're doing it in teams, and each time your team guesses correctly, you have run over to me and get the next word to act out."

The game fit Sarah's personality perfectly. She liked control, so she came up with all the word clues, and she didn't like being the center of attention so she wouldn't have to act anything out herself.

"So if the movie was *Sixteen Candles,* I might do this." She mimed blowing out candles on a birthday cake and acted out some other ridiculousness to demonstrate the number sixteen. "Everyone got it?"

And the games began.

The whole thing was a giant clusterfuck because Becca guessed so loudly that the other team could hear her from across the yard and using her guesses to help them. And Finn was such a perfectionist that he kept starting to act something out, and then he'd come up with a better way to do it.

I laughed my ass off for about an hour straight and felt pretty pleased when their mom correctly guessed my charade for *Dead Poet's Society.* "That was a hard one," I admitted, impressed she'd nailed it based on my charade of a dead guy reading a book.

"Braden, but you and I, we're—" She pointed two fingers at her eyes and then at me.

"Seriously, I thought the movie was *Death by Book* or something," Cherry trilled.

Every so often, I'd lock eyes with Sarah across the yard and find it impossible not to smile at her.

Where did we stand? I couldn't have said for certain, but if Finn was right, this was more than temporary. She had to feel it too.

A bit later, things were quieting down, and I started cleaning up the table, taking a few stray glasses into the house. I hadn't realized Sarah had gone into the kitchen with Isla until I reached the patio door and heard them talking.

"I miss our hikes," Isla was saying.

"Oh, I need a hike badly," Sarah said. "We'll be able to do it soon. When I get back to the real world."

"Perfect. I'm holding you to it."

I turned and went back outside, still holding the glasses. I left them on the table and went over to pour some of that Scotch Finn had been drinking. I needed something more potent than wine.

"When I get back to the real world." She actually said those words. Her time in Carolwood was still a vacation from her real life, a little suspended animation that allowed her to indulge in a fling with a fireman.

While I'd been wringing my hands and sweating over telling Finn the way things were between us, explaining that I wasn't just messing around, admitting that I was falling in love with her, Sarah was planning to go hiking as soon as she got back from fantasy land.

As it should be.

Sarah dreamed of being a tenured professor. She'd worked for ten years, studying her way through a PhD program and working her tail off on the tenure track. What seemed like a deviation from her path wasn't a deviation at all—it was proof she deserved to get the tenured position she wanted. Everything she'd done had followed her plan—she'd told me that the first night she was here.

The only thing that didn't fit into her plan was me.

Of course this was only temporary. Brilliant scientists on the tenure track with plans for how their lives will unfold don't give up their dreams to live with guys who give them great orgasms.

"Hey, are you okay?" Finn asked as I took a long sip of the Scotch. I usually didn't drink this shit, and it burned my throat going down.

"Yeah. Great."

I was an idiot.

Finn didn't press me for details, but from his look, he sensed something was up. "We'll talk later, okay?" He nodded and clapped me on the back. "Whatever it is, I'm here for you, you know that."

Sarah and Isla came out of the house right then, and I watched her laugh at something Isla said. She was so beautiful, made even more so by the presence of her family. Even though she said they drove her crazy, they lifted her up—I could see that.

In the time she'd been here, I'd narrowed her world, and it wasn't her reality, not the one she should have.

I couldn't keep her here, waylaying her from doing something fabulous with her life back in Berkeley. If she stayed, she might continue to enjoy herself for a while, but eventually, she'd resent the deviation from her goals.

A woman like her deserved to have everything, much more than I could give her.

So even if it killed me, I had to let her go.

CHAPTER THIRTY-TWO

arah

I HADN'T SEEN Braden in two days.

By the time my family finally rolled out at two in the morning—after a lot of wine and more rounds of running charades that even I wanted to play—Braden had cleaned up the whole kitchen and headed up to bed, exhausted.

I just slipped between the covers and curled up against him. My happy place. "You cleaned up everything. You're amazing."

He didn't answer, and I fell asleep quickly. But when I woke up in the morning, he'd already worked out, showered, and was heading to the station to work a double shift. He hadn't done that once since I'd been in town.

Still, I didn't worry.

I just missed him.

We texted, but there was none of the usual sexy banter. He didn't call me Damsel.

Something was up.

A couple days later, my phone rang, and because I'd been thinking nonstop about Braden, I assumed it was him. It took me a moment to shake off the disappointment when it wasn't. It took me another moment to realize the person calling was the department chair at Berkeley.

After I hung up the phone, I sat motionless at my desk. Stunned.

Then I texted Braden.

Me: Hey, you home?

The flicker of three dots on my phone made me happy.

Braden: Just got here.

Me: I'm coming home early. Can't wait to see you.

Braden: You too.

Me: PS—a neutron who walks into a bar and asks How much for a beer?

Braden: ??

Me: For you, no charge.

That earned me a smiley face, and even though our text exchange felt lackluster, I told myself Braden was probably wiped out after a double shift. I didn't want to think about what else it could mean.

I found Braden in the kitchen doing dishes. It looked like he'd made an omelet or something, and cheese had burned on the pan.

"Hey." I wrapped my arms around his waist and tipped my head up to kiss him. "I missed you. How was your double shift?"

"Long. Exhausting. And I missed you too." His kiss was warm, sweet, and he tipped his forehead against mine. I really was so damned happy to see him.

"So, I just got a crazy phone call. I'm still kind of in denial it even happened, but you were the first person I wanted to tell."

He moved back to look at me while I told him I was offered a full professorship at Berkeley, a good two years ahead of when I thought it *might* happen.

"Not just tenure track, but full tenure! The chair just called me," I said, still blinking and shaking my head in disbelief.

He put the pan down and stared at me, a smile pulling at his lips. "Sarah, that's amazing. You deserve it. I've seen how hard you've worked. Congratulations." He reached for me and pulled me into a hug.

His reaction seemed sincere. He seemed really happy for me.

But I felt distance between us.

If anything could knock the wind from my sails after the phone call, it was Braden's measured response.

"Tell me more. What did they say?" he asked, his voice sounding calm but strained. His almost-forced smile made it seem like he was working hard to convey interest.

Maybe all my physics talk wasn't that exciting to him. He'd been nice about taking an interest, but maybe other than a prelude to sex in my office, he could take it or leave it.

I gave him the broad strokes, shaking my head because I was still processing it. "Well, they got an opening because a professor is leaving, so there's an unexpected pot of money and the chair said he's been impressed with the progress on what we're doing at the lab. He said I'd earned a permanent spot on the faculty, and they were lucky to have me." Even as I heard myself say the words, I was having trouble believing them.

Braden released me from his grasp. "I'm so proud of you. You're going to do great things." He kissed the top of my head. It almost felt like a goodbye kiss, like a parent was sending me off to college.

I was so confused. "Thanks."

He nodded.

I persevered, determined to get him out of whatever post-work funk he seemed to be in. "So, things have been going well at the lab, and I think we'll finish ahead of schedule. I might have a couple weeks of unexpected free time."

He leaned against the countertop with his arms crossed. "Right. I overheard you tell Isla you're wrapping up a little early at the lab. You didn't mention it."

"No, because there were still a few boxes to check, but now it's more certain. The team will continue using the lasers for welding after I leave. So I was wondering . . . if maybe you'd want to take a weekend away with me. Maybe a very long weekend."

He smiled, and if I didn't know him at all, that smile would have launched a thousand rockets with its heat. But I knew what he looked like when he was happy, and this wasn't it. He wasn't locking eyes with me. He wasn't even looking at me.

"I don't think I can get the time off." Braden turned away from me and started to wash the dishes in the sink.

Slipping behind him, I wrapped my arms around his waist and tipped my head against his back. For a second, I thought I felt him flinch at my touch, but I decided I'd imagined it. But Braden didn't turn around. "Hey. Do you have to wash those right now?" I ran my nails along the skin at his waist, teasing him.

"I really should."

He really should?

This was a man who had no problem leaving dishes for days when he had a shift. How many times had he run out in the morning and told me he'd wash the dishes when he got back —tomorrow?

Something was different. He was keeping his distance. It didn't take a tenured professor to know that.

I took a step back. Now I was the one leaning against the counter with my arms crossed. "Braden, what's wrong? Did something happen at work?"

Turning off the water, he motioned me into the den and sat on the couch. I perched on the ottoman. It didn't feel like he wanted me next to him.

"Nothing's wrong at work."

"So tell me. What is it?"

"Nothing. Things are exactly as they should be."

I threw my hands in the air. He was so stoic and exasperating. It was like the Braden from five months ago was back. "I have no idea what that means. Please explain."

He looked at me calmly and pushed a hand through his hair. "We're good. We made it through our six months, roomie." He smiled, but it didn't reach his eyes. "Hope I didn't annoy you too much."

"No, not at all . . . in fact, I've loved being here with you. So things feel different to me now. I guess I'm asking . . . should I take it?"

"Take what?"

"Should I take the position they're offering?"

He looked stunned at the question. "What? Of course, you should. That's your dream job. Why wouldn't you?"

It was the loaded question I'd been pondering from the moment I got the news. Yes, I still wanted the coveted tenure track position at a top university. But I wanted him too.

Maybe more.

But I couldn't say that. In the face of his stoic indifference, I couldn't be the girl who gave up everything to stay with him, especially if he didn't want me. I had more self-respect than that.

And let's face it—he'd never given any indication he wanted me to stay or wanted more of a relationship. Ever. He was sweet and loving toward me, but that wasn't the same thing as love, was it? We were temporary. We were fun. And pretty soon, we'd be over.

I nodded, confirming my answer to his question. "I guess there's no reason not to take the position." I inhaled a deep breath and made a decision I hoped was the right one. "And I guess since I'm pretty much done at the lab, I can let you have your spare bedroom back. Surprise—you get your freedom back a month early. I can commute down here if I need to finish up."

I tried to smile past the sting of tears in my eyes. They'd be full-on rolling tears if I stayed here another second. So I stood up and did my level best to look Braden in the eye. His face was stony. "I really can't thank you enough for letting me crash here. You're a good man, Braden."

I turned to go toward the stairs, and I heard his voice behind me, "Wait."

Gulping over the lump in my throat, I looked at him.

"You can still stay here. The room is yours. I'm not going back on my word to offer you a place to live while you're finishing up at the lab."

It was my last chance to tell him how I felt, so I went for broke.

"I don't need the room, Braden. I need you. I...I love you." My voice caught in my throat when I said it. I closed my eyes to hold back tears building there. I didn't want to open them and see the look of disappointment on Braden's face because I'd done exactly what I'd promised not to do.

I swallowed hard and faced him. "If you'd given me even the smallest indication you wanted me to stay here for something more . . ." What was the point? He didn't want me. "I can see that I'm the only one who feels it here. So I'm gonna go before I feel even worse about myself."

He closed his eyes for a long blink, and I had a final glimmer of hope that he'd look at me the way that stirred something deep in my heart and tell me he wanted me to stay.

When he opened his eyes, I could see that he'd shut down. "Okay." His face was a mask of indifference, his tone void of emotion.

Hearing the single word only proved what I already knew—Braden and I weren't a couple. Never would be.

I went up to my room to pack. Then I left without saying goodbye.

CHAPTER THIRTY-THREE

raden

GOING to the winery had always made me happy, but not today. Not now that every bit of the place reminded me of Sarah. How had that happened?

She and I had only been there a handful of times, and I'd been working weekends at the place for years. The math didn't add up. This was my retreat from the world. It had been long before I'd ever met Sarah, and it would be for years to come.

Why did the crunch of the gravel under my running shoes remind me of the way she danced with Bella in front of my truck? It was just gravel.

But it wasn't. It was her.

I'd driven Bella out for the day because she needed some real exercise, and I didn't feel like jogging outside. With other humans. I'd pounded out eight miles on the treadmill in the dark hours of the morning while Bella snored under my bed. Now, with the leftover endorphins still trying to elevate my mood, I watched the streak of golden fur charge through the vineyard and marveled at her boundless optimism.

In the cruddy shed behind the pressing room, I was cursing a blue streak at the drip system that had stopped watering sixteen rows of plants, which were now withering on their vines. The crew who tended the grapes a couple times a week hadn't said anything, so they either didn't notice, or it happened since they'd last worked.

Now it was my problem unless I wanted a bunch of dead plants.

The scrape of tires made me pick my head up, but the billowing dust from the driveway had already obscured whatever car had pulled up to the vineyard property.

Bella came barreling out of the vineyard in excitement, probably hoping to see Sarah. She seemed to figure out before I did that the car in the drive wasn't going to get her what she wanted, and after a moment, she sulked off and sat down in the shade.

I had to wait for the dirt to settle and the air to clear before identifying whether the visitor was someone I knew or a wrong turn off the highway. When I recognized Mitch's white pickup, I groaned. A map-challenged stranger would be more welcome than a half-brother who no doubt came armed with opinions about my life.

Without waiting for him to walk up the drive and push through the gate, I went back to examining the drip watering system as though I were a plumber and had any fucking clue how to fix it.

"Dude, I thought you owned a bar. What's this giant garden all about?" Mitch stood in front of me wearing jeans, a denim shirt with rhinestone snaps, and a belt with a huge silver buckle that sparkled.

For the first time in a week, my spirits lifted enough that I laughed. Hard. "What in the fucking name of bedazzlement are you wearing?"

He looked down at his outfit and up at mine, which was a pair of workout shorts and a long-sleeved T, and seemed to realize he'd missed the mark. "I thought you had a ranch. Doesn't that indicate horses?"

"It's a vineyard, not a ranch. And even if it were, you wouldn't show up looking like a sparkly urban cowboy. Where'd you even get these clothes?"

He shrugged. "I have clothes."

"So you do." I stared at him, wondering if he'd feel the need to tell me why he'd suddenly shown up when he'd never been set foot on the property in the time I'd had it. "Mitch?"

"Yeah?"

"What's up? Why're you here?"

"You invited me."

I did? When had I done that? I was losing my mind.

"Regardless, now's not a good time."

"Oh, I beg to differ. It's the perfect time. Now, where's the wine? And not the cheap stuff you give to strangers. I want the good vintage stuff."

He walked past me into the pressing room like he owned the place. I followed him because I was confused.

Once my eyes adjusted to the dark room, I saw Mitch walking down the rows of wine barrels thumping on the occasional side and whistling at the vastness of the place. I felt a surge of pride at how much I was producing this year, though he had no frame of reference since he hadn't seen the place at the beginning.

Leaning against the cold stone wall, I waited for him to finish his self-tour and explain his unannounced visit. "Well?" he asked expectantly, looking around. "Where's the booze? Or is all this just for show?"

He threaded his thumbs into his belt buckles and thrust his hips forward like a Halloween cowboy.

"Mitch, why are you here? If all you want's a free glass of wine, you can have that at your house. It's hardly worth the drive out here."

He smacked the back of my head. "I know that, you stupid jerkoff. I'm here to help you extract your head from your asshole because clearly an intervention is needed."

This again? He'd been harping on me for a week to stop acting like a depressed asshole, but I'd refused to indulge him in a conversation.

"Incorrect. Nothing is needed, so I'll grab you a couple of bottles to go, and you can drink on someone else's time. I've got a wonky drip watering thing that needs sorting out."

He held up a hand. "Say no more. I installed one at my mom's house a while back. I can take a look at yours, so you're not dicking your way out of the conversation."

"I don't even know what that means."

"It means grab us some wine and let's go water some grapes."

BEFORE WE WORKED on the drip problem, I gave Mitch a tour of the place, trying to block the memories of walking down the same rows of vines with Sarah a couple months earlier. It was just one of a host of thoughts I'd been blocking, trying forcefully to keep my mind focused on anything but thoughts of her. What was the point in letting my mind go there now?

"All good with Molly?" My voice came out monotone like I didn't care.

With anyone else, I'd worry about sounding like a dick, but not with Mitch. "Yeah, we're solid. Thanks for checking in."

It was one of those ideal Saturday afternoons when the powder blue sky seemed to reject the idea of clouds. All I saw for miles were rows of green vines twirling around their posts and sunning their grapes like points of pride.

Mitch had finished one glass of cabernet and was halfway through his second, and we'd walked up and down a dozen rows of vines. There were probably a hundred more, and I wondered how long he planned to wait until he started giving me shit about Sarah.

As it turned out, not that long.

We sat down in the shed, and Mitch refilled his glass and topped off mine. The first thing he noticed was the valve. "You know this is turned off, right? Is it possible you're that dumb?"

"Normally, no. But I don't have my head on right."

"I can see. Now, what are we going to do about that?" He turned the valve until it was completely open and turned on the water. We waited for a minute, and then a trickle of water started flowing out through the pipe.

"We? We're going to drink our wine, and then I'm calling you an Uber."

Mitch pointed to the valve and smiled, impressed with himself for saving my vines from an unnecessary drought.

Then all hell broke loose. Out in the fields, one of the hoses went flying up in the air, waving around like one of those air puppets outside a car dealership, water spraying everywhere. Bella popped her head up, apparently thinking we were throwing some kind of party, and began racing around after the hose, trying to bite the water.

Mitch indicated an orange bucket. "Something tells me one of your guys was trying to fix the problem, hence the valve being off."

"Yet he said nothing." Irritating. I turned off the valve. The one requirement I had of the guys tending to the vines was that if they found a problem, they needed to let me know or get it fixed without my involvement. It might cost me a little more, but neither of those had happened here.

"Maybe he figured he could fix it before you saw the problem. Kind of like someone else I know."

I emptied the bottle into my glass and drank half in one gulp. "You don't know what you're talking about."

"Asshole."

"What's with the name calling?" I was too irritable to figure out what had crawled up his rectum and died.

"Just because I'm younger than you doesn't make me unaware of what's going on."

His directness left something to be desired. "What's going on?"

"You're punishing yourself for something that wasn't your fault. For two years, you've closed yourself off from having any kind of a real relationship with a woman, and I can't fault you for that. I get it. Ellie left, and you convinced yourself you deserved it. Then you decided if you ever did open yourself up and love someone else, it would happen again. But Sarah . . . she's different and I'm here telling you not to screw it up."

"I hate to break it to you, but she left days ago. And she's not coming back."

"So you fucked it up." He shook his head at me.

"I faced reality is what I did. Which is that everybody leaves. And even if she thinks she wants to stay here, eventually she'll come to her senses and resent me even more for all the lost opportunities in her life. And then she'll leave. I saved us both the trouble. I love her too much to see her sacrifice her life for me."

"She wanted to stay?" Mitch asked, incredulous.

"Yeah, believe it or not." I huffed out a hollow laugh.

"What I can't believe is that you'd let her go. That's not what you do when you love someone."

"It's what I do."

Mitch rolled his eyes and hauled off and punched me in the arm with his fist. Hard.

So I tackled him to the ground, and pretty soon, we were rolling around like a couple of middle schoolers, trying to throw punches and wrestle each other to offset their raging hormones.

Because I'm bigger, I got him into a headlock, but the little fucker was fast and landed another punch to my jaw.

"Fuck!" I threw him off me and sat up.

"Yup. You think that hurts, you should try being me and having to look at your ugly face."

"I should deck you again." I lunged for him, but he moved.

"No, you should not. You should pour me some damned wine and work your shit out. Whatever you did, man, fix it." Mitch got up and brushed himself off. "You deserve to be happy, and that's not me telling you as the son of the same dad who fucked everything up with our moms. I'm saying it as a guy who sees that you're a better man than him." He wagged a finger in my face. "If you choose to be."

His words hit me hard. Almost as hard as his damn fist.

But they were just words. I still wasn't sure I believed them.

CHAPTER THIRTY-FOUR

raden

THE SCREAMING fire bell woke me out of a deep sleep during which I'd thrashed so hard both of my pillows were on the floor, and my blankets hung off the sides.

Like a zombie on autopilot, I jumped into my pants and boots and pulled on my coat. We'd been anticipating getting called out to a brush fire that was still zero percent contained, but the dispatcher reported a second incident and asked that we share resources.

Mitch and I strapped on our oxygen tanks for the apartment fire in Pleasanton and jumped in the ladder truck with Logan. I sent an engine with a different crew to the brush fire.

The smell of smoke hit me from two blocks away, which was a bad sign.

Flames licked the second floor of the building, and smoke was visible through the windows of the upper floors. A couple of the tenants were on the street staring up at the flaming building as Logan parked the truck in front.

"I was up reading, and my light went out. Right after, I started to smell smoke," a woman in a yellow nightgown gasped, clutching a small dog in a reindeer sweater.

The battalion chief from the Pleasanton department gave me the rundown. "Electrical fire in the basement, working its way up through the walls. Two guys went into the basement twelve minutes ago. Manager says there are thirteen units total. He's accounted for only half the tenants."

"Shit, okay."

"Prep for search and rescue on upper floors." That was why we all had oxygen tanks. Mitch and I strategized how to enter the building to avoid the flames.

Logan was attaching hoses to the fire hydrant, working fast, and Duke extended the ladder so he could take out the windows and let some of the smoke out from the upper floors. From what we could see through the closed windows on the upper floors, the smoke was already getting darker, so speed was crucial.

Thick smoke like that would kill anyone in the building if we didn't get them out.

Mitch and I went in through a first-floor window, hoping the flames were contained in the basement and the smoke wasn't horrible there yet. But we couldn't see shit.

"Manager hasn't accounted for two residents on this floor," Mitch said.

Stopping to listen, all I heard was the hiss of flames destroying everything beneath me. I'd trained for years in these situations, so I took every precaution, covering the front of my oxygen mask with a wet towel and crouching as low as possible to stay beneath the smoke.

Then I heard it.

Mitch did too. He pointed to the apartment in the corner. Not a voice, but a whimper.

The locked door wouldn't budge and from the heat emanating from the other side, I feared what we'd find when I raked through it with the blade of my axe. The whimpers grew louder as we crawled from room to room, finding two tenants prone and barely breathing in a tiled bathroom with the shower running. It was clever, but they'd still die of smoke inhalation in a matter of minutes.

One at a time, we shouldered them and carried them to the open window where Duke was waiting at the top of the ladder to help them down.

I started for the stairwell to the third floor. Two steps along, it was already much hotter.

Mitch grabbed my arm and yanked hard. "Hey. We need them to open the roof or the windows before we go any further. It's too hot."

He was right. I could feel it on the exposed skin on the back of my neck.

But my adrenaline was running high, and I felt the jones of a dangerous situation. Mitch knew the protocol as well as I did, but we were geared up, and I thought we had a little time.

"I'm going up," I barked impulsively.

I didn't have time to think about why I was so insistent on staying in the building longer than was probably safe. I just knew it felt good that I was already sweating beneath my gear.

My muscles ached from the heavy tank on my back. And I was going to give my all—and maybe my life—to help other people.

That was the job. That felt good.

If I wasn't deserving of love and a lasting relationship, which time and experience had proven I wasn't, then at least I could earn my worth on this planet by giving everything I had to help someone else.

Mitch pulled me back once more. "Braden, enough. It's too damn hot in here. We've got to get out. Let 'em break the windows first, let the smoke out. Then we can go back," he begged. I didn't look him in the eye. I couldn't. I knew I wouldn't find judgement, only concern, and I wasn't sure I could take it.

"Go. Get out. I'll be right behind you. I just need to check this floor. I won't stay longer than it's safe."

"Dude. Please . . . it's already not safe." He was urging me to be sensible, and I could see from the sadness in his expression that he knew I wasn't listening. Still, he tried with the one piece of ammunition he believed he had. "Sarah would not want you to do this."

His words were a gut punch. I'd promised Sarah I'd never take unnecessary risk.

Sarah's gone.

I left Mitch behind and worked my way up the stairwell through thick smoke, finding a few apartments where all the doors were open, hopefully because everyone had already left and made it down the stairs.

But I had to check them all.

I lucked into a pocket where the air was thinner, which helped me navigate. I could hear the water hitting the ceiling of the floors below me, dousing the flames at their source, but with an active fire crawling through the walls and ceiling crawl spaces, I had another problem—an unstable floor that could give without warning.

By the time I got to the third apartment, I was sweating like the devil and feeling the burn from scalding steam coming from the floor below—even with the mask on, my airways were swelling. I could feel the heat burning the back of my neck and ears.

But if I bailed out and someone died, I'd never forgive myself for getting this close and turning around. I stayed focused.

The smoke was so thick I couldn't see anything but an orange glow through dark grey smoke, but I banged on the door. "Hello? Anyone inside?" I shouted, banging harder. "Hello?"

Listening, I could hear only the shouts of the firefighters outside and the blast of the hoses, but with the door closed, there was no way to be sure no one was trapped unless I got in.

The axe was heavy in my hands as I swung. Splinters from the doorjamb shot out in all directions when I made contact with the wood and broke the lock. Flames shot at me from inside the room, and I dropped to the floor to avoid the effects of the back-draft. I had to army crawl on my stomach to stay low and avoid as much of the smoke as I could, but it was a losing battle as I pulled myself deeper into the apartment.

My voice was muffled by the oxygen mask to make much of a sound, but I tried again to reach out. "Anyone here?" My voice was a croak.

Then I heard it, a quiet cough, barely audible but enough to direct me to that back room, where I reached for the knob, worried about what I'd find inside. I also knew that each time I opened a door and drew oxygen into a room, there was a good chance of tiny flames raging up into life-ending ones. I'd been here before and had always escaped with my life. But I'd never done it without backup.

Mitch was right. This was too risky, and I was falling on my sword like a coward instead of being smart.

Huddled on the floor was a teenage girl holding an infant wrapped in a blanket. The terrified look in her eyes told me there was no way she was getting out of here alive without my help. She looked paralyzed with fright. I'd seen it before. All the regular fight or flight instincts freeze when they should propel a person to safety. There was a window above her head, but she was staring straight ahead, her small body shaking.

Her cough sounded hoarse and jagged, and without the benefit of a mask or even a cloth to soak up the particulate matter, her small lungs were no match for what she was inhaling.

The way she sat with her back straight up against the wall reminded me of the way Sarah was sitting in my kitchen the morning after her car accident. Thinking of her sent a sharp pang of agony through me.

Between where the girl sat and where I crouched, an enormous hole burned through the floor, making it near-impossible for me to get to them.

I signaled to her to come toward me—there was a tiny ledge of floorspace remaining, too small to support me, but she was tiny. Forcing a hoarse scrap of a voice out, I called to her. "You can do this."

She shook her head, clutching the baby tighter. Then her head lolled to the side and her eyes closed. No!!

Like hell, I was going to let a baby and girl barely old enough to be her mother die when I was six feet away. I had to get to them.

Looking down into the fiery hole between us, I saw a cannon of water barreling through as the firefighters in my unit made every attempt to extinguish the blaze. There was a scrap of a pink bedspread hanging off the end of the bed nearest to where I crouched. If I could grab it and it held my weight, I might be able to balance on the ledge long enough to get to her.

"I'm on the second floor, northside bedroom, two people trapped. Heavy smoke." I radioed, needing someone to break out the window and get us out of here.

"Coming to you now," someone responded.

One chance, and I took it. The fabric held, and I used the momentum of my jump to swing across the dead space and over to the corner of the floor where she sat.

The girl was getting pale from lack of oxygen, and I made a split-second decision that was the only thing I could think of to save her. I released the mask from my face and held it to her small one, hoping to see a sign of breath. We could share for a minute or two until someone got to us.

"Come on, come on," I urged, still not seeing her chest inflate.

I coughed and sputtered. My lungs burned in agony, seared by the smoke and whatever particulate clogged the thick smoke. Sarah would probably want to talk about its atomic mass and tell me about the reason certain matter could pass through other matter.

Sarah . . .

I couldn't bear the idea that I'd never see her again. Mitch was right—this was a suicide mission, one I shouldn't be on.

Because I should be with her. Wherever she was or however she wanted things to play out, I should be there. That was the only correct answer when you loved a person as much as I loved her.

I coughed again, this time gasping when I tried to breathe. My airways were closing. I didn't have much time left before the lack of oxygen did me in. My lungs folded in on themselves, and my throat closed up. I tried to inhale, but nothing got through. It felt like I was choking on my own tissues.

"Hey, here, in here!" I heard the voices below me where the blazing flames seemed to have subsided, but it didn't matter. I'd taken my last breath.

The last thing I saw before passing out was Sarah's beautiful smile. Even then, I didn't know if I deserved it.

arah

THERE WEREN'T enough mojitos in the world to erase the pain I felt every waking hour since I'd gotten back to Berkeley.

I know. Because I tried.

Fortunately for my health and my sanity, Finn had redirected me away from the rum bottle and dragged my sorry self out onto the San Francisco Bay, where we currently sat in a kayak for two.

He was doing most of the paddling.

I was dead weight and an occasional hindrance whose only function seemed to be dousing him with water when I remembered to use my paddle.

After the third time I splashed him, he stopped paddling and turned around to glare at me. "Do you mind? You're soaking me every time you do that."

"Sorry. I'm not focused," I said, slumping against the backrest that I hadn't noticed for the half hour we'd been out on the water. "Ooh, that's comfortable." When we'd rented the kayak, Finn insisted on paying extra for the backrests, which were sort of like our life vests, only shaped like a small chair that fit into each of our kayak seats.

I'd been leaning forward over my paddle the entire time, lost in my head and not enjoying a single moment of our time on the still waters that were the whole reason he'd forced me up at seven in the morning.

That, and the fact that I hadn't been sleeping since I moved back to Berkeley. Finn was the master of persuasion, so what was the point of arguing?

"I know you're not. Do you even know what day it is? Or where you are?" He was smiling at me, but I saw the concern in his eyes.

I let out a long exhale and finally took in the scenery around me. "I'm on the bay in a kayak at the ass crack of dawn, thanks to someone who's even more of an irritating morning person than I am." I glared at him.

He deserved worse for dragging me out here and trying to force me to enjoy myself. There was still far too much wallowing to do before I could be expected to embrace things like pretty views of the Marin headlands.

"And you're enjoying yourself. You forgot that part," he chuckled, assessing me from beneath the brim of a vintage San Francisco Giants baseball cap as he paddled gently.

"I like your hat," I told him.

"What?"

"The retro thing. It's cool."

His hand went to the brim. "Oh. Thanks. I can tell you where to get one. Isn't retail therapy good after a breakup?"

"It isn't a breakup. We were never in a relationship." I figured if I said it enough times, it would finally sink in. Braden and I were never a couple. We were a sex marathon that was destined to run its course.

Finn slid his paddle into the kayak and turned around in his seat, so we were face to face. "Not what I saw. Not what he told me."

I vaguely recalled that Braden and Finn had slipped away the night my family came to dinner, but things went sideways right after that, so we hadn't talked about their conversation. What did it matter? He'd stuck to our rules—rules I laid out—and it wasn't his fault I'd fallen for him anyway.

Doing my best to block the memory of him—something that required a daily battle with my heart—I focused on a layer of moss that seemed to be growing on the bottom of the kayak. "D'you think they ever clean these things?" I asked, scraping at the moss with my paddle. It didn't budge.

"I try not to go there. I figure the kayaks spend their days in water, so how dirty could they be? There's probably a non-zero probability it's toxic."

"God, you're such a nerd."

"Takes one to know one." We were still twelve.

Finn looked out over the water and I followed his gaze. For the first time, I took in the scenery around us. We'd paddled pretty far from the Berkeley marina, and our orange kayak bobbed on the surface of the bay near Angel Island, where I could see a few mountain bikers on the rutted trails.

It was a gorgeous morning for anyone who could see past the cloud of doom hanging over her head. In the distance, a few snowy white seagulls sat on the surface of the water, riding the gentle current beneath them and lazily waiting for something worthy of breakfast.

The spires of both the Bay Bridge and the Golden Gate soared into the sky above the bay, framing San Francisco's peninsula of land with twin feats of engineering. Normally, sitting out here would bring me peace and a sense of well-being. Today, it just made me feel depressed. The world around me was shimmering and gorgeous, and I couldn't see past my own mood.

Finn nudged me with his paddle. "You know he's crazy about you, right? He didn't want you to leave."

"Not the impression I got." My words landed with an angry thud. I reached for a scrap of plastic floating on the water.

He laughed, actually laughed in my face. "Oh. Okay."

"You're laughing at my misery? Nice." There wasn't anything funny about what I'd said. I didn't need to be ridiculed by my older brother, especially if I wasn't in on the joke.

But the look on his face was pure concern. "I'm only laughing because you're an idiot if you think the man isn't in love with you. I could see it the second I walked in the door. And that guy doesn't do love."

"Exactly. He made that pretty clear. So I don't know where you're getting your ideas."

Finn dipped a paddle in the water and swirled it around, making our kayak rock gently from side to side. "Did he tell you about his ex?"

"Yes. I asked about her. Sounds like a bitch."

He laughed. "Yeah, that was the takeaway. Anyway, it messed with him. I mean, severely. He went into such a downward spiral of self-loathing when she left, convinced he wasn't good enough for her. I spent a couple weeks living on his couch until he was fit to get back to work again, and he swore he'd never put himself in a position to be left behind again."

A pang of awareness shot through me. "But I didn't want to leave him. I wanted to stay. I told him I loved him and he pushed me away. I don't see how it's the same." Heartbroken for Braden despite my own hurt, I pressed my fists to my cheeks.

"Sar, you have a life here. And a job that you've worked hard for. Don't you think he wanted that for you?"

Realization dawned on me. "I know he did."

"Exactly. He isn't the kind of guy to be selfish by letting you give up your dream for him. Think about it. The guy's a living hero. It probably felt like the right thing to let you go."

In all the wallowing I'd done and questioning how I'd misunderstood what Braden seemed to feel, it never occurred to me that he was pushing me away because he thought it was best for me. It only made me love him more.

Neither one of us spoke for a while, and eventually, the gentle lap of water against the kayak seemed louder than my thoughts. "He has the biggest heart of anyone I know, but he protects it fiercely," Finn said, finally. "When Ellie left, it proved all the worst things he thought about himself, and he loves you even more. Probably felt like you could hurt him even worse."

"Knowing that doesn't help anything if he's determined to push me away." Angrily, I chucked a floating stick as far as it would fly.

"I guess not, but I thought you should at least understand where it was coming from." He sized me up from his perch in the boat. "You're a wreck, by the way."

"Thanks. I'm aware."

"So, what are you going to do about it?"

"There's nothing to do. Eventually, I'm going to be distracted enough by work and hobbies and whatever else that I'll stop thinking about Braden for every minute of every goddamned day, and I'll start to feel like a normal human again. Until then . . ." I had no idea. "I guess I'll just be a wreck. Is it hurting anyone? No. Have I missed a deadline or a day of work? No. So just let me wallow until I'm done wallowing."

"I don't accept that as a solution." Finn shook his head and started poking me again with the paddle. It was starting to piss me off.

"Quit it. Seriously, Finn. Stop." But he didn't stop. His paddle was wet, and he was hitting me right in the stomach, which both tickled and hurt from the jabs. I tried to scoot away to escape the onslaught, but the kayak didn't allow for much wiggling. "I'm serious. Cut it out."

"No." He only poked harder.

"Fine, you want to get into it? Someone's gonna end up in the water, and it isn't going to be me."

"So you say." He jabbed my armpit. I picked up my paddle and splashed him first, then went in for a jab under his ribs.

The second Finn stood up in the kayak, there was no turning back. "Finn, no, we're gonna—" I didn't have time to get any more words out before the kayak listed to one side, dumping both of us overboard. He howled. I cursed. We both ended up plunging into the water, but the buoyancy of our life vests popped us to the surface almost immediately.

"Fuck, that's cold!" he yelled.

"Whose bright idea was it to come out here?" I yelled. I don't care how many people occasionally swim out here—the waters of the San Francisco Bay are an ice plunge. There was a reason most escapees from Alcatraz never made it out alive.

"I think it was mine." He laughed. "Kind of feels good once you get used to it."

"It feels horrible. It hate you!" I screamed. But I didn't. I could never hate him.

"You love me."

"And I also love you. But I can't believe you capsized us in this frigid water."

Inexplicably, his hat was still on his head. The brim stood up like a tiara. When he smiled, the sun glinted in his eyes, making them sparkle like tiny stars. He looked like a slightly possessed fairy godmother. "You've been puttering around like a zombie for a week. Have you noticed that Tater Tot is still living in your house?"

It made me laugh. "I did notice that. And I'm glad to have the company, so I kind of hope she stays."

"I heard her say you made her co-owner."

That didn't sound like something I would do, but what did I know about myself anymore these days? I never thought I'd be willing to stay in Carolwood for love either, so I was just a surprise a minute.

Finn swam over to my side of the kayak. "Come on, let's flip this thing and go back."

"In a minute," I said, leaning back and letting the life vest float me on the surface of the water with minimal effort. "This is the first time in two weeks that I've been able to feel anything besides misery. I want to enjoy that before I continue my wallowing."

Closing my eyes, I let the morning sun hit my face. Even though my teeth were chattering, there was no escaping the beauty of my surroundings and the reality that the new day had unleashed a new chance to pick myself up from the pavement and decide to return to the living.

"Hey." Finn's voice called me out of my haze. I opened my eyes. "You okay?"

I nodded. "Not yet, but I will be."

"You gonna fix this thing and make yourself happy?"

"No comment."

Together, we launched ourselves onto the bottom of the kayak and pulled the far edge back toward us. In one swift motion, the plastic vessel flipped right side up. Carefully, I held it steady while Finn climbed over the edge and sat on the far side. Then I swam around and collected the paddles we'd strewn into the water and handed them to him.

He leaned back toward the far side, so I wouldn't dump the whole thing back into the bay when I leaned hard to climb in. When I'd settled back in my seat, Finn handed me a paddle but made no move to pick up the other one.

"C'mon, let's go back, and I'll buy you some breakfast," he said.

I waited for him to pick up the paddle, but he didn't. "What's up? Why aren't you paddling?" I accused.

"I did most of the work on the way out here while you were sulking. I think you'll feel better about yourself if you do the paddling on the way back."

Being the oldest, Finn did a lot of bossing around in our house growing up. The only male, he had the deepest and loudest voice. Plus, he was smart. Translation: he could do things like dumping a person into the San Francisco Bay and demanding to be paddled back to shore while he lazed in the sun.

But not today.

"Not doing that, dude. I know I didn't pull my weight coming out here, but the tide shifted. I can't get both of us back in this current."

He folded her arms over his chest. "Sure you can. You still need to burn off some steam. Start paddling, and I'll jump in when you're gassed."

"Fine." He pissed me off, but he had a point. Since I'd been back home, I'd intentionally tortured myself, which meant I hadn't been to my pole dancing class, I hadn't looked for vistas where I could see the sun setting over the bay, I hadn't ridden my bike, I hadn't done anything except work myself to the bone.

As I slid my paddle through the water, it didn't take long before I found my rhythm. After a while, a bead of sweat dripped down my forehead, and I inhaled a deeper breath into my lungs.

Even though a part of me wanted to surrender to the ease of wallowing in sweatpants, the crisp morning air and the proximity to the water had the effect of chilling me out and making me want more than the lowest possible state of human existence.

When my arms started to ache, I pulled the paddle harder. When I felt my breathing get heavier, I leaned into the discomfort. The only way I would get past Braden was by going through all the stages of grief, so I willed myself to move from inertia to claiming my life back.

The only way out is *through*.

It pained me to hear the echo of his words, but I reasoned that maybe he'd been telling something I wasn't ready to hear at the time. He had helped me. He'd made me realize I was ready for a relationship, and I didn't need to compartmentalize my life into neat boxes and stages. Sometimes they overlapped. Sometimes life got sloppy and unmanageable.

I just needed to find someone who wouldn't freak out at the first sign of a mess.

We hadn't reached the marina yet, but when I stopped paddling, Finn turned around to look at me. I could see from his satisfied expression that wearing me out had been his intention all along.

"Did you plan to throw me overboard?" I asked quietly. I no longer felt angry, just drained.

His eyes twinkled. "I'm not gonna lie. I thought about it the whole time your lazy ass was making me paddle." He pressed his lips together. "And I just may have invited you out here with the idea that you needed an ice bath to pull you out of your stupor."

I nodded, and he ducked, maybe afraid I was going to throw the paddle in my hands at him. "Thank you."

Smug, he picked up his paddle and turned back around. "You're welcome." He started paddling, and I joined the rhythm. With the two of us working, we made it back to the marina quickly.

Our clothes had mostly dried by the time we got back and returned the kayak, so we went straight to breakfast at Bette's Oceanview Diner before going across the street for some Peet's coffee to take back to my house.

Finn drove and I looked out the window, amazed at how much better I felt than when I'd woken up that morning. For the first time since I left Carolwood with my heart in my throat, I believed I could find a way to be happy with or without Braden. I still had a lot to sort out, especially if what Finn said was true. But either way, I had a sense that something better was on the horizon.

With that slightly adjusted mindset, I nodded to myself. "Okay, I'm ready to get out of my sweatpants."

Finn laughed. "Good girl." When we turned on my street, I was looking at him, so I didn't immediately see the white pickup parked in front of my house. But I saw the questioning look on Finn's face.

Then I saw Mitch leaning against my front door.

CHAPTER THIRTY-SIX

arah

I ASSUMED he'd come on an errand. That was the only reason I could fathom for Mitch standing there. Sadly, I'd noticed I accidentally packed that damned hoodie Braden loved so much, and a couple of his T-shirts had gotten mixed up in my laundry. No doubt I'd left some things behind as well.

"If you're here for the ritual exchanging of breakup items, you can forget it. I'm burning his hoodie, and he can do the same with my stuff."

He walked toward me, the look in his eyes heavy and laced with sadness. "Sarah . . ."

My heart started thundering. Something had happened to Braden—I knew it in an instant. "Tell me. What's wrong?"

A slew of thoughts bounced through my mind, possibilities ranging from sadness about our breakup to something much,

much worse. But my mind couldn't go there.

Then I took in Mitch's face and posture, the totality of it—the dark circles under his eyes, the defeated slump of his shoulders, the soot staining his cheeks. The man hadn't showered. He hadn't looked in a mirror. After whatever had happened to Braden, he'd come straight here.

"What happened?"

Finn had parked the car and heard enough to understand something was wrong. He put an arm around me protectively.

"We got called out to an apartment fire. They're complicated, high heat, poor visibility." I nodded rapidly because I'd learned enough over the past few months to understand all the variables at play. "People were trapped inside. Braden stayed inside longer than he should have. He saved two people's lives."

Mitch swallowed hard, and I stood frozen, feeling a knot of bile rise into my throat. My legs started shaking, and my breathing went shallow, waiting for the final edict. Even without him saying so, I knew what he was about to tell me couldn't be good.

I grasped his arms and focused my eyes on his. "Mitch. I need to know. Please."

"He got everyone out. They wouldn't have made it without him. He always said fighting fires was the hill he'd die on. I think he went into that blaze expecting it might be his last." I gasped and immediately felt like I needed to heave. And almost as if he could read my mind, he shook his head. "I tried to stop him. It's important to me that you know that."

I felt the sting of tears in my eyes. Mitch sucked in a breath and sighed. "He's still alive. But he lost consciousness and suffered from smoke inhalation. He wasn't out of the ICU when I left, but I wanted to tell you in person."

Nodding, I shuffled through the myriad thoughts competing for dominance in my mind, trying to decide if any of them deserved to be said out loud. I blamed myself for leaving. I blamed him for taking unnecessary risks.

Finally, I said the only thing that felt like it mattered. "I love him."

Finn's grip tightened on me. "Can we go see him? Can he have visitors?" he asked, knowing I was too stunned to come up with logical next steps.

Looking dazed and exhausted, Mitch nodded. "Once he's out of the ICU, yes." He looked at his phone. "Not sure when that will be."

"I don't care. I'll sit there and wait. Is that okay?"

Mitch nodded, and I eased out of Finn's grip to pull him into a hug. He clung to me like he needed the contact as much as I did. "Thanks for coming to tell me," I said.

Despite the worry and concern, his lips tipped up into a smile. "Of course. You're family."

"You want me to drive you down there?" Finn put an arm around me. I knew he had to teach a class in two hours and would probably rather wait until after that to go.

"Thanks, but I'm okay. I'll take my car." I wanted to leave immediately. And unlike a regular drive, I knew nothing would distract me from getting to the hospital.

CHAPTER THIRTY-SEVEN

raden

BLUE WAVES the color of sapphires washed over me as I floated on a sand-scuffed surfboard, but I had no plans of riding any of the breakers to shore. It felt too good to bob there, safe from sinking into the sea and relieved of the need to paddle to stay afloat.

In the distance, voices at the shoreline spoke in hushed tones, telling me a story about a hedgehog who dreams of going on a space mission. Then he goes on the space mission because he's the only one small enough to fit in the rocket capsule.

It made no sense.

But I didn't fight it because the lilting voice telling the story sounded familiar and calming to me.

I also had other wild, technicolor dreams—images of Mitch yelling to people around me and carrying me someplace, the inescapable feeling that I was flying higher and higher in the sky without a parachute or a way to get down to earth. Sounds of sirens. The screech of tires on asphalt. Lots and lots of coughing until I couldn't speak.

But someone else was speaking, and it was the only sound I wanted to hear.

"Braden? Can you hear me?"

Yes, I can hear you. Keep talking because I don't want to forget the sound of your voice in case I'm dead and I need to tuck this memory away.

Moving felt impossible. So did speaking.

There were beeps and some buzzing and the general feeling of people surrounding me, talking to each other, and rattling of data and numbers.

The first thing I became aware of was a pair of peaceful blue eyes that saw into my depths, even when I wasn't sure I had any. Creamy skin that was creased with concern. Plump lips whispering the words to a ridiculous story about a hedgehog.

I'd need to ask her about that later.

I fought against my sadness and the fear that I could only see Sarah's face because I was dead, and somehow the afterlife had given me something beautiful to look at for all of eternity.

The second thing I became aware of was the warm brush of her fingers against the back of my hand, calmly soothing my nerves and reminding me what love felt like.

"Damsel," I tried to say, but the words stayed buried for some reason.

She shook her head. "It's too soon. You can't talk. There's damage to your airways. But of course, I want you to talk to me. So much.

Just not right now. Let me talk instead." She was so calm, a vision I wanted to stare at forever. I didn't need to speak in order to do that.

"They had you in an induced coma for two days. They tried to bring you out yesterday, but your lungs were still too swollen to breathe on your own, so they had to wait another twenty-four hours."

I nodded. Speaking wasn't an option, but I managed a grunt. My throat felt like someone had used it for char-grill barbecue and hadn't swept out the hot ash.

Words couldn't do justice to the swell of emotion I felt at looking into the clear eyes of the woman I'd fallen in love with despite myself. She was my serenity, and as long as she kept her warm hand clasped around mine, I knew I'd heal.

"Mitch wanted you to know the two kids you saved in that apartment survived. They're alive because of you, and if you hadn't gone in there, they probably wouldn't be. So you should feel proud." Her voice caught on the last word. Tears welled in the corners of her eyes, but she swallowed them back, trying to be tougher than I knew she was.

I reached for her and cupped her face with my hand. I took her other hand and held it to my heart. She'd know the words even if I couldn't say them.

"I'm going to stay with you until you're discharged. Mitch arranged it so I can sleep here." She pointed to a pink chair that looked like the world's most uncomfortable place to sleep. All I could do was nod.

I wanted to say so much more. Ironic that when I was finally desperate to tell her how much I loved her, I couldn't speak at all.

"Now that you're awake, I'm going to run home and shower. Trust me, you'll like me a lot better when I don't smell like the San Francisco Bay." I had no idea what that meant, and I didn't want her to leave, but her reassuring smile told me she'd be back.

I just hoped she'd stay long enough for me to tell her everything I needed to say.

CHAPTER THIRTY-EIGHT

 arah

ONE WEEK Later

WITH A LITTLE BIT of pulmonary therapy and a few days on a liquid diet, Braden made a full recovery and was discharged from the hospital. He had to be wheeled out in a chair—hospital rules —but the second he'd crossed the threshold, he stood up and squinted into the sun.

The guy hadn't been outside in a week, and his eyes were probably having trouble adjusting.

That was okay. I'd just wait—leaning against the side of his truck wearing a pair of sunglasses in the roundabout in front of the hospital. I folded my arms across my chest even though my biceps were unimpressive.

Bella, wearing a red handkerchief around her neck, sat at my feet, her tail wagging so hard she was sweeping up a mini-tornado.

The sun was out and the sky was that medium blue, cloudless color that seemed to hang over Carolwood and the surrounding towns. Perfect grape growing weather.

When Braden finally saw me, his face broke open—literally stretched beyond what I'd ever seen his cheeks do before—into the biggest smile his features could hold. We were only a hundred feet apart, but he ran the distance between us and pulled me into his arms.

"Sarah . . ."

I buried my face in his long-sleeved shirt, which was, of course, so tight that I could feel every muscle in his chest. I didn't want to let go.

But I also wanted to see his face. I'd seen him every day since the fire, but I'd never gotten tired of looking at him. Never would. So I leaned back. His eyes fixed on mine, and we had one of those crazy moments of connection we always seemed to have.

"You look good, fireman. Glad to see they let you out."

"I'd have clawed my way out to get to you, Damsel."

I knew he'd want to drive, so I tossed him his keys and went around to the passenger side. Then I waited until Braden came around and opened the door and held out his hand because I knew he'd want to do that too. When I'd stepped up and settled on the passenger seat, Braden leaned in and ran his fingers along the side of my face.

"If I didn't say it when I was doped up on pain meds, I want to make sure I say it now. Thank you for being here."

I nodded.

We still hadn't discussed anything about us.

With the pain Braden was in from burns to the back of his neck and his inability to speak for several days, we agreed to table all serious discussions. So I read him more books I'd gotten from the kids' section of the library, and he mostly closed his eyes and listened with one hand resting on some part of me at all times.

But we needed to talk.

I assumed Braden would drive straight to his house, so it surprised me when he got on the highway instead. "Where're we headed?" I turned to look and saw that he was smiling.

"Field trip."

Quirking an eyebrow, I thought about our last field trip when I ended up pole dancing in the station. "Okay, I trust you. Your field trip ideas in the past have proven to be to my liking."

He smirked. "Mine too."

Since it seemed like he wasn't going to share our destination, I tipped my head back against the headrest and closed my eyes. I hadn't slept well for the past week, between worry about Braden's condition to trying to sleep curled up in the uncomfortable hospital chair.

The next thing I knew, Bella was licking the back of my hand, and Braden was smiling at me through the open door of the truck. He extended his hand to me, but I was so groggy it took me a minute to unlatch the seatbelt and get my bearings.

"How long did I sleep?"

"About forty minutes, give or take."

"Wow. Sorry. You're the one who just got out of the hospital. I didn't mean to fall apart on you."

He was still holding out his hand, so I took it and stepped down, fixed on Braden's face. Bella loped off the seat and sat down next to him. "First of all, never apologize for being tired. And second, falling asleep isn't falling apart."

"Okay, I guess I exaggerated." I gave him my deep-voiced imitation of how he sounded when he was grumpy. Then I looked past him when I realized we were apparently at the destination of our field trip.

And lo and behold, it was another firehouse.

"Aha, do I detect someone who's interested in a little pole dancing action?" I smiled seductively, but I had my heart under lock and key. It wasn't healthy to feel things for him when I didn't know if we had any chance of a future.

"Not exactly, no." He folded his arms across his chest, making his biceps look insanely sculpted.

"Okay, I've never asked you this, but I'm sorry . . . do you do that because you know how hot it makes you look?"

"Do what?" He actually said that. How could he not know?

"Nothing. Never mind. So why no pole dancing?"

He started walking me toward the front of the station. "Well, this particular station doesn't have a pole. Most of the newer ones don't. It's only two stories. Doesn't take that long to go down a flight of stairs."

And yet . . . we were still standing at the front door.

"Okay, so what are we doing here?"

"I'm told it has a backyard. I wanted to see it, and I thought you might like to see it with me."

Had he damaged his brain in that fire? What the hell was this man talking about?

He texted someone, and a minute later, the door opened, and a firefighter in the same blue uniform Braden wore welcomed us. "Captain Michaels, I was told to show you out back."

"Thanks so much."

Thoroughly confused, I followed him through the fire station that looked a lot like the one in Carolwood where I'd done my pole dance. And for that matter, what part of town were we in now?

The backyard was big. Pretty with a wide-open grass area. Bella took off, running circles around the perimeter, and Braden led me to a bench under a tree.

"This is a great yard," I said, still waiting for an explanation. When I didn't get one, I had to ask. "Why are we here?"

Braden took my hand and interlaced our fingers. "Couple reasons. For one, last week, there was a moment when I stared down into a flaming hole that I was pretty sure would be the last thing I'd ever see, and I got some pretty good goddamned clarity. I figured out a few things."

He looked at me, the calm in his eyes something I hadn't seen before. I'd never thought of him as troubled, just sad. But the absence of something that had weighed him down was now gone.

I felt bad that I hadn't known it was there when I could have asked about it.

"What'd you figure out, fireman?"

"I'm done taking unnecessary risks. I'm selling the motorcycle. My job comes with enough adrenaline that I don't need to push the envelope. I don't want to risk my life unless it's for you. I'd run into a hundred burning buildings for you. But that's it." He squeezed my hand. "Only for you."

The thought warmed my heart, but the idea of him running into danger still made the hairs on the back of my neck stand on end. "I hope you never have to do that," I insisted, my eyes pressed shut at the image of him facing fire and danger for me.

"All that matters is that you believe—that you know—I would. I will."

"Thank you." The quiet solemnity of my tone was at odds with the intensity of my love for him and his desire to be there for me in the worst of circumstances. That was not lost on me.

He shook his head and looked around like maybe he was noticing our surroundings for the first time. It was a really nice yard, almost like a park. I could hear neighborhood noises like maybe a school was nearby.

Braden turned on the bench, so he was facing me more squarely and brought my hand to his lips. When his breath warmed my skin, I felt a chill that I'd missed so much since I'd left town.

"The woman I described to you when we were hanging out on that night after you moved in, the one I said I was looking for, my idea of perfect love—that woman is you. It's been you since the moment you insisted you could carry your book boxes after a car accident and told me you cared whether I died in a fire. You didn't even know me, and I could tell it mattered to you—that I . . . mattered to you." His voice broke as he said it, and my heart clenched at the soft vulnerability I so rarely saw. I reached up and cupped his cheek in my palm, feeling the soft scruff on my hand. A tiny muscle in his jaw popped, and he swallowed.

"Of course it mattered. And you matter—more than I think you know."

"You blew into town and turned my world upside down. I never planned on wanting more than a life alone in the same town where I've lived for a decade, and you've got me wanting it all."

He was saying things I'd needed him to say while I was still there. Before, I made myself believe he didn't feel them because he'd so easily let me go.

"I love you, Sarah. I love you so much. And I want you with me on the journey—wherever it takes us—even though I don't deserve it."

I put a finger over his lips. I melted at his words, but I couldn't take it anymore. "Stop saying you don't deserve it. If you don't deserve to be happy, then neither do I. And I won't stand for that. I deserve it. And I want you. So there's nothing left to discuss. You've got me. And I'm not letting you go."

I didn't know how it was going to work with him living an hour away and me being a disaster in a car, but maybe . . . maybe we'd figure something out.

He crushed my lips with his kiss, pushing his hands into my hair. Our tongues tangled, and he wrapped me in his arms. Things could have escalated quickly from there if we hadn't both realized we were in a fire station yard.

Speaking of which . . .

"Braden, how'd you find this place? What town are we in?" I asked. It was certainly picturesque.

"Richmond."

"Where?"

"Woman, please get a map. It's one town over from Berkeley."

"No, I know where Richmond is. I'm asking why we're here."

He raised an eyebrow. "Captain Michaels was offered a transfer."

My brain whirled as I put the pieces together. "Wait, here? You're going to work here? So I can keep my job at Berkeley and still live with you and not have to get in a car?"

He nodded, and my eyes welled with tears.

As he blotted them with his thumb, he grazed my neck with his lips and whispered in my ear, "There's beauty in the unexpected, Sarah. Love is the beauty."

He was right. I loved him. And it was beautiful.

EPILOGUE

arah

Three Months Later

I RUSHED through the door to our new bungalow north of campus and only cast a passing glance at the photo of us on the entryway table. It was a candid photo of us at the beach, Braden shirtless, me in a straw hat. I loved the photo. It reminded me of one of my favorite days together.

We'd hiked to the Point Reyes National Seashore, which was only reachable via the hiking trail on foot or horseback. On the particular weekend we went, we crested the bluffs above the beach to find it nearly empty. We spent the rest of the day walking along the shore, collecting driftwood to make a campfire on the beach, and thoroughly, responsibly extinguishing the fire before we slipped into our tent. Each time I looked at the photo, it brought back the memory of the cloudless sky, warm end of summer weather, and gentle Pacific surf.

"This is what it feels like to be happy," Braden had said to me that day. Maybe that's why I'd used it as a touchstone ever since, a daily reminder that all I needed to be happy was him.

But today, I didn't stop to admire the photo. My heart pounded with the panic I'd felt for the past hour as I raced through the small craftsman to find Braden in the backyard. He'd never ended up building a firepit at his house in Carolwood, so it became his first project after we moved in here.

He'd dug the pit itself in a corner of the yard and flanked it with low-slung deck chairs and outdoor pillows. The pile of rocks surrounding the pit, however, was in constant need of tweaking, according to Braden.

The second he stood up from the rocks he'd already arranged and rearranged countless times, I flew at him and wrapped my arms around his neck. His body automatically absorbed me like a second skin. "Hey, you okay?" His voice came out muffled as he kissed the top of my head.

It wasn't unusual for me to practically jump him the minute I arrived home—often I spent the short drive from campus imagining exactly how and where I wanted him and put my desires into action the second I saw him.

Today, I had a slightly different goal—not to pass out from sheer nerves and anxiety. And because he knew me so well, he sensed something was up.

"I'm … not gonna lie. I'm freaking out." I didn't let go of him. He held me up and rubbed circles on my back until my rapid breathing returned to something resembling normal, and I leaned away enough to look at him.

I exhaled a lungful of air while his eyes roamed over my face, assessing. "Talk to me, Damsel." The nickname had stuck and would always remind me of the day we met beside the firetruck for Engine 97.

I inhaled again and loosened my grip around Braden's waist. He spun me around and gently lowered me into one of the chairs. Sitting in his own, he slid it closer until our knees were touching and picked up my hand. His other hand went to my cheek and stroked, turning my face toward his.

Swallowing hard, I steeled myself to blurt out my news without any more leadup or subtext. "I'm three months pregnant."

Puffy white clouds filled the deep blue of the late summer sky. I had the wherewithal to notice the perfect day and the even more perfect way Braden continued stroking my cheek. Glancing at his face, I looked for signs of shock or dismay. I saw neither.

The serenity of Braden's beautifully angular face cracked as a smile took over. His teeth were so damned white and straight that I caught myself staring at them and wondering what kind of orthodonture he'd had as a kid. So blinded by his smile, I almost forgot what I'd just told him.

As the deep gray of his eyes shifted to a lighter, brighter hue, the crinkles at the corners of his eyes deepened more than I'd ever seen them.

"That's the best damn news I've heard in my life." He leaned in and grazed my lips with the barest whisper of a kiss before sitting back and watching my expression. "Your eyes are huge. You look grim," he assessed. "You're not happy about this."

"No … it's not … I *am*. I'm happy. It's just sudden and a little bit shocking and *very* unplanned."

He nodded, his hand never leaving mine. He knew how I felt about *unplanned*.

We'd talked about kids—briefly. We both wanted them, both loved our big families, but that was about as far as we'd gotten. Already in my thirties, I knew I didn't have the luxury of waiting for years and years, but I'd officially begin my tenure the following semester, and I hardly felt like I should start by taking maternity leave.

Forget unplanned … I didn't even *have* a plan for a future version of this.

But for as much as I felt freaked out by that, Braden's smile never waved from his face. Not for a second.

And that made me certain I'd be okay. "I just earned tenure. I don't know if my work schedule will change. Or how I'll feel…" My shoulders sunk as I accepted these unknowns. I'd have to deal with them, and I wouldn't be able to control every outcome.

"I've got you," Braden said quietly, bringing my hand to his lips. He cupped my chin and turned my face toward his. "You're amazing, and you can do this. And in the moments you think you can't, I'll remind you." He put his arm around me and held me tight.

I loved that he knew it was all I needed. And I loved this man— who rushed into danger when most people ran from it, who made a career of managing situations outside of his control—I love that he had my back. He had me. I could do this.

"We'll figure it out," I agreed, leaning my head against his shoulder.

Braden and I were solid. Even as I'd grown to feel more comfortable with events I couldn't control, I had a long way to go before I could embrace the unknown. Doing it by the side of someone I loved made the journey bearable, even enjoyable.

I knew we'd be together forever.

"This is good news. I'm so, so happy, Sarah. I love you." Tears pricked the corners of his eyes, and my strong heroic firefighter looked like he'd just rescued a hundred people from a burning building. In reality, he'd rescued one—me.

THANK you so much for reading The Spark Between Us!

Want a little more Sarah and Braden? You can read an exclusive BONUS SCENE HERE by signing up for my mailing list. Only the good stuff, I promise, including a monthly free book from one of my author colleagues and other goodies!

AND...there's more of the Finley sisters! You can read Tatum and Donovan's book, Playing for You NOW! Read on for a Sneak Peek!

ACKNOWLEDGMENTS

Readers, thank you. I'm grateful for every word you read, every kind review, every thoughtful click and comment. I could not do this without you.

Jay, Jesse and Oliver: thank you for walking the dogs and doing your dishes so I could tap tap away on the computer. Big love to you three giant men with the best hair ever.

Amy Vox Libris and Nancy Smay - the edits, the feedback and the SOS phone calls got me through this one. Thank you.

Mike Noone, my firefighter/paramedic friend, thank you for answering all of my questions and providing expert knowledge of your field. You are a true hero.

Shannon, this cover is gorgeous - thank you, thank you. Thank you Jenn and the Social Butterfly team for expert advice, brilliant execution, and other superpowers. Catherine and Shan, I'm happy to have you in my corner - you make the PR part a breeze.

Bloggers and bookstagrammers—thank you for embracing my books and exposing my writing to readers. I couldn't do it without your help. Glad to have you in my village.

And to my fellow authors: you lift me up. Thank you.

ABOUT THE AUTHOR

Stacy Travis writes sexy, charming romance about bookish, sassy women and the hot alphas who fall for them. Writing contemporary romance makes her infinitely happy, but that might be the coffee talking.

When she's not on a deadline, she's in running shoes complaining that all roads seem to go uphill. Or on the couch with a margarita. Or fangirling at a soccer game. She's never met a dog she didn't want to hug. And if you have no plans for Thanksgiving, she'll probably invite you to dinner. Stacy lives in Los Angeles with her husband, two sons, and a poorly-trained rescue dog who hoards socks.

Facebook reader group: Stacy's Saucy Sisters

Super fun newsletter: http://bit.ly/3nvgkcunews

Tiktok: https://www.tiktok.com/@authorstacytravis

Website: https://www.www.stacytravis.com

Email: stacytraviswrites@gmail.com - tell me what you're reading!

facebook.com/stacytravisromance

instagram.com/stacytravisauthor

bookbub.com/authors/stacy-travis

goodreads.com/stacytravis

ALSO BY STACY TRAVIS

The Summer Heat Duet

1. The Summer of Him: A Mistaken Identity Celebrity Romance

2. Forever with Him: An Opposites Attract Contemporary Romance

The Berkeley Hills Series - all standalone novels

1. In Trouble with Him: A Forbidden Love Contemporary Romance (Finn and Annie's story)

2. Second Chance at Us: A Second Chance Romance (Becca and Blake)

3. Falling for You: A Friends to Lovers Romance (Isla and Owen)

4. The Spark Between Us: A Grumpy-Sunshine, Brother's Best Friend Romance (Sarah and Braden)

5. Playing for You: A Sports Romance (Tatum and Donovan)

6. No Match for Her - an Opposites-Attract Friends-to-Lovers Romance (Cherry and Charlie)

Standalone Novels - Adult Contemporary Romance

French Kiss: A Friends to Lovers Romance

Bad News: An Enemies to Lovers Romance

SNEAK PEEK - PLAYING FOR YOU
A SPORTS ROMANCE

Chapter 1.

Tatum

My competitive streak runs hot. Like melted cheddar under a flaming broiler—that kind of hot.

Maybe it derives from birth order, given that I have five older siblings. I always had to compete and chase after them.

Or I just got the racehorse equivalent of serenity in our family gene pool.

Either way, I've never considered it a problem. Good old competitive spirit saw me through calculus and computer science classes with the smart kids' high school. A lot of them were guys. A lot of them held it against me.

I didn't date much in high school.

In college, I found my merry band of fellow strivers and achievers, so no one looked twice when I rode my sputtering used red moped to the science lab on campus in the middle of the night to check my results and record them in real time. No one found it odd that I ran a bunch of solitary miles at five in the morning to train for sprint distance triathlons—for fun.

Ah, to be a nerd among nerds.

Study dates with electrical engineering and computer science guys almost qualified as actual dates. After we'd finished our problem sets, they wanted to score as much as the frat boys. And missionary style sex lined everything up at nice orderly angles.

Scientific. Unimaginative.

Is that all there is? Probably.

Why I got engaged at age twenty-one to a fellow coder named Warren and broke it off a year later. Story for another time.

Let's just say I lost my mind for a minute because of an eggplant, and not the kind that goes in baba ghanoush.

Sitting in my programming pod at the Silicon Valley tech campus where I work, I twirl a purple pen and consider the results of all my competitiveness. The desire to outdo my peers has landed me here, at an ergonomically designed desk on wheels which can slide around the open-plan office for impromptu meetings with the design pod or the marketing pod. Infinite configurations of potential productivity.

Productivity makes me almost as happy as competition. It's its own sort of measurable achievement.

"Hey, I hear we have another challenge." It's not information—it's a taunt. My colleague and best friend Terrance splays one hand on the gray surface of my desk and plucks a browning leaf from my potted ivy plant with the other. His longish brown hair hangs over his forehead and into his eyes, but if it bothers him, he finds tending to my plant more important.

"Ooh, yeah? Tell me." I bend my neck trying to see his light brown eyes, whose sparkle tends to mirror the potential prize for the winner of any challenge within the company. He's fixated on my plant, now testing the soil's dampness, so I won't know the magnitude of the challenge bounty until he finishes fussing.

So I type a few lines of code and wait. When he still doesn't speak, I press my lips together to buy a little more time before my impatience makes me blurt, "Terrance! Enough with the plant. What's the challenge?" The company where we work regularly pits us against each other in design or programming challenges in a race against the clock. They keep our adrenaline racing which leads to some creative ideas.

He looks up at me and smirks, cheek dimples popping in his round face that looks like it hasn't seen the sun in a decade. Terrance doesn't run at five in the morning, doesn't stay at work past six at night, and insanely, doesn't care about the challenges so he refuses to waste his time on them. "Um, let me try and recall..." He stares at the ceiling.

His methodical persistence amazes me sometimes. He works carefully, thoroughly—but so slowly. Unlike me. I approach every assignment and new project like the Tasmanian Devil, bent on coding the hell out of it.

And it's working. I've gotten pay raises and a better position at a better company, but I still want so much more. We couldn't be more different. Maybe that's why we make such good friends. That, and the fact that there's zero spark for either one of us, something we admitted in the early days of our friendship.

A junior programmer, Terrance started with our company, Vivi-Tech, a year after I did. He should have earned a promotion to senior programmer by now, but he's happy taking orders from other people and seems to be missing the hyperdrive that might get him a better job.

We've talked about it. I sometimes try to give him a push because he's smart and I see his potential, but he's happy doing workaday programming and not stressing about staying late to climb the company ladder.

I really have no idea what that feels like.

"Oh, you recall. Just tell me." It's not that I don't have a sense of humor. I can appreciate his game. I just intend to win at it.

Terrance grins like a cat who's got his mouse cornered and is settling in for a nice long session of fuckery. "I don't know the prize. Something related to a pet project of Charlie's, and you know that could be anything..." His voice trails off and he looks for something else on my desk to mess with.

But really, he's messing with me.

"That's all you know? Wow, too bad you can't tell me more. I have about three hours of coding busywork and I've been looking for someone to hand it off to." I smile sweetly at him and let him know—not for the first time—that he's about to come out on the losing end of this bluffing game.

I twirl my pen a few times like I have all the patience in the world to wait him out. Really, my stomach acid is threatening to digest all my internal organs, but I smile.

Then I see it, the telltale twitch in his right eye that indicates he has no interest in three extra hours of busywork. He nods. "Fine. It's a VR functionality competition. Not sure what the prize is, but I'm sure it'll be good."

"And you know this how?" I squint my eyes at him, not willing to let him off the hook with a bum lead or something he made up—yes, he's pulled one of those and only let on after I'd spent an hour on a wild goose chase. Hence the need for me to have reams of busywork at the ready as a threat.

He laughs. "You're such a hardass. I just delivered the code files to Charlie, and he told me himself."

Charlie is the king of ViviTech, the company he created to revolutionize virtual reality so NASA scientists could essentially be the rovers on Mars and examine the planet with all the simulated land conditions that they'd encounter if they were there.

Charlie then made a big bet in gaming, designing VR sets that had become the gold standard. But the technology can do so much more, and that's what gets me excited—the idea of helping people deal with phobias by simulating those environments in therapeutic settings. The applications are endless.

At five foot six with light brown hair and light brown eyes, Charlie doesn't cut an imposing figure physically. But the second he opens his mouth, the stream of consciousness visions of tech world building makes it clear he cleared his first billion before age thirty for a reason.

He regularly creates challenges—impossible-seeming designs, programming using minimal lines of code, physical products using recycled materials—and rewards the winners with perks like tickets to pro basketball games, sailing lessons, and cases of wine.

Big surprise, I never care as much about the prizes as much as the idea of winning.

I swivel my chair around to face Terrance head-on, dying to know more. Pulling my messy curls out of their pony, I stare a hole into him while I wait for him to give me the rest of the details.

Enjoying his scrap of power, Terrance backs a few steps away. "I believe Charlie will be sending an email about it soon. You should watch your inbox."

"Terrance," I warn, looking around my desk for something to throw at him. Absent something heavy, I use the purple pen. He catches it and pops it into the pocket of his khakis. Now I'm down a pen and I'm losing patience. I have actual work to finish, after all.

"Yes?" he asks, batting his lashes.

"The lash thing, not a good look for you. Spill." I swivel the mess of my hair up into a bun and glare.

Terrance leans on the corner of my desk and crosses his arms. "Okay, I've had my fun for the day. Here's the deal. Charlie's going to ask for an enhance avatar model based on a real person. So, all the facial expressions and movements have to match exactly."

I narrow my eyes, trying to see something that doesn't exist. "We already do that. It's the whole point of VR, to mimic real people."

He shakes his head. "I'm not explaining it right, then. It's going to be based on specific people, like celebrities or whatever, so you can be that person in the game. That's what I understood him to mean."

"Oh." Oh. We'd never done anything like that before. And the idea of getting to move and think like a real known person sets off little thrill bells of excitement ringing in my veins. Even if the idea of studying the expressions and verbal cues of celebrities doesn't float my intellectual boat, the technology piece gets me seriously hot and bothered.

Terrance frowns at me and his lips turn down in disgust. "I don't need to see your O face at work, Tatum."

"What? Jesus, Terrance. I don't have an O face."

"Well, that's another problem altogether. I'm sorry, but maybe we should address that challenge instead of talking about some dumb thing Charlie dreamed up." Now he's winking at me. If I didn't know he was married—adorably, happily married to an adorable, happy high-school sweetheart—the wink might bother me, but on Terrance's baby face, it never does.

I wave a hand at him. "Stop. That's not what I meant."

"I know, but I don't care. Besides, it wouldn't kill you to go on a date every once in a while."

"Thanks, Mom."

"I can set you up with someone. I know single people."

"Do you? Really? I thought you had to renounce your single friend membership when you said, 'I do'." The sarcasm drips from my voice.

Maybe I've picked the wrong person to unload on, given that Terrance has his work-life balance finessed perfectly. But he's my closest friend in an office where I barely have any friends. Most of the people I work with I consider colleagues, but I'd never invite one over for coffee and I definitely wouldn't confide in them. Confiding is the kiss of death in a cut-throat business.

So Terrance is my person, even though we diverge when it comes to drive.

He grins. "You're so much fun to play with. It makes me really sad that I have to go back to my desk and do actual work."

"I'm sure." Time wasting aside, he's done me a solid with the early heads-up about the competition. Even though his explanation of what Charlie's planning sounded vague, it's enough to start my wheels turning. Plus, now I can work on clearing other tasks, so I'll have time to take on the challenge.

"Thanks for the info, Terrance. If you want to send a chunk of your programming to me, I'll knock it out for you."

He looks at the floor with a guilty smile. He was counting on easing his workload with his insider information and he knew who'd take the bait. The truth is, I can get through the programming he's tasked with in less time than it takes him because I've done so much of it that I've gotten efficient.

A few minutes later, Terrance sends me some coding, and a few minutes after that, Charlie sends a company-wide email alerting us that the challenge is on.

***

Charlie's email rounds out the information Terrance didn't tell me. It says that ViviTech's newest gaming project will be a sports reality competition where we'll be creating avatars of real athletes. Gamers will become the athletes they choose and simulate competing in their sports.

"Imagine scoring the winning three point shot as Kawhi Leonard or intercepting a pass as Patrick Mahomes," Charlie's email enthuses. "It's next-level gaming, combining a workout, tactical decision-making, and fantasy play with a sports franchise."

I'm all in for that, especially since I've heard rumors that Charlie is planning on having ViviTech become a major sponsor of a football team. He hasn't said anything officially, which is typical Charlie. He fans the flames of rumors on social media with little

340

hints to whip the gaming community into a frenzy but gives no confirmation until he's ready.

He has a strict policy of announcing company business to his employees at the same time he announces it to shareholders and the media, so no one leaks anything early and he controls the narrative.

Still, I hope there's something to the rumor.

The idea of studying football players for the sake of game design sounds way more interesting than building avatars in the likeness of violent auto thieves or world-destroying killers armed with knives and grenades.

Been there, done the savage murdering.

As a peace-loving person, I sometimes go home sick to my stomach after testing the coding for those games. They're that real.

I'd much prefer to craft an avatar with every sinewy muscle and intense facial feature of a pro athlete. It hardly feels like work to conduct interviews with the players, getting to know their mannerisms and speech patterns, the way they think about the sport.

Plus, I love football. College, pro, doesn't matter. I'll watch pretty much any team play on TV and I regularly catch Stanford home games since the stadium is less than a mile from where I live in Palo Alto. My siblings don't know about that part. With Finn, the oldest, and Sarah, the second-oldest sister working at Berkeley, I know better than to advertise attending the games of their biggest rival.

I almost get so sidetracked thinking about a new potential football VR division that I'd give my right arm to run that I stare at my screen for a full minute without writing a single line of code. Not exactly the way to win a competition.

But my daydreaming has actually given me an idea. I scrap my original plans and pull together a new configuration for the avatar's backend design.

I test it.

I test it again.

It works both times.

And so far, no whoops or hollers have indicated that one of my colleagues has presented a winning design to Charlie. I tee up my design, write a few lines summarizing how it works, and press send.

Not ten minutes later, a text from Charlie blinks at the top of my screen.

Boss Man: Come to my office please

Me: Coming

Sending my chair spinning, I fly from my desk toward Charlie's office, the only one in our shared workspace that has a door. I always appreciate that he says *please*. Charlie has socially awkward quirks and an oddly fascinating brain, but he never lacks for courtesy.

Smoothing my clammy hands down the legs of my jeans, I glance around to see if any of my colleagues notice where I'm going—to claim bragging rights for beating them! Not a single person looks my way.

Typical.

Most of what I do at work doesn't merit much attention, since most of my colleagues regularly hit their projects out of the park like they're doing a Sudoku. No one's worried about me stealing focus. I'm not flashy and I let my work speak for itself.

I've also been told I dress like a tech druid—older sisters are nothing if not brutally honest—in baggy jeans and a hoodie most days, with my hair piled on top of my head so it doesn't get in my face while I type. Makeup seems like a waste of time, especially when I spend my days wearing dark-rimmed computer glasses and looking at no one. So again, I make myself practically invisible to everyone except my married best friend.

Unfortunately, the only other person immune to my cloak of invisibility seems to have it out for me. "What's the rush, Finley?" Paul Peters jeers, standing up from his desk to block my path. He's my direct supervisor and he's always up in my business.

"Just walking by, Paul." I use his actual name even though he insists on being called Pauley. He's not a Pauley. Pauley would have a softer approach and he'd be a team player.

Paul Peters is not that guy. He's the worst kind of human to have as a boss—paranoid about being outsmarted and replaced, vindictive toward anyone who has an idea better than his, and quick to take credit for other people's 'work. I have the great misfortune of working directly beneath Paul in the company chain of command, and he lords that over me regularly, giving me extra work to do and boasting about his brilliance to Charlie when one of the projects bears fruit.

"You're going to Charlie's?" His accusatory tone tells me he knows exactly why.

I fold my arms over my chest and fight my instinct to tell him to mind his own business. "It would appear so."

"Good luck with that." His eyes assess me, trying to figure out if I really came up with a solution to Charlie's challenge and calculating how he can take the credit for it.

I bump his shoulder with mine, startling him with the affection. "Thank you so much." I leave him reeling, unsure if I meant it.

"Um, sure. You're welcome." He puffs out his chest, willing to take any praise, even the passive-aggressive kind.

As I stride toward the corner glass-walled office, I tuck the stray flyaway strands behind my ear and swallow thickly. Charlie makes me nervous, mostly because I never know what will come out of his mouth.

"Tatum, greetings," Charlie says, standing to shake my hand in the oddly formal way he always says hello, no matter the time of day or whether we've seen each other an hour earlier.

"Hey, Charlie. How are you?" I try to make eye contact, so he'll know I really do want to know about him. I feel like a lot of people who work for him do it because they like the cachet of working for a sought-after tech company, but they don't really like him. I worry that he doesn't seem to have many friends. He always eats lunch alone in his office, and when other tech pioneers around Silicon Valley have their calendars filled with venture capitalists and serial entrepreneurs jockeying for their time, Charlie chooses his solitude.

Plus, I like understanding people because it helps when programming VR experiences. In his case though, I really want to understand the puzzle that is Charles Walgrove. He's genius-level smart when it comes to understanding what technology people need and how to build it, yet mundane daily tasks trip him up. He'll spend fifteen minutes in front of the vending machine deciding between regular chips and barbecue because he's weighing the salt variables, the number of bags of each kind in the machine, and weight distribution in the machine that will result from choosing one bag over the other.

Case in point, he looks at me, two fingers pinching his lips together, eyes crinkled under a furrowed brow. He tilts to the side as though he's determining something that has nothing to do why he called me into his office.

I watch him and wait.

"Your hair is different. It was in a…" He flips his hands around pantomiming a ponytail. "And now it's up."

"Sometimes I switch it around."

"Why?"

With some people, I'd shrug and say I don't have a reason. With Charlie, I know he really wants to know. "Sometimes I get a headache, so I pull the band out. Then it gets in my face, and I pull it up again. Maybe a bun, maybe a ponytail. It's an unconscious decision."

His face opens into a grin, as though he's gleaned valuable information he'll use at a later time, and he nods.

"Well, you've completed my task, kudos, and I'd like you to come up with a few other iterations of the algorithm because I have a hunch you can improve on the performance speed. Based on what you submitted, I saw some opportunities for efficiencies. Of course, I wouldn't expect you to address all of those in a competitive environment so for these purposes I'm prepared to hand over the prize for this particular game."

Everything is a game to Charlie. The wild success of his company seems to baffle him sometimes because he's just in it for the fun.

I'm playing an entirely different game. I want to run this new VR project. I've been dying for the chance to prove I can run a division of the company, and if using VR for therapy isn't at the top of Charlie's list, I'll joyously throw my hat in the ring for the new game. I know football. I can do this job.

I don't get a lot of solo time talking with Charlie in his office. So now feels like the right time to ask for what I want.

"I don't need the prize, but I would like to put myself up for running—"

He cuts me off. "That response confuses me. The offer of a prize was not about need—of course no one needs a prize and if that was your supposition, it's faulty. Needs imply basic human requirements like food, shelter, clothing, family. Though arguably we can create family where one doesn't exist biologically, so I might remove it from the list, but nevertheless, it puzzles me that you'd turn down a prize, without knowing what it is."

I swallow hard.

Play his game.

"True. I was getting ahead of myself. I just meant that I didn't compete in this in order to win a prize. I did it because I'm really interested in—"

He shuts me down again by raising a hand. "I know. I know why you compete in all my little games—you're ambitious and you like to win. But part of winning is enjoying the fruits of your labor." With a nod, he gestures for me to sit in one of the leather club chairs opposite his desk.

I want to tell him that winning is only part of the prize for me. I want more job responsibility. I want to head up a division, but I have a feeling he already knows. He's trying to make a point, and he won't consider me to run the new project—or even discuss the new project—until I do what he wants.

I lean against the arm of a chair, perching like a bird ready to flee instead of sinking into its depths. Fleeing sounds great right about now.

The furniture in his office reminds of a well-appointed pub—not a dark, messy English pub with beer-sticky floors and dartboards, but a finer place that serves good food. His desk has a glass top and the walls are lined with hardcover books.

"As you know from my email, we're taking VR to the gaming space, starting with a few football clubs whose players have mostly signed on to have their likenesses included in the games. I've invested personally in the Strikers, and their jerseys are currently being redesigned with our logo on the front. All of this has allowed me to offer a pretty exciting prize to our competition winner."

My brain crunches through information I don't understand. I'm expecting him to present me with a pair of tickets to a game but now I'm puzzling through what football team he's talking about since I know there isn't an NFL team called the Strikers.

"I hope you're free this evening because there's a banquet in the city to announce the naming rights and they'd like someone from ViviTech to attend. It's being held at the Edmunton Hotel and I'm told they have a Michelin-starred chef. So go, eat some caviar, be affable, geek out over VR, get the people involved with the team excited. I don't do well in these situations—public...gatherings... very stressful and I'm an introvert. I'll either clam up or say something that will get me in trouble with the SEC, no telling which..." He looks at the ceiling and grimaces as if recalling a particularly bad instance. "Anyhow, I'm pleased you're the one I can send in my stead because you're very personable. You'll represent us well."

Before I can process half of what he's telling me, Charlie is standing from his desk and herding me to the door like a corgi with a flock of sheep. "Wait, Charlie, I've got a lot of work to finish. I'm not sure I can make it to a...banquet..." I cross my arms over my chest, not liking the idea of going to a dinner where I'll probably not be let through the door in a hoodie, let alone having to make small talk all night with people I don't know, even football players. "I'd be willing to step aside if you'd like to send someone with more experience at these things."

Make it sound like you're taking one for the team.

Charlie has herded me ten feet out the door and he turns and walks back into his office and closes the door without saying goodbye.

With no other options, I get the requisite information on where I need to be and when and shuffle back to my desk so I can google this mysterious football team I've never heard of.

It only takes me about a minute to understand why—the San Francisco Strikers play European football—otherwise known in this country as soccer. I know next to nothing about the sport, save what I remember from playing in a youth league at age eight —ball goes into the net and parents rejoice, trophies are liberally distributed.

That paltry knowledge won't cut it here.

If I want a shot at running the new VR team, I have exactly two hours to learn enough not to embarrass my boss, our company, and myself. Or just two out of three.

———

Playing for You is available HERE!

Made in the USA
Coppell, TX
18 October 2022

84791875R10203